THE ROME OF FALL

Borne Back Books
West Egg, New York

This book is a work of fiction. Any references to historical events, real people, or real places are used fictitiously. Other names, characters, places, and events are products of the author's imagination and any resemblence to actual events or places or person, living or dead, is entirely coincidental.

THE ROME OF FALL
Copyright © 2020 by Chad Alan Gibbs

First Borne Back Books trade paperback edition March 2020

Cover Design: Phil Poole (https://jestyr37.wixsite.com/philpooledesign)
Author Photo: Selfie ¯_(ツ)_/¯

Manufactured in the United States of America

Publisher's Cataloging-in-Publication Data
provided by Five Rainbows Cataloging Services

Names: Gibbs, Chad Alan, author.
Title: The Rome of fall / Chad Alan Gibbs.
Description: Auburn, AL : Borne Back Books, 2020.
Identifiers: LCCN 2019918567 (print) | ISBN 978-0-9857165-6-1
     (paperback) | ISBN 978-0-9857165-7-8 (ebook)
Subjects: LCSH: Rock musicians--Fiction. | Football players--Fiction. |
     Alabama--Fiction. | Bildungsromans. | Shakespeare, William, 1564-
     1616. Julius Caesar--Adaptations. | BISAC: FICTION / Coming of
     Age. | FICTION / Southern. | GSAFD: Bildungsromans.
Classification: LCC PS3607.I2255 R66 2020 (print) | LCC PS3607.I2255
     (ebook) | DDC 813/.6--dc23.

THE ROME OF FALL

chad
alan
gibbs

For Tricia,
forever and ever.

If music be the food of love, play on;
Give me excess of it, that, surfeiting,
The appetite may sicken, and so die.

—William Shakespeare, "Twelfth Night"

Dear Brutus

From Wikipedia, the free encyclopedia

Dear Brutus was an American indie rock band formed in Austin, Texas, in 1996, consisting of Marcus Brinks (lead vocals, guitar), Porter Clayton (drums, xylophone, accordion), Wade Barker (guitar, zanzithophone, backing vocals), Kyle Craven (bass guitar, banjo, backing vocals), and Piper Van Pelt (piano, pipe organ, synthesizer, bullhorn, backing vocals).

After signing to Geffen Records in 1997, the band released its only album, an eponymous debut, known as the *Beige Album*, which sold over 500,000 copies, was certified gold, and hailed by *Rolling Stone* as "a gut-wrenchingly confessional, lo-fi power-pop masterpiece."[1] Widely considered to be inspired by *The Giver*, Lois Lowry's young adult dystopian novel, and by lead singer Marcus Brinks's breakup with his college girlfriend, the *Beige Album* received universal acclaim and holds a perfect score of 100 on the aggregate review website *Metacritic*.[2][3]

The group disbanded in 1999, when Brinks, citing stress, abruptly walked off stage during an Amsterdam concert, though after months of eccentric behavior followed by years of reclusion, it is generally believed the lead singer suffered a nervous breakdown.[4]

ACT I

"On the strength of their demo, hastily recorded in lead singer Marcus Brinks's dorm bathroom, Austin-based indie rockers Dear Brutus have signed a deal with Geffen Records. Their first album is due out later this fall."

—*The Austin Chronicle*,
April 1, 1997

Chapter One

"Dude, you like Weezer?"

Those were the first words Jackson Crowder ever spoke to me. I was sitting in the front row of Mrs. Nero's twelfth-grade homeroom, on the first day of my senior year at Rome High School, and Jackson took the seat next to me. The cool kids sat in back. We were both front-row sort of kids.

I glanced at my Weezer T-shirt then back at Jackson and said, "No, not really."

This was my first day at Rome, and I didn't want to be there. I wanted to be back in Texas, with my friends. But Mom moved us here in July, without even consulting me, so in the spirit of petty teenage retribution, I decided not to make friends at my new school. I'd be mysterious and depressed. A miserable loner. My plan was to sulk through senior year until I graduated in May and moved off to college and got on with my life. So, on day one, I wore the T-shirt of a band I figured no one in this backwoods school had heard of yet, in hopes they'd leave me alone. But five minutes in, this guy was asking if I liked Weezer and totally ignoring the go-to-hell vibe I was trying and apparently failing to emit.

"Oh," Jackson said, pointing at my T-shirt. "I just thought … since you were wearing that shirt and all … that maybe you …"

His voice trailed off, and I looked at him. Jackson was tall but skinny. He weighed less than me, and I was a featherweight. His full face was mostly nose with a dash of mouth and black eyes, and he had a DIY haircut, shaved on the sides, unmanageable brown waves on top.

"I mean, yeah, I like them all right," I said, because he looked hurt, and I was shitty at being a miserable loner.

"Me too," he said with the eagerness of a Labrador puppy. "Do you have the "Undone" single? Julia, my sister, works for the college radio station in Jacksonville, and she gave me copy back in the summer. She gets me all the new stuff before it even comes out."

"A friend in Texas made me a copy," I said.

"Awesome. "Mykel & Carli" is my favorite B-side," Jackson said then added, "Hey, they're coming to Birmingham next month. It's on a Thursday night, but maybe we could still go. I bet my sister would drive."

It was hard to imagine a world, even in the multiverse where all possible worlds supposedly exist, where my mother would let me go to Birmingham with Jackson Crowder and his sister to see Weezer on a school night. But Jackson's optimism was contagious, so I said, "Yeah, maybe."

"Sweet," Jackson said. "So, do you like "Buddy Holly" or "Say It Ain't So" better? My sister thinks—"

"Good morning, class," Mrs. Nero said, walking into the room and kicking off the school year, and while she stood at her desk, shuffling through papers, Jackson continued in a whisper, "My sister thinks "Say It Ain't So" is better than half the songs on the *White Album*, and she loves The Beat—"

"Marcus Brinks," Mrs. Nero said, and I looked up to see her scanning the room. "Is there a Marcus James Brinks here?" I raised my hand and she said, "There you are. Welcome to Rome, Marcus. Why don't you stand up and introduce yourself to the class?"

New kids want, more than anything else, to blend in. To merge slowly into the fabric of a school until people forget we weren't there all along. I wanted to tell Mrs. Nero this, but causing a scene would have been counterproductive, so I half-stood and said, "I'm Marcus Brinks," but before I could sit, Mrs. Nero said, "And will you please tell everyone where you are from, Marcus?"

Again, I half-stood and said, "We moved here from Texas," then added, "League City, it's near Houston," in case Mrs. Nero demanded specifics.

"Class," Mrs. Nero said, "please say hello to Marcus."

The class mumbled, "Hello, Marcus," in uninspired unison, and Mrs. Nero added, "I do hope you will all try to make Marcus feel at home in Rome. Jackson, you two seem to have hit it off already; would you be a dear and show Marcus around today?"

Jackson said he would, and he did.

~ ~ ~

At our lockers after homeroom, Jackson and I compared schedules. We had five of our seven classes together. "I've got gym when you have study hall," I said, "and when I have sociology—"

"Move, dick."

A literal giant passed by us, elbowing Jackson headfirst into his own locker. I wanted to run, but my fight-or-flight response malfunctioned, and I stood there, staring.

"What are you looking at?" the man-child asked me.

I was looking at the quarterback of the football team. How did I know this? Well, quarterbacks just have a look, don't they? This guy was tall, six-foot-four at least, with a head one size too big for his body. Good looking guy too, which typically isn't the sort of thing straight guys admit about each other, but this dude, I think we all realized if we looked like him, getting dates would not be a problem. Also, the front of his T-shirt said, "ROME QB," which might have tipped me off.

"Nothing," I said, averting my eyes.

"Good," the living Ken doll said, "'cause I don't like your face." Then he shoved Jackson in the back again before walking away.

"Deacon Cassburn," Jackson said after the quarterback was out of earshot. "He plays quarterback."

"Yeah," I said, "I figured."

We walked on to our first class of the day, precalculus, and after we took our seats, I said, "Your schedule says, when I have sociology, you have football. There's a class here called football?"

"It's just gym," Jackson said, "but for football players."

"Okay," I said, "but why are you in it?"

"I'm on the football team," Jackson said, almost embarrassed about it.

I didn't laugh because I'd already hurt his feelings once that morning, but Jackson looked less like a football player than the Sharks and Jets looked like gang members.

"I am," Jackson said, reading the doubt on my face. "Everyone here plays football. I mean, everyone. It's kind of a big deal."

"I moved here from Texas. I know when football is a big deal."

Jackson shrugged and said, "I'm telling you, man, it's a big deal. It's probably too late; we've already gone through two-a-days and all, but Coach P might still let you join the team. You'll have to get a haircut, but—"

"I'm not joining the football team," I said, louder than I meant to, and some people stared.

My dad all but forced me to play football in seventh grade because he'd mistaken my admiration of Houston Oilers' quarterback Warren Moon as a desire to put on shoulder pads and crash into other thirteen-year-olds. Those two months were, without question, the worst of my childhood, and this from someone who spent half his freshman year wearing orthodontic headgear to school. I played linebacker because, like most linebackers, I too was a carbon-based life form, but our similarities ended there, and I spent most of that fall sulking and begging to quit. Dad wouldn't let me, but halfway through the season, my mom, who could be cool sometimes, took me to lunch and said, "When we get home, we'll tell your father we've been to the doctor and you have a heart condition, and if you play football again, you could die." I had to quit soccer too, which I did enjoy, but it was a small price to pay.

"Oh shit. I'm sorry, man," Jackson said, after I told him my heart condition story. Well, the part about me having a heart condition, not the part about it being imaginary. "Are you okay? Are you going to … I mean … you're not going to …"

"I'm not going to die," I said to Jackson. "I can't play sports, that's all."

"Oh, good," Jackson said, as more of the football team drifted into class. They wore all manner of Rome Football T-shirts, since it was way too hot to break out their letterman's jackets, and as the classroom filled, I realized I was the only able-bodied male in the room not on the team. I felt like a draft dodger.

Mr. Titus, the precalculus teacher, entered the room as the bell sounded, and he switched on an ancient window air conditioner that rumbled to life and pumped arctic air exclusively on the student sitting next to it, leaving the rest of us to sweat and struggle to hear as, over the course of the next hour, he worked through dozens of football-related word problems on his whiteboard.

"What do people around here do for fun?" I asked Jackson in the hall after class.

"Like, on weekends?"

I shrugged and Jackson said, "Well, everyone will be at the first game on Friday. We're playing Helvetii Hills. You should go."

"Maybe," I said, "but I don't know anyone to sit—"

"Beyotch!"

A gangly blond-headed kid spitting Snoop Dogg lyrics whacked Jackson across the back of his knees with one of his forearm crutches, knocking him into me, and me to the ground, and as I stood up, I thought it didn't bode well, socially speaking, that my only friend in Rome was bullied by both jocks and disabled kids alike. But Jackson, laughing and pointing toward the guy who'd just flogged him, said, "Marcus Brinks, meet Silas Carver."

"'Sup, Brinks," Silas said, setting a precedent of almost everyone in Rome ignoring my given name.

"Hey," I said, not sure about the logistics of shaking his hand, but Silas shifted his weight and raised his hand, and when I hesitated, he rolled his eyes and explained, "I've got Becker's. It's not contagious."

I shook his hand and asked, "You've got what?"

"Becker muscular dystrophy," Silas said.

"It's an STD only virgins can get," Jackson added, and Silas whipped him across the shins with his left crutch.

"Shit, that really hurt," Jackson said, rubbing his legs.

Silas smiled at me and said, "My muscles are deteriorating, so I've got to pick on him while I can."

"Yeah, well," Jackson said, still rubbing his shins, "Brinks doesn't have anyone to sit with at the game Friday, so he's sitting with you."

Silas looked me over, sighed, and said, "Fine, but you've got to make my concession stand runs."

"Deal," Jackson said, and Silas half-heartedly swung a crutch in his direction then laughed when Jackson nearly tripped jumping out of the way.

"I'm out," Silas said, grabbing both crutches with his hands. "Welcome to Rome, Brinks."

"Silas is a good guy," Jackson told me on the way to our next class. "He's listened to nothing but Dr. Dre and Snoop Dogg for the last year, so he calls me bitch way more than I'm comfortable with, but he's a good guy." We took our front-row seats in Mr. Galba's world history class, and Jackson said, "You'll have fun with him at the game. I've seen him scream at the refs so much he passed out."

My memory of what happened next is certainly faulty. I had a garage band back in Texas, and I'd just asked Jackson if he played guitar, when the lights dimmed. This was possible, if not likely—Rome High School was built sometime between world wars, so the lights dimmed all the time. But then a spotlight lit the doorway, and everything in the room, the students, the walls, the blackboard, the pencil sharpener, inhaled in anticipation. A second lasted a thousand years, and at long last, through smoke and falling confetti, she entered the room.

Her short blonde hair fell in lazy curls from her pretty head, and she wore an open plaid shirt that failed to hide the curves below her tight Weezer T-shirt. No dress code in human history allowed for shorts as short as hers, but her long tan legs strode across the room, confident no teacher would dare send her home. The goddess took no notice of me as she passed, ignoring my prayers for her to come sit next to me, and after she made her way to a desk in the back, I looked at Jackson, who'd been watching me with amusement.

"Becca Walsh," he said.

"Becca Walsh," I repeated and glanced back at her but this time looked directly into her electric blue eyes and quickly spun back around.

"Yeah, Becca Walsh," Jackson said, nodding toward Deacon Cassburn, who'd just entered the room. "Now watch this." I watched Deacon swagger across the room with a confidence known only to high school quarterbacks then turn down the last row and take the seat in front of Becca Walsh but not before kissing the top of her head—a gesture she acknowledged with a quick wink that would kill a lesser man.

I looked back at Jackson and said, "Shit."

Jackson laughed. "Shit indeed. Welcome to Rome, Brinks."

Chapter Two

"How is your sweet mother, Mr. Brinks?"

It used to weird me out that teachers never referred to each other by first names. They were always saying things like, "Can I borrow your projector, Mr. Galba? Of course, Mrs. Nero, but remember to bring it back. I'll need it fifth period." I'd always assumed, in error it seems, that in the teacher's lounge things were less formal. Granted I'd never been inside a teacher's lounge, but just that word, *lounge*, evoked images of a smoke-filled room where educators sat at candlelit tables, sipping cocktails and complaining about students, while on stage a finger-snapping crooner worked through Sinatra's catalog. In reality, the teacher's lounge at Rome consisted of four round tables, two vending machines (one with soft drinks, the other with candy bars), a television tuned to either CNN or Fox News (depending on the political leanings of the teacher who bothered to turn it on that morning), and a bulletin board with a sign-up sheet for homecoming dance chaperones and a stern reminder from the Rubicon County Board of Education not to have sex with students. Along with realizing you never stop getting pimples, the teacher's lounge was one of the greatest disappointments of my adult life.

"Not too good," I said to Mrs. Nero, whose homeroom I'd been in twenty-three years earlier. She'd retire in May, after twenty-five years at Rome, which meant she was in her mid-twenties when she taught me all those years ago. I think we both felt ancient.

"Well, she's a sweet lady," Mrs. Nero said. "Will you please tell her I asked about her?"

"I will, Mrs. Nero," I said, not because after ten minutes on the job I was already referring to my co-workers exclusively by surname, but because I still thought of Mrs. Nero as my teacher, and it would seem weird to call her Tonya.

We sat at one of the four round tables in the lounge, and I sipped my coffee wishing it was something stronger, like hemlock. I flipped through a recent edition of the *Riverton Times* someone had left in the lounge. Jackson Crowder, head coach of Rome, was on the front page, and after skimming the article, I asked Mrs. Nero, "Are there any other teachers here I'd remember?"

Mrs. Nero set her mug on the table and said, "Let me think … Mr. Galba, Mrs. Nerva … was Mrs. Leo here when you were in school?" I shook my head no and Mrs. Nero said, "That's it then. Most of us retire after twenty-five years, start drawing our pension, then work in Georgia for a few years to double-dip. Some people you went to school with teach here now though. Mr. Carver teaches pre-calculus and algebra."

"Mr. Carver?" I asked, and Mrs. Nero said, "Silas Carver," whispering his first name like it was her social security number.

"No shit," I said, and Mrs. Nero frowned at my profanity. "I haven't seen Silas since …"

I didn't finish my thought, and Mrs. Nero said, "He usually stays in his room between classes, but you should drop in and see him."

I said I would, and while Mrs. Nero refilled her coffee across the room, she said, "And of course Coach Crowder is here." She returned to her seat and added with a quick roll of her eyes, "Though he rarely descends from his ivory tower to grace us with his presence."

I laughed, but Mrs. Nero looked embarrassed and said, "I shouldn't have said that. You two are friends."

"Were friends," I corrected, and the concern melted from her face.

"Still," she said, "that was unprofessional. I shouldn't talk bad about other teachers. It's just that he … well, give it a few weeks, you'll see." Then, before I could ask her to expound on her vagueness, she said, "Now who would you know at Rome Middle? I believe you were in school with Ms. Wal—"

The morning bell, louder than I'd remembered it, rang out, and I was sick to my stomach. "Shit," I said. "Tell me what to do."

This time, Mrs. Nero didn't flinch at the profanity. She stood up, patted my back, and said, "Just be yourself. You're going to do fine, Marcus. Have a great first day."

~ ~ ~

I had a twelfth-grade homeroom, which meant for the first ten minutes of each school day, thirty seniors sat in my classroom and listened to morning announcements. When I was in school, we watched *Channel One News*, but after they showed two men kissing during a same-sex marriage story ten years ago, a group of concerned Rome parents demanded the school drop the news network. Now we had two minutes of announcements, followed by eight minutes of sitting around, and Principal Trajan told me it was best to enforce a no-talking policy on day one. This seemed a little strict though, so after the second bell rang and everyone found a desk, I said, "It's okay if you guys talk in here, but I need you to listen during announcements," but they were all texting each other and paid me no attention. A minute later, when Principal Trajan's disembodied voice crackled through the speaker mounted above the door, ten seniors slept through his announcements, nineteen did not look up from their phones, and one kid, in a trench coat, in August, stared at me for ten straight minutes.

"I'd like to welcome you all back to Rome," Principal Trajan said, "and I hope you all had an outstanding summer full of enriching …"

Principal Trajan spent ten years in the United States Army before starting his career as an educator. He kept his hair cropped short, wore a short-sleeved shirt with a wide tie every day, and said the word "outstanding" a lot. I know having a former military man as your principal sounds scary, but Principal Trajan was a pushover, and the students loved him.

"This being day one," Principal Trajan said, "here are a few reminders for veterans and recruits alike. No student allowed off campus without a pass. No student allowed in the hallways or bathrooms during class periods without a pass. Students possessing, using, or under the influence of alcohol at school or any school sponsored event will face immediate expulsion. Student attendance at pep rallies is mandatory ..."

Once it became clear Principal Trajan intended to read through the entire student handbook, I sat back and watched my homeroom sleep and play on their phones, while trying not to make eye contact with the trench coat kid who was still staring at me.

"Finally," Principal Trajan announced, "as you all already know, Rome plays its first football game of the season this Friday, here at the Colosseum, against Riverton." A couple students looked up from their phones long enough to make whooping noises. "I know Coach Crowder wants a loud and rowdy crowd, so I hope to see you all there. Remember, student admission is free, so no excuses. Again, welcome back to Rome, and I hope you all have an outstanding first day." The speaker clicked off, and seconds later, the bell rang and the students shuffled out of my room toward their first-period class.

I followed the last student from my classroom, though at a safe distance because it was the trench coat kid, and stood in the doorway watching a river of students course through the hallway. It was like a dream, or maybe a nightmare, being back in my old school, and as I flashed back to roaming those same halls over two decades ago, I became aware of someone standing right in front of me. I glanced down at a mousy-looking girl and realized I was blocking her and half a dozen others' paths into my classroom. I mumbled an apology and went to my desk and took deep breaths while the room filled up.

This was my first of three periods of freshman English literature, and I was terrified, until I noticed the students. Unlike my homeroom, they were not talking or sleeping or playing on their phones. They squirmed and fidgeted, placed their notebooks on their desks just so, and checked and double-checked the sharpness of their pencils. Then it hit me; these were freshmen, on their first day of high school, and they were even more terrified than I was, and this gave me a small boost of confidence. The bell rang, and one last student sauntered in and said, "Sorry, Teach," over the giggles of his classmates, before taking a seat near the back. I took one last deep breath, then three more, and wrote my name on the blackboard because that's what teachers on television do. I turned around and said, "Good morning class," and pointing toward my name on the board, said, "I'm Mr. Brinks, though I suppose I could have just told you that without writing it on the board." A couple freshmen laughed, and I felt encouraged, until the mousy-looking girl on the front row raised her hand.

"Yes?"

"That says 'Mr. Brins'."

I turned around to more giggles and realized I'd misspelled my own name on my first day teaching English literature. I reached for the chalk, dropped it, picked it up, hit my head on the eraser rail, then squeezed in a *k*.

"There," I said, "Brinks, with a *k*," and more students found the courage to giggle, though now I wasn't so sure they were laughing with me. "Okay," I said, trying to regroup, "this is English literature, which covers everything from Shakespeare to J. K. Rowling—"

"Ain't you in a band?"

The boy who'd run in after the bell raised his hand to indicate he'd asked the question, which wasn't exactly how this worked, but whatever.

"I was in a band," I said, ignoring his use of "ain't" for the time being.

"What sort of band?" the boy asked.

13

He had the look and attitude of a quarterback, but there was no way Rome would start a freshman under center, so I figured he was just too dumb to know freshmen were supposed to be scared on their first day of high school.

"A rock band," I said. "Well, indie rock, I guess."

A short blonde girl sitting by the air conditioner said, "My mother said your music was obscene," then blushed and tried to disappear in her seat.

"Did she really?"

The girl nodded and I said, "I've never heard anyone else refer to our music as obscene, though Tipper Gore did slap a parental advisory sticker on our album; maybe that's what your mother was talking about."

"Tipper who?"

"Al Gore's wife used to ... never mind ... not important," I said, and the girl shrugged. "Obscene ... our album wasn't obscene. It was ... authentic, you know. The lyrics were confessional and about real life, and sure, a couple songs were perhaps a bit graphic ... but, you know, in real life, people have sex." The students laughed, and I wished I hadn't said "sex" only three minutes into my first class, then I continued digging my hole. "And sex is not obscene," I said. "I'm here, and so are you, because two people had, well ..."

"Laura was adopted," said a guy with glasses sitting by the wall.

"Okay," I said, "I'm not sure what—"

"She's adopted," the kid with glasses repeated, "so no one had sex to make her."

"That's not exactly how adoption—"

"People had sex to make Laura, you moron," said the guy behind the bespectacled kid. "It's just her parents have never had sex."

"Again, that's not exactly—"

"I don't understand." A curly-haired girl by the door asked, thankfully changing the subject, "Why would people want to listen to music about real life? I mean, we all live normal lives. Why would we want to listen to songs about other people's normal lives in our free time?"

"Great question," I said, sitting on my desk. "So you believe all art should be pure escapism?" I'd hoped this would initiate an interesting discussion, but now, feeling the focus of her classmates, the curly-haired girl sank into her desk and shrugged.

"My dad said you're a millionaire," said the tardy kid who'd first steered the class off course.

I laughed. "No, I'm not a millionaire."

"Well, how much do you make when someone streams your song?" asked the short blonde girl sitting by the air conditioner.

"I have no idea," I said. "I'm not sure if anyone streams our songs. We sold half a million records, but that was back in the late nineties."

There were gasps around the room, and the guy in glasses who believed adopted kids were produced asexually said, "CDs used to cost thirty bucks each, so you are a millionaire."

"First, CDs cost like sixteen bucks each, so—"

"That's still eight million dollars," said the guy behind the guy in glasses, who was surprisingly quick at math.

I shook my head and walked over to the blackboard. "This isn't math class," I said, "but before you all run around Rome telling everyone I'm rich, I want you to see this." I began writing numbers on the board and explained, "The band had a royalty rate of 12 percent, but our producer took three, so 9 percent. Not 9 percent of sixteen bucks though—half of that went to the retailer—we got 9 percent of eight bucks, which is seventy-two cents per album, times half a million is …"

"$360,000," said the guy behind the guy in glasses before I could do the math.

"That's still a lot of money," said the short blonde by the air conditioner.

"But then the record label took their cut," I said, "and we had to pay the studio, and the engineer, and session musicians, and there were five of us in the band, so by the time we split—"

"This says you are worth 1.3 million dollars," said the tardy kid on the back row.

"Wait, what says that?"

"This celebrity net worth website," he said, holding up his phone like I could read it across the room.

"Okay, maybe after the tour, and the money we got from Nike when they used one of our songs in a commercial ... Yeah, I probably made somewhere around that."

A murmur of million-dollar excitement passed over the room again, and I held up my hand and said, "But ... but what you're forgetting is I'd made most of that money by the time I was twenty-three, and I'll be forty-one in December, so tax it by 30 percent, then divide it by eighteen, and ..."

Around the room, students typed the numbers into the calculators on their phones, and one by one raised their heads in disappointment.

"Wow, my dad makes more money than you do," said the tardy kid.

"I'm sure he does," I said.

"My mother does too," said the curly-haired girl who didn't want to listen to music about real life.

"Yes," I said, now feeling the need to defend my career choice to a bunch of high school freshmen, "but the band still has a bit of a cult following, particularly in Paraguay for some reason, and we have a promising plagiarism suit against a boy band I've never heard of, and—oh, forget it. Take out your textbooks and let's talk about William Shakespeare, a man who, I remind you, never came close to making as much money as me."

"Heartbreaking and haunting. Power pop never gut-punched this hard."

—*SPIN*, 10/10 review of *Dear Brutus* by Dear Brutus, November 22, 1997

Chapter Three

On Fridays in the fall, pep rallies replaced my seventh-period chemistry class, which isn't a big deal until you consider there are roughly 180 days in a school year, and that includes the last day before Christmas break, the last day before spring break, the last week of school, and a dozen other days when no one does shit. A hypothetical state championship run would necessitate fifteen pep rallies. Fifteen mandatory pep rallies. Meaning Rome High School, whose chief aim was supposedly to educate the youth of Rome, insisted, under penalty of three days' suspension or beating with a paddle, that I miss roughly 10 percent of my chemistry instruction to stand in a sweaty gymnasium and implore a cavalcade of meatheads to go, fight, and win tonight.

Rome fielded girls' and boys' basketball teams, a baseball team, softball, and track. The school competed in over two dozen sports, and those teams trained and competed hard, but not once was I required to skip a day of balancing chemical equations to rally them with pep. And not to mention the debate team, or scholars' bowl, or any number of academic squads that were never sent into battle with an ass-shaking routine from the Rome cheerleaders.

I sound bitter. I'm not. It's Alabama, and it's football. I get it. If I'm bitter about anything, it's that Silas was unable to climb to the top of the bleachers where we could hide behind the crowd until the pep rally was over. No, Silas stood on the front row, the floor, and I stood next to him because, apart from Jackson, he was the only person I knew in Rome.

This is how Rome did pep rallies. At two p.m., the bell rang and students from the high school and the middle school next door sprinted toward the gymnasium, which was brand spanking new, while the old school building would likely crumble in a stiff breeze. "You know they didn't build this for the basketball teams," Silas told me as I followed him inside. "It's so the football team will have a nice place to practice when it rains. That's why they named it after Coach Pumphrey, even though he hates basketball and has suggested shutting down the program more than once."

High school students filled the home bleachers, middle schoolers sat on the visitors' side, and we waited in silent anticipation until the crack of a snare drum split the air. The students rose as one and clapped in rhythm as the marching band, dubbed the Rome Marching Legion, marched in, taking its place across the court from the stage. Band in place, the lights cut out, and a kid on the middle school side shouted, "Victory or death!", which seemed a little intense coming from a twelve-year-old. His classmates cheered him on but soon fell silent as the Rome cheerleaders entered the gymnasium single file, wearing red cloaks and holding candles.

"Are we going to sacrifice a virgin?" I whispered to Silas.

"Good luck finding one in that bunch," Silas whispered back.

The cheerleaders floated toward the far end of the gym, lined up in front of the stage, and one by one blew out their candles. When the last cheerleader extinguished the last candle, and the gym was dark as a tomb, a bass drum boomed, and the crowd whooped and jumped as one.

"What the hell?" I asked.

"Just watch," Silas said.

A second bass drum sounded, and again the crowd shouted and jumped as one. Another drum hit followed, then another, and another, each one closer together, each one accompanied by jumping and shouting students until the drumbeats and the jumps and the shouts were an indistinguishable blur of motion and sound. The room lit up, and now on stage, as if they'd teleported, sat the Rome High School football team, Coach Pumphrey in his purple windbreaker front and center. At the sight of their heroes, the crowd reached hearing-loss decibel levels, while the cheerleaders dropped their cloaks and spread out around the gym to lead cheers, and the band struck up Rome's fight song, which was a complete rip-off of Michigan's "Hail to the Victors," but in their defense, almost all high school fight songs are rip-offs, and, this being Alabama, at least it wasn't "Dixie." I watched in reluctant awe as students and teachers alike belted out, *"Hail! to the victors valiant. Hail! to the conqu'ring heroes. Hail! Hail! To Rome High School, the champions of the state!"*

After the fight song, some seniors performed a skit where a Roman gladiator beheaded a hapless Confederate soldier— Rome played the Helvetii Hills Rebels that night—then five minutes of cheers followed, one where fans on the high school side informed fans on the middle school side that we, indeed, had spirit, before inquiring about them. Next, the cheerleaders treated us to a routine involving more writhing around on the floor than most adults in attendance were probably comfortable with, and finally, the team captains addressed their subjects.

First, a three-hundred-pound man-child wearing number 69 grabbed the microphone and screamed, "This is our house!" The crowd roared, and the behemoth raised both arms in triumph.

"Marshall Ford," Silas said to me. "Dude says the same garbage every week. He's about to inform us that no one comes into our house and pushes us around."

Marshall Ford stepped back to the microphone and screamed, "And no one comes into our house and pushes us around!" The crowd erupted again, and Silas shook his head and laughed.

Deacon Cassburn stepped to the microphone next, and girls squealed and screamed until the blond god blushed, stepped back, and stared at his cowboy boots, which made the girls scream and squeal even louder.

"This happens every week too," Silas said. "That dick slap loves it."

Deacon's adoring fans finally stopped screaming—they may have all passed out—and again he stepped to the microphone and said, "If y'all come out and see us tonight ..."

The screaming and squealing resumed, but this time Deacon commanded silence with a single raised finger.

"If y'all come out and see us tonight," Deacon repeated, rolling up the sleeves on his jersey and pointing at his comically large biceps, "I promise you, I'll let slip these dogs of war!"

The Ronald J. Pumphrey Gymnasium shook following Deacon's promised dog slipping, and as he and Marshall walked back to their seats high above, I thought about how pissed I'd be if I died in a pep-rally-induced building collapse. The roof held though, and everyone sang the alma mater with absurd reverence. Then the lights cut once more, and the cheerleaders, re-cloaked and again holding candles, left the room. When the lights switched back on, the team and the band were gone, and school was over for the week. It was perhaps the most ridiculous use of an hour imaginable, but I couldn't help appreciating the spectacle of it all. That said, a year later at college, in my freshman chemistry class, I did not find the experience very useful.

~ ~ ~

"How do you like the bitch seat, Brinks?"

A sign on the first row of the student section, installed by the Rome Quarterback Club, of which Silas's father was a member, stated that seats 1 and 2 were reserved for "Silas Carver & Guest." I suppose it was the least they could do for a kid with muscular dystrophy.

I laughed and asked, "The what?"

"You heard me," Silas said, pointing toward my seat. "That spot is usually reserved for one of my bitches, but I'm letting you sit there tonight because you're new and all."

"It's nice," I said.

"It's the best damn seat in the house, Brinks. Show some appreciation, man, or I'll make you sit with the rest of the plebs."

"It's life changing," I said, and Silas replied, "Damn straight."

We were, for the time being, alone in the student section. Our classmates were all on the field, forming the human tunnel the team would run down once they'd burst through a gigantic victory banner depicting Roman soldiers preparing to crucify Jefferson Davis, first president of the Confederate States of America.

"That banner is a little ... intense," I said to Silas.

"Yeah, I imagine the school will get some angry phone calls next week—here we go."

"Here. Comes. Rome!" the PA announcer bellowed through a massive speaker system stacked atop the press box, and the Rome football team poured out of the locker room wearing their famous red—Tyrian red if you want to get specific—jerseys, with gold numbers and *SPQR* across the chest. Their golden helmets, painted by the cheerleaders the night before, sparkled as they crashed through the crucifixion mural and sprinted to the home sideline where they jumped around like rabid animals while the crowd stood and roared.

Rome won the coin toss, elected to defer, and as the kicker approached the ball, the crowed thundered, "Victory or death!", which was, apparently, a thing people yelled a lot around here.

The kick was awful, low and bouncing, and a Helvetii Rebel scooped it up around the twenty-yard-line and took two steps to his left, where Marshall Ford hit him so hard crucifixion didn't seem so cruel and unusual anymore. The ball fell to the ground, and a guy named Fletcher Morgan recovered it then received a fifteen-yard penalty for unsportsmanlike behavior after he spiked the ball on the Helvetii player, who appeared to be unconscious. One play later, Deacon Cassburn rolled right and found an open man in the back of the end zone. Just like that, it was 6-0 Rome.

From there, things only got worse for Helvetii Hills, and between plays, Silas and I got to know each other. He loved Dr. Dre and Snoop Dog, hated Eazy-E, and did not have a strong opinion regarding Ice Cube. He wanted, more than anything, including, I think, a cure for his disease, a 1964 Chevy Impala. "It'll need hand controls because eventually I'll lose use of my legs," Silas told me and I nodded, "but they could install those when they put in the hydraulics." He also shared with me his plan to drive to California during spring break. "Long Beach, Watts, and I really want to see Compton."

"That … would be fun," I lied.

"So what brought your family to Rome anyway?" Silas asked, after he'd spent the better part of the first quarter recounting the rise and fall of N.W.A.

"My mom is from Rome, and my dad sort of ran off with his secretary, so we moved back here."

"What a punk-ass bitch," Silas said. "Someone needs to pop a cap in your dad."

"Yeah," I said and tried to change the subject. "Do you wish you could have played?" I asked, pointing at the field, where Rome led Helvetii Hills 27-0 with two minutes left in the half.

"Beyotch, I did play," Silas said. "I was the starting quarter-back in seventh grade."

He saw me glance at his crutches and said, "I wasn't diagnosed until freshman year."

"Oh," I said and wasn't sure what to say after that.

"I was the shit, Brinks," Silas said. "Deacon knows he'd have never beat me out, and he hates me for it."

I wouldn't have thought of Silas as an athlete, but now I could see it or at least shadows of it. He held up a crutch and said, "I didn't need these damn things until last summer." Then he laughed and added, "Even with them, I could probably still beat Jackson out for third string." He was probably right.

"I'd like to coach one day," Silas told me, pulling an index card from his wallet. "I draw up plays when I'm bored at school. This is my best one. It's called Convulsion." He pointed at an X on the card and said, "See, the quarterback acts as a decoy, and if he sells it, the defense will never know what hit 'em."

"Yeah," I said, not having any idea what he was talking about.

At halftime, the Rome High School Marching Legion performed a spirited, if unrecognizable, medley of Rolling Stones hits, and the second half was no more interesting than the first, minus one interaction.

"Hi gorgeous," said a girl, interrupting Silas as he contrasted the rhyming techniques of Nate Dogg and Snoop Dogg. I looked down to see Becca Walsh wearing overalls over a Nirvana T-shirt and Deacon Cassburn's number 7 painted on her left cheek. She reached up and squeezed Silas's hand, and I made a mental note to wear my own Nirvana T-shirt to school on Monday.

"Your man is playing well tonight," Silas said.

"Silas, you're my man," Becca said with a wink.

"Well," Silas said, "your side dude is playing well tonight."

Becca looked at the field like she'd forgotten about the game then turned back to Silas and said, "Oh, is he? I try not to watch since he'll spend the rest of the night telling me about it anyway."

Silas laughed, and Becca looked at me and asked, "Who's this in my seat?"

"This is Marcus Brinks," Silas said by way of introduction. "He just moved here from Tennessee."

"Texas," I said.

"Or Texas," Silas said. "He has terrible taste in music and a deadbeat dad. I'm only being nice to him as a favor to Jackson, but next week, he's on his own."

I summoned the courage to look Becca Walsh in her terrifying blue eyes, and she smiled at me and said, "Hello, Marcus. Welcome to Rome."

"Hi," I said and extended my hand to shake hers, but she'd looked away and didn't see me, so I awkwardly pulled it back hoping Silas hadn't noticed. But he did, and he laughed.

"What's so funny?" Becca asked, turning around.

"Oh nothing," Silas said. "I think Brinks has as thing for you though."

I turned to Silas with wide eyes then looked down at Becca, who was laughing. "Sorry, Marcus, I'm spoken for."

"I didn't—"

"But," she whispered, "my boyfriend is always busy on Friday nights, so maybe you can be my boyfriend during games."

"Friday Night Boyfriend, that's a solid offer, Brinks," Silas said. "You should take it."

"I'm not—"

"It's a deal," Silas said. "Brinks is your FNB."

"Deal," Becca said with a wink, then she patted my knee and said, "See you next Friday, Marcus."

"What the hell?" I said to Silas after Becca joined her friends in the bleachers above us.

"Calm down, Brinks. It was just a joke. But she will insist on sitting by you next week, and that's a good thing, because having you in the bitch seat is cramping my style. Just don't get your hopes up because, and I mean this in the kindest way possible, that girl is the biggest tease in human history. Also, she has a boyfriend who'd enjoy turning your face into abstract art with his fists if he saw you two together."

"Oh, I'm well aware," I said.

Mercifully, the game ended with Rome scoring forty-eight points and Helvetii Hills managing only 6. Jackson played a little in the fourth quarter at defensive back, and he even made a tackle, which he'd recount for us half a dozen times on Monday. And as the scoreboard clock hit triple zeros, I was totally unprepared for the dozens of Roman candles shot from the home bleachers into the night sky.

"What the hell?" I said, ducking as a Roman candle behind us misfired into our section.

"Tradition," Silas said. "The school outlawed them six years ago, but people still sneak them in. Oh, and speaking of tradition, everyone goes to Pantheon Pizza after the game." He nodded toward Becca and repeated, "Everyone."

"You told me not to get my hopes up."

"Yeah, but I can tell it's already too late. You want to ride with Jackson and me?"

Of course I did, but I'd promised Mom I'd come home right after the game, and I wouldn't start lying to her for another two weeks. So I told Silas to have fun, and, despite his warning, went home, strummed my guitar, and dreamed about a girl I had no business dreaming about.

Chapter Four

"You rock star," Silas Carver said, rolling into my room. "You motherfu—"

My eyes widened, and Silas covered his toothy grin with a hand after he noticed two students sitting in the back of my classroom, but they paid him no attention, so he finished in a much lower voice, "Brinks, you mother effin' rock star. You've been here five days and haven't bothered to come see me?"

I laughed. "You know, I heard you taught here, but I thought it was just an urban legend, like the clown that lives under the school."

"There is a clown living under the school," Silas said, as we shook hands. "I've seen him, Brinks, and he's terrifying."

"He couldn't be more terrifying than that Fu Manchu," I said.

Silas rubbed his face and said, "You're just jealous you can't grow one."

He was in a wheelchair now. A giant, robotic-looking ride with big off-road tires, and an Atari joystick he used to move around. He'd pimped it out with an iPad, some speakers, and there was an oxygen tank on the back, but I don't think it was hooked up.

"You look good," I lied, "facial hair notwithstanding."

"No I don't," Silas said. "I look like I'm wearing a sexy Stephen Hawking Halloween costume."

A student stopped in my doorway and said, "Hey Coach, what time do we need to be at the field house?"

Silas spun around and said, "Four, Mac. You need to be there at four. The same time you've needed to be at the field house for every game you've ever played."

"Oh right, thanks, Coach," the kid said and walked away.

"I'm surrounded by morons," Silas said.

As he spun back around, I asked, "Coach?"

"Yeah, I'm the offensive coordinator."

"No you're not."

"Oh, you think just because I'm in this chair I can't call FB West Right Slot 372 Y Stick? That's ableism, you bipedal ass-hole."

"Sorry, man. I just …"

"Shut up, Brinks," Silas said, laughing. "I'm joking. No one would look at us and guess I'm an offensive genius and you're a famous rock star."

I smiled and said, "I was famous for half an hour, twenty years ago." Then I asked him, "How'd you end up coaching?"

"My football coach in college took me under his wing and—"

"Wait, you played football in college?"

Silas gave me his best are-you-a-dumbass look and said, "No, Brinks, the coach at the little college I went to heard about me. His brother had muscular dystrophy, the really bad kind. He brought me on as a manager for four years then a graduate assistant for two. By the time I left, they were running some of my plays. I've been back at Rome for ten years now, running the offense."

"No shit," I said then covered my mouth and looked to the back of the room where the students still paid us no attention. In a lower voice, I said, "That's awesome, man. Mom never tells me much news from Rome." This was a lie. I'd called Mom every Sunday night for the last thirteen years, and she talked almost exclusively about Rome; I just tuned it out.

"We led the state in scoring last year," Silas said, "and we'll be even more explosive this year, assuming Jackson stays out of the way and lets me do my thing. Are you coming to the game tonight?"

"God no," I said.

Silas laughed. "Brinks, we expect a little more school spirit from the faculty around here."

I sighed and asked, "Do they still expect all teachers to attend pep rallies too, or is that just a suggestion?"

"Oh no, you've got to go to the pep rally. Principal Trajan doesn't care, but Jackson wants everyone there, and Principal Trajan does whatever Jackson tells him."

I rolled my eyes and said, "Well, I guess I'll be there."

Silas glanced at his watch and said, "All right, better get back to my room before the halls flood with kids who have no respect for the disabled. See you at the pep rally, Brinks. Bring your spirit."

"Rah. Rah," I deadpanned as Silas left the room.

~ ~ ~

As required by law, the football team, which consisted of every male student and one female, the backup kicker and star of the girls' soccer team, wore their jerseys to school on Friday. Even Karl, the small, thoughtful boy in my second-period class whom I could tell read his assignments, not just the CliffsNotes, wore a jersey. After class, I stopped him and asked, "Karl, what position do you play?"

"Third team free safety," he said, and I laughed, not that Karl was third string, though he looked the part, but that a school as small as Rome had a football team large enough to go three-deep.

First period was disjointed. Attention spans were shorter, more notes were passed, and the students not playing on their phones stared blankly out the window toward the Colosseum. It felt like the last day of school, but it was only the fifth, and after ten minutes of teaching to blank faces, I said, "Look folks, I know there is a football game tonight, but Rome will play at least ten this year, maybe as many as fifteen, and I don't intend to lose 10 percent of the school year to a stupid game."

The students looked hurt, like I'd just unfriended them on Snapchat or something. I sighed and said, "Come on, guys. I went to Rome. I know how important you think this is. But I moved away from Rome too, and hear me on this, it's not that important. Unless you get knocked up, or knock someone up, nothing that happens outside of class during these four years matters much. Not in the long run. I know you don't believe me. Maybe you can't believe me no matter how hard you try. Maybe someone broke your heart last week, and it's all you think about, and it's all you think you'll ever think about from now until the end of time, but I promise you, you won't. You'll go to college, you'll get jobs, you'll move on, and one day, you'll realize I was right."

I'm not sure if I believed any of this, but I was on a roll now and felt like a teacher in a movie, so I held up my textbook and said, "This stuff, this is the stuff that matters. Algebra matters. Chemistry matters. Drop the winning touchdown pass tonight, and ten years from now, no one will care, and if they do still care, they're losers, so why do you care what they think anyway? But drop the ball in here and you're screwed. Look at you guys. I mean, I hate to break this to you, but none of you are NFL material. You know Marshall Ford, right? We were in school together, and he is still the only player from Rome to earn a DI scholarship. He was the biggest, most talented player ever to come through here, and he warmed the bench at Auburn for two years before transferring. But there are dozens of doctors and lawyers and nurses and engineers and teachers who went to Rome. When they were here, they focused on what needed focusing on, and that's why they're not sitting in Pantheon Pizza right now, talking about a pass they dropped two decades ago. Okay? Okay. Now, *Julius Caesar*, page twenty-seven, who wants to read for us?"

The cocky kid in the back of the room raised his hand, and

I asked, "Kyler, you'd like to read?"

"Naw, Teach," he said. "I was just wondering if you played football when you was at Rome."

"It's Mr. Brinks," I said, turning my back to the classroom before taking a seat behind my desk. "And no, I was only here for my senior year, and I did not play football."

The kid smirked, and I wanted to throw my book at him but instead asked, "Is there anything else, Kyler?"

"Naw, Mr. Brinks," he said with a laugh, "that's all we need-ed to know about you."

I considered telling them about my heart condition—that I had one, not that it was fake—but instead silently petitioned God to consider letting Kyler single-handedly lose the game that evening. Then I spent the rest of the day teaching Shakespeare to a disinterested hoard.

~ ~ ~

Though my attendance was mandatory, I had no duties at the pep rally, so I found a spot on the wall opposite the stage and near the door, so I could leave as soon as it ended. Waiting there, I checked my phone. I had an email from Wade, the rhythm guitarist from my old band, asking how I'd been, which was code for, "Why don't you write some new songs so we can get the band back together and make a little money?" I deleted the email and slipped my phone into my pocket just as the snap of a snare drum brought the student body to a collective hush. As the band marched into the gymnasium, I felt the paw of a small bear on my shoulder and looked up to see the oversized blond head of Deacon Cassburn. He wore dark jeans and a tan blazer, the official uniform of middle-aged men who want to look wealthy yet casual, and I flinched because I fully expected him to shove me into the wall.

"Marcus Brinks," Deacon said, squeezing my shoulder too hard but otherwise not turning violent, "welcome back to Rome, my old friend."

"Hi, Deacon," I said, not mentioning that we were never

33

friends and that he was about to break my collarbone. He let go
with one last knee-buckling squeeze, slapped my back a couple
times, and when I realized he intended to watch the pep rally
with me, I asked if he had kids on the team because I couldn't
think of any other reason a grown man would be here if he
didn't have to be.

"No, no," Deacon said, "not yet. My oldest is a seventh-grad-
er. Starting quarterback on the JV team. Kid's got a damn cannon."

"Good for him," I said, still not sure why Deacon was here.

"I'm president of the Quarterback Club," he offered, and
with a dismissive wave at the spectacle before us, added, "Gotta
be at these things."

"Silas told me Jackson disbanded the Quarterback Club," I
said, and Deacon glared at me and said, "Jackson isn't as powerful as he thinks."

The band, which was half the size it'd been two decades ago,
took their place in front of us, and the lights cut as the cheerleaders entered the door to our right, wearing dark red cloaks and
holding electric candles.

"Fake candles?" I whispered to Deacon.

"Few years ago, a girl's hair caught on fire," Deacon said.
"Now the fire marshal makes 'em use those. I suppose it's safer,
but kinda ruins the effect."

The cheerleaders filed into the darkened gym, took their po-
sitions along the stage, and switched off their candles. The room
took a collective breath, and a spotlight hit center stage to reveal
Jackson Crowder, wearing a purple windbreaker and sitting high
upon a throne I recognized from the drama club's production of
Macbeth.

"That's new," I said to Deacon, who shook his head and said,
"They wanted him to do that last year, but he kept acting all
modest. The asshole. A lot of things are different around here,
Brinks. This isn't the Rome we loved."

The spotlight pulled back to reveal the entire Rome football team seated below their leader, and when Jackson raised his arm, a bass drum hit, and the crowd jumped and shouted as one.

The rest of the pep rally was indistinguishable from one twenty years ago. Cheerleaders gyrated, seniors performed skits, and team captains informed the crowd that this was their house, and no one walked into their house and lived to tell about it. But then one of the captains handed Jackson the microphone, and he addressed the adoring crowd, something Coach Pumphrey never did.

Jackson motioned toward his team below and said, "These sons of Rome sacrificed their summer for you. While you lounged poolside, they were on the field of battle, puking their guts out … for you … for Rome! They are prepared. They are coiled and ready to strike. But they cannot do it alone. They need you; I need you—every one of you—in the Colosseum tonight." The crowd roared their intention to attend, and Jackson began to shout, "We need you there early, and we need you loud. It's the least you can do for these who've given so much to you! Now, who is ready to die for Rome?"

The crowd roared even louder, and Jackson shouted, "Victory or death!" before dropping the mic. Deacon turned to me and said, "Your friend thinks he's the damn king of Rome."

"He's not my friend," I said.

Deacon raised an eyebrow. "Good to know."

After the alma mater played, the team, led by their coach, exited the gym to the rhythmic clapping of their classmates, and just as Jackson reached the door, an old man standing next to us shouted, "Watch out for Middlesboro, Coach!"

For the briefest moment, Jackson looked our way, then he was out the door, and Deacon turned to the old man and said, "We don't even play Middlesboro, you old fool."

The old man stared at us with wild eyes then walked away, and Deacon shook his head in bemusement before turning to me and asking, "You going to the game tonight?"

"No," I said. "I'm not much of football fan."

"Well, all right then," Deacon said, slapping me on the back with his bare hand. "I'll see you around, Brinks."

There was a flyer taped to the wall behind us from Rome First Baptist, asking everyone to invite their friends to hear Coach Jackson Crowder share his testimony on Wednesday, September 6. Deacon ripped the flyer from the wall and stuffed it into his pocket before following the last player from the gym like he was part of the team. I wasn't sure if I could leave yet or not, so I turned to find someone I could ask and ran smack into Becca Walsh.

"Oh, I'm sorry—Marcus!"

"Becca!" I said, then my brain overheated, leaving my mouth to fend for itself.

She hugged me and said, "Oh my God. I heard a rumor you were teaching this year but didn't believe it. It's so good to—" Like a ninja, Becca grabbed a kid by the arm and shouted, "No running, Tyler!" She turned back to me and said, "Sorry, Marcus, I've got to make sure these hellions get back to the middle school. Will you be at the game tonight? We've got to catch up!"

"I wasn't … uh … yeah," I said. "I'll see you there."

Becca smiled and said, "It's a date," before sinking into a river of preteens flowing back toward Rome Middle School, leaving me there, hating myself.

"There's a tension here, an album that rhythmically all but begs listeners to their feet then lyrically knocks them right back down."

—*Rolling Stone*, 5-star review of *Dear Brutus* by Dear Brutus, November 23, 1997

Chapter Five

"Brinks, you're coming with us Saturday night, right?"

It was Thursday, pizza day, the week after Rome's first football game of the season, and I sat across a lunchroom table from Jackson.

"It's either that or the game on Friday," I said. "My mom has a weird one-night-out-per weekend rule. What exactly are you doing Saturday again?"

"*We* are cruising, Brinks" Silas said, collapsing less than gracefully into the seat next to me. "All three of us."

"I don't know," I said. "I sort of wanted to go to the game because—"

"Because Becca Walsh said you were her Friday night boyfriend?" Silas interrupted. "Homie, that was a joke. Skip the game. Cruise with us."

"Maybe you should go to the game," Jackson said. "I'll get to play most of the fourth quarter, and—"

"Skip the game; cruise with us," Silas repeated.

"I'm leaning toward Saturday," I said, "but I still don't know exactly what we're doing."

"Okay," Jackson said, soaking up the extra grease from his pizza with a stack of napkins, "have you seen that old George Lucas movie?"

"*Star Wars*? Yeah, I've seen *Star Wars*."

"No, not *Star Wars*, dumbass, the other one. Silas, what's it called?"

"*American Graffiti*," Silas said, after shaking his head at Jackson's ever-growing pile of grease-soaked napkins.

"Right, *American Graffiti*. Have you seen *American Graffiti*?"

I pointed toward Jackson's napkins and said, "You've ruined pizza day for me."

Jackson shrugged and asked again, "Have you seen *American Graffiti*?"

"I don't like space movies," I said.

"It's not a space movie. It's about teenagers driving around and talking to each other."

"Han Solo is in it," Silas said, "but he's not Han Solo."

"Indiana Jones?" I asked.

"No, I think his name is Bob."

"Focus, people," Jackson said. "On Saturday, we're cruising, and you're cruising with us."

"Okay, let me get this straight," I said. "The two of you drive up and down, what street is it again?"

"Main Street, in Riverton," Jackson said.

"The two of you drive up and down Main Street, and girls get in the car with you?"

"What?" Silas asked.

"You said something about picking up chicks," I said.

"No, dumbass," Jackson said, "we don't literally pick them up. We're not running a taxi, Brinks."

"We just flirt with them," Silas said, "and sometimes we get a car full of girls to pull over, and then we pull over too and talk to them and stuff."

"And stuff?"

"Yeah," Silas said, without offering details on said stuff.

"Okay," I said, "how many times have the two of you cruised Main Street?"

Jackson and Silas looked at each other, and Jackson said, "Maybe twenty times."

"Twenty or thirty," Silas added.

"And of those thirty times, how often has a car full of girls pulled over and talked to you ... and stuff?"

They hesitated, looked at each other again, and Jackson said, "There were those girls from Glencoe last summer."

"And those two girls from Hokes Bluff."

"Oh right, they were hot, but they had that ugly dude with them. And last week, we talked to Maggie Duncan and Rachel."

"Yeah, but they don't count, since they go to Rome."

"True."

I stared at them until they looked at me and Jackson asked, "What?"

I laughed. "I want to make sure I've got this straight, because this is my weekend we're talking about here. You've cruised Main Street thirty times, and you've talked a car full of girls into pulling over exactly twice, and one of those cars contained 33 percent ugly dudes? I mean, playing the percentages, wouldn't we be better off sitting on the interstate waiting for a car full of hot girls to get a flat tire in front of us?"

"Playing the percentages, there's a zero percent chance of a hot girl showing up in your bedroom on Saturday night," Silas said.

I sighed in defeat. "Good point. I'm in."

~ ~ ~

Jackson scored a touchdown in Rome's second game of the season—another blowout win, this one 56-0 over the hapless Butterflies of Pinkerton High School. In retrospect, his reaction to the garbage-time score offered a glimpse into what success would do to his psyche, but I only recall wishing he'd shut up about it.

Because he was one of the few guys on the team smart enough to learn all the plays, Jackson was the emergency third-string quarterback behind Deacon's backup, Jake Norton. But when he actually saw the field, which was rarely, Jackson played strong safety, not because he was strong, but because he wasn't fast enough to play free safety or cornerback, couldn't catch well enough to play wide receiver, and wasn't big enough to play any other position without risking serious injury. He claimed to be second string, and perhaps on some long-forgotten depth chart he was, but as far as playing time went, he was behind the starter, Fletcher Morgan, and a sophomore named Jimmy Anthony. Jackson only played in these 56-0 type games and twice, as a junior, bore sole responsibility for allowing a late touchdown that blew Rome's shutout. But not this week.

Rome's defensive coordinator, Mr. Titus, blitzed Jackson a lot in late game situations, because it relieved him of coverage duties and significantly decreased the odds Jackson would screw up. There were less than two minutes to play, and on second down, Pinkerton's quarterback set up to throw and was almost decapitated by Mark Porter, a Rome freshman the size of a Mini Cooper. The ball flew straight up, and as if controlled by a puppeteer, fell into the rather unsuspecting arms of a blitzing Jackson Crowder. It was, perhaps, the only imaginable scenario where Jackson would ever score a touchdown, because he was already running full speed in the direction he needed to go, and after he caught the ball, there was nothing for him to think about. He crossed the goal line before he knew what happened, and as the referee's arms went up, Jackson dropped the ball and stood there, dumbfounded, until the rest of the defense piled on top of him in celebration. I know this version of the story because Silas told me on our way to pick up Jackson Saturday night. Jackson's version had more details.

"I mean, I saw Mark hit the quarterback, and I could tell by the way he held the ball it would fly back and to the left, so I adjusted my angle, and jumped a lineman on the ground, and caught the ball at its highpoint like we're coached to do. I would have high-stepped, like Deion, but we get into so much trouble if we're flagged for unsportsmanlike conduct. So, I just took it to the house and stood there with my hands on my hips like, 'Yeah, bitches!'"

This was the third time in the last fifteen minutes Jackson had recounted his touchdown, though the detail about jumping a lineman was new. I suspect, when he tells the story now, Pinkerton had fifteen men on the field, and Jackson juked them all twice during his high-stepping ninety-nine-yard run.

"Pull over, Brinks!" Silas said. "I think I see some girls lining up to give Jackson congratulatory blow—ouch!"

Jackson smacked Silas upside the head with my mom's umbrella while I laughed.

"Never mind," Silas said, rubbing his head. "They were lining up for some other third-string safety anyway."

We were on our way to cruise Main Street in my mom's 1992 Buick Roadmaster station wagon—an unfortunate necessity since we wouldn't all fit in Jackson's Chevy S-10, Silas didn't own a car, and just before leaving that evening, I'd noticed my Mazda 626 had a blown headlight. The Roadmaster wasn't the ideal cruising vehicle, but we hoped the novelty would play to our advantage.

"I know you both think my touchdown was meaningless," Jackson said, "but forty-nine points was our largest margin of victory ever against Pinkerton, and now it's fifty-six because of me."

"Well, because of Mark Porter," I said. "If he hadn't hit the quarterback—"

"—I would have stripped the ball and scored anyway," Jackson said.

"And I would have kicked the extra point," Silas said.

"And I would have made out with Becca Walsh," I added.

"Screw you guys," Jackson said as we reached the bumper to bumper traffic of Main Street.

How to describe cruising Main Street to someone who never went? Main Street was a social network, only in real life. There were hundreds of cars, each with two or three or more people inside, trucks with a dozen kids piled in back, SUV's packed beyond any reasonable measure of safety, and one wood paneled station wagon. Everyone from Rome was there, yet we made up less than 5 percent of the traffic, which means the rest of the kids were strangers from other schools, other cities, other counties even. I suspect—and I have no way to verify this—on Saturday nights, Main Street contained 75 percent of the teenagers from a five-county radius.

"Cop," Jackson said, pointing toward an officer standing near the crosswalk.

There was always an overabundance of police around, writing tickets to anyone who turned without signaling or got stuck in an intersection when the light turned red.

"I see him," I said, waiting for the car ahead of me to make room before I dared to cross the intersection.

Main Street traffic violations were a steady stream of income for the city and had been for decades. When I told her of my evening plans, my mom laughed and said she used to cruise Main in high school. But for reasons I cannot comprehend, the city of Riverton put an official end to cruising two weeks later.

"Riverton is always threatening to shut this down," Silas said from the backseat, "but I can't imagine why. It's nothing like it was when our parents cruised. People don't fight or anything. They just come here to hook up."

This was true. Years ago, streaking, mooning, and egg and shaving cream fights were the norm. But now, all that anyone on Main Street ever did was drive two miles per hour up and down the same stretch of road all night, talking to the inhabitants of every car they passed. No one dared do anything illegal because you were never more than a few yards from a cop. The police had every high school kid in Northeast Alabama confined to a ten-block radius, but they dispersed us back to our boring towns, and twenty-three years later, Riverton is the meth capital of the United States. I do not believe these two things are unrelated.

So, though I didn't know it at the time, that night, I hit Main Street for the first and last time, behind the wheel of the ugliest car in automotive history.

"What exactly do we do now?" I asked once we were stuck in the middle of traffic, with two lanes of oncoming cars creeping to our left and another lane on our right.

"We talk to skirts," Silas said then leaned out the window and shouted, "You girls look bangin' tonight," at the two blondes in the Toyota Celica next to us.

The girls laughed but otherwise paid us little attention, and when they moved on, Jackson tried his luck with the girls behind them in a white Ford Bronco. "Good evening, ladies," he said. "Want to ride with us? OJ wants his Bronco back."

This time, the girls didn't laugh, and Silas hit Jackson upside the head and yelled, "You've tried that OJ joke a dozen times now, and it never works!"

We moved on, and I was about to say hello to some girls in a Geo Metro, when my view through the driver's side window was eclipsed by the massive shape of Marshall Ford.

"Good evening, dicks," Deacon Cassburn said, leaning in Jackson's window, and he was soon joined by Fletcher Morgan, grinning like a psychopathic kid who'd just learned what a magnifying glass can do to ants.

Traffic crept forward, and the girls in the Metro were gone, but Deacon and friends continued to walk with us down Main Street.

"Any luck with the ladies tonight?" Marshall Ford asked, and I shook my head no.

"Well," Deacon said, slapping Jackson's cheek a little harder than necessary, "there's a girl up there in a Chevy Blazer who wants to meet the guy who scored the last touchdown tonight."

Jackson turned to us in wide-eyed excitement, and before we could tell him there wasn't girl, here or anywhere, who wanted to meet the guy who scored the last touchdown in a 56-0 blowout, he said, "Later, losers," and jumped from the car.

We watched Jackson follow Deacon and the others up Main Street on foot, because football stars can do whatever they want, and then I turned to Silas and said, "Great, now it looks like I'm your chauffeur."

"Yes, it does, Jeeves," Silas said, then he turned to the girls in the blue Eagle Talon next to us and said, "He's my chauffeur. I'm extraordinarily rich."

Before I could remind Silas we were in a Buick, not a Bentley, someone called my name, and I turned to see Becca Walsh smiling at me from the back seat of a red Ford Probe.

"Where were you last night?" Becca asked. "I thought we had an arrangement."

"Becca, hey, sorry … I … my mom said I could only … I'll be there next Friday. I promise."

Becca smiled. "That's what they all say." Then she pointed toward the backseat and asked, "Are you chauffeuring Silas tonight?"

"Jackson was with us, but supposedly, some girl in a Chevy Blazer wanted to meet him."

Becca raised a skeptical eyebrow, and I shrugged.

"Well, have fun tonight," Becca said with a wink, as the car she was in moved on, "but don't forget, you're mine."

"I won't forget," I said then turned to check on Silas, who'd just made the girls in the Talon laugh with a Grey Poupon joke. He was about to talk them into pulling over, so we could talk and 'stuff', but a commotion up ahead distracted us, and in unison, we both said, "Oh shit!"

Many things go through your mind when you see your best friend running down a crowded street wearing only his tighty whities, first and foremost, 'Thank God that's not me.'

Jackson jumped into the passenger seat, sinking low into the floorboard, and Silas deadpanned, "Looks like things went well with the girl in the Blazer."

"The sons of bitches," Jackson yelled, "they got me in Marshall's truck and stripped me down and threw me back out on Main Street."

I stifled a laugh, and Jackson screamed at me that it wasn't funny, which was patently false, but I can understand his struggle to see the funny side.

"Just get me out of here, okay?" Jackson begged, and I tried, but in the bumper to bumper traffic of Main Street, going any-where fast was impossible, so for the next half hour, we creeped down the road, past all the cars Jackson had just sprinted by in his skivvies, and more than a few people stopped and got out for a look at the boy in briefs hiding in the floorboard of a 1992 Buick Roadmaster.

We spent the rest of that night in Silas's garage, playing NHLPA '93 on Sega. Well, Silas and I played Sega. Jackson, wearing a Dr. Dre T-shirt and some sweatpants Silas let him borrow, spent the next two hours inventively combining curse words while pummeling a punching bag hanging in the corner.

It's a night I'll always remember, not because it was the only time I ever cruised Main Street or because I saw my friend sprinting half-naked through a teenage traffic jam, but because minutes before curfew, as 16-bit Mario Lemieux lay bleeding on the ice, Jackson first gave us the idea of bringing down Deacon Cassburn.

ACT II

Chapter Six

"Brinks, get your candy ass over here."

I'm a songwriter, so my imagination pays my bills—or at least it used to. And yet, six months ago, I couldn't have imagined a future where I'd attend another Rome High School football game. Perhaps a lack of imagination explains why I hadn't written a new song in decades, because here I was, paying five bucks and walking through the gates of the Colosseum, and there was Deacon Cassburn, telling me where to get my candy ass. Marshall Ford, who I'd last seen twenty-three years ago half-naked on the balcony rail of a Montgomery hotel room, was with him, as was Fletcher Morgan and the rest of the now defunct Rome Quarterback Club. Men who preferred watching games while leaning against the South end zone fence, because they believed themselves a bit too important to sit in the bleachers among the commoners. Well, that, and they could mix bourbon into their Cokes from the privacy of Deacon's truck, which was always parked behind the goal post. I was there to see Becca, but I couldn't just ignore the waving hoard, so I walked over, and after receiving back slaps and handshakes, joined them along the chain link fence as they stared out at the only green grass in Rome.

The grass wasn't real. It was monofilament polyethylene fibers, installed two years ago for half a million dollars.

Deacon gave me the place of honor at his right hand, and throwing an arm around me, said, "Brinks, you've been in town for days. Why haven't you been to see your friend who loves you? We are still friends, ain't we, Brinks?"

I could smell the bourbon on his breath and assumed the alcohol was inquiring about my lack of visits, not Deacon. The closest thing we'd ever shared to even a friendly gesture was a reciprocal shake of our heads at a party twenty-three years ago. We even had what you could loosely describe as a fight, until Becca broke it up.

"Sorry, man," I said, "I've just had so much going on with Mom that I—"

"We was sorry to hear about your mama, Brinks," Deacon said, squeezing me with the arm he still had around my shoulders. "We all thought a great deal of her. She was a fine lady."

"Well, she's still alive," I said, "just on hospice."

"Right," Deacon said, not the least bit embarrassed, and when he took his arm off my shoulder, I saw the holster under his sport coat. He must have noticed the look on my face because Deacon said, "Did Trajan not tell you? Rome is an open-carry campus, Brinks. If you ain't packin', you're the only teacher who ain't."

While I tried and failed to think of a reply to that, most of the students filed past us onto the field, forming a spirit tunnel for the team to run through, and I asked no one in particular, "Were we ever that young?"

"Hell, Brinks, you still look young," Deacon said and slapped Marshall Ford's belly. "But we've all gotten old and fat, ain't we, Marshall?"

"I was always fat," Marshall said, "but I've sure as shit gotten old."

Farther down the fence, Fletcher Morgan said, "I ain't fat," and spat on the ground.

"Because he takes enough Percocet to kill a horse," Deacon whispered to me, and I believed him.

The students on the field and the crowd in the bleachers roared, and I turned to see the double doors to the locker room opened wide and backlit for dramatic effect.

"What's this?" I asked Deacon, who, like the rest of the Rome Quarterback Club, hadn't turned around to watch whatever was about to happen.

Before Deacon could answer, the silhouetted form of Jackson Crowder stepped into the doorway, and the crowd showered him with noise. Someone unseen flipped on a smoke machine, and just as he faded from view, Jackson Crowder burst through the fog, followed by his team, through the victory banner and onto the field where they jumped and shouted and head-butted each other as football teams are wont to do.

I shook my head and said, "So the team doesn't mind that their coach breaks through the victory banner for them? I always thought that was half the reason anyone ever played football to begin with."

"He started doing that last year," Deacon said, glaring across the field where Jackson stood with arms crossed over his purple windbreaker, "and nobody said shit. Jackson could stab these people's mamas and they wouldn't hold it against him."

"Well, I did read in the paper that Jackson's had Rome in the playoffs for three straight seasons."

"Playoffs," Deacon shouted. "Brinks, the playoffs are our God-given right. Gettin' in the playoffs ain't no damn accomplishment; it's the starting point for Rome. If these fools are satisfied with the playoffs, then their settling asses are what's wrong with the world. Ain't nobody striving for excellence anymore. Playoffs. Shit." He motioned toward the statute of Ronald J. Pumphrey behind us and said, "The state championship. Coach P won the state damn championship." At this, Marshall and Fletcher raised their state championship rings toward the graven image of their old coach, and Deacon said to me, "That's a man worth worshiping, Brinks, not the great Jackson Crowder and his 0-3 playoff record."

I considered pointing out that Coach Pumphrey would not have won the state damn championship without Jackson Crowder, but that felt hazardous to my health among this crew, so instead I just said, "Weird," more about being at a Rome game again than anything else, but Deacon heard it a different way, and he looked at me and said, "You see it, don't you, Brinks?"

"See what?"

"What's going on here in Rome, with Jackson," Deacon said. "Hell, I played ball at 'Bama, Marsh played at Auburn, you're a damn rock star. Mandy Duke's little sister is on Fox News. A lot of people from Rome have done a lot of cool shit, Brinks, but this town goes and throws up a statue of that dickface." He pointed across the field to the statue of Jackson in the North end zone, the end zone where Rome Quarterback Club members used to stand and watch games. I didn't have to inquire as to why they switched ends. "They throw up a statue for that dickface," Deacon repeated, "and why? 'Cause he crossed the road without looking both ways and got run over by immortality. Shit. You guys remember when we went to Atlanta on that field trip in seventh grade and Jackson pissed his pants?" I laughed and Deacon said, "It's true, this god pissed his pants. Jackson was nothing, Brinks. Hell, even senior year he was third string. Now he dyes his damn hair and works out a little and people worship at his feet." Deacon motioned toward the rest of the Quarterback Club and said, "Our daddies, they'd have burnt this school to the ground before they let Coach P get away with half the shit Jackson Crowder's tried to pull off."

I didn't reply, because I preferred not to delve into the politics of Rome football, but Deacon wasn't finished. "Hell," he said, "changing grades is one thing. I know I didn't deserve some of the grades I got in school."

"I earned every D I ever got," Fletcher said and spat on the ground.

That was debatable but not something I cared to debate.

Deacon laughed at Fletcher and said to me, "But bumping a

test score up a letter grade now and then to keep a player eligible is one thing, Brinks. You know how it is around here. Some of these boys, football and memories of football is all they're ever gonna have. To take that away because they failed chemistry is a sin. Ain't like they're ever gonna use chemistry anyhow."

"Mark Porter used chemistry," Marshall said, laughing to himself.

"Yeah," Deacon said, "and now he's on a ten-year paid vacation in Atmore."

"Wait, what?" I asked.

"Sheriff busted him running a meth lab in his mama's basement. Hell, it's probably safer not to teach these kids chemistry. But like I was saying, Brinks, changing a test score or two is just part of the game. It don't hurt nobody, and nobody is gonna turn you in, because everybody else is doing it. But what's going on now is systematic. Jackson's got every teacher at Rome involved, and I can tell you, the other schools in the county won't stand for it. They'll turn us in, and when the state finds out how big the operation is, they'll shut down this football program, and then what'll we have?"

Conspiracy theories at the local level aren't nearly as popular as the vast global ones, in part because they are much easier to debunk. "Deacon," I said, "I teach at Rome, and no one has asked me to change grades."

Deacon stared at me. "Not yet."

Rome, who'd taken the kickoff and marched down the field in six plays, was now on the ten-yard-line in front of us, and I hoped proximity to the action would shut Deacon up for a bit, but he kept on about Jackson. "Hell, grade fixing ain't the half of it, Brinks. Some of the horse steroids he's got the team taking ain't even legal in Mexico."

Rome's quarterback lofted a perfect fade into the back corner of the end zone where his receiver made a diving catch. The home crowd went wild, but none of the men standing along the fence even clapped, so to avoid awkwardness, I stopped clapping too.

"Wait, that kid is in my class," I said, after the quarterback took off his helmet and jogged to the sideline. "Rome is starting a freshman quarterback?"

Deacon chuckled. "Who, Kyler? Naw, his parents held him back a year for sports, then he failed kindergarten. He should be a junior."

"Wait, he failed—good lord," I said then flinched as the sky filled with celebratory fireworks after the extra point split the uprights. "When did Rome get pyrotechnics?" I asked.

"Those were the brainchild of the great Jackson Crowder," Deacon said. "He thought it was safer than fans shooting their own Roman candles."

Of course it was safer, but I held my tongue.

"We're gonna have to shake his ass, Brinks, or worse days are coming."

I didn't reply, and after Rome kicked off, Deacon said, "You know, Brinks, we'd love to have you at a Quarterback Club meeting one Thursday night."

If given enough time, I could easily list over one million meetings I'd rather attend than the Rome Quarterback Club, but on the spot, all I could muster was, "Yeah, that sounds fun." A few minutes later, I excused myself to the bathroom and never went back.

~ ~ ~

I walked the length of the home bleachers, looking for Becca while trying not to look like I was looking for her, all the while hoping she, or anyone not affiliated with the Rome Quarterback Club, would recognize me and ask me to sit with them. No one did though, so I found a seat and watched the rest of the first half by myself.

Silas was in the press box, calling plays into his headset, which were then relayed to the quarterback through an absurd combination of hand signals and random images on giant placards. After big plays, and there were plenty of them for Rome, I'd turn around to catch Silas's reaction, but he was always calm and already sending in the next play. He really was good at this, which reminded me that I was not very good at what I did, at least not anymore, and then I didn't want to be there anymore. I stood up to leave, and that's when I saw Becca walk by on her way to the concession stand. I decided I needed a Coke.

I caught her just as she joined the back of the line and cleared my throat twice, but she didn't notice, so I tapped her shoulder and she turned and smiled and said, "Marcus, you made it!" She hugged me again and, when she pulled away, said, "I still can't believe you're back in Rome. Oh my gosh, look at my hand shaking. Marcus, I don't typically run into famous rock stars in the concession stand line."

"I'm not a famous rock star. I'm a forty-year-old single teacher." I cringe after saying this because Becca was a forty-year-old single teacher as well, but to my relief, she laughed and said, "Who isn't? But hey, the Quarterback Club did vote me Rome's most eligible bachelorette at last year's Valentine's Banquet."

We moved up in line and Becca said, "Now tell me, Mr. Brinks, how was your first week of school?"

"I survived."

"That's my goal most weeks. Seriously though, your students must love having a rock star for a teacher."

I smiled and said, "There are literally two kids in school who care. One guy who never takes off his trench coat and this crazy girl who takes selfies with me every day. The rest of them would have no idea who I even was if their parents hadn't told them. All of that happened before they were even born. So, you teach at the middle school?"

"Sixth grade," she said. "Thirty sweaty, smelly, puberty-going-through monsters. They're so awkward, it's kind of awesome."

"God, it's hard even to remember those days," I said.

"I know. When'd we get so old, Marcus?"

"We're not old. Deacon just told me I look young."

"He must want something from you," Becca said then ordered three Diet Cokes and three hotdogs and waited on me to order my Coke. I followed her to the condiment station and she said, "The team looks pretty good this year," which was an understatement, considering the 42-0 halftime score.

"Not according to the concerned citizens of Rome standing along the fence."

Becca sighed. "And what imaginary threat to our republic concerns them on such a beautiful night?"

"Mostly him," I said, pointing up at Jackson's statue, and Becca shook her head.

"Before Jackson came back, we won one game in three seasons. I don't know what those idiots want."

"Access, best I can tell. He closed practice, and he doesn't come to their Thursday night meetings, and, well, he's still the most famous person in Rome, isn't he? Deacon played for Alabama, but no one cares about him. It must drive him crazy."

"He walked-on at Bama for one season," Becca said, "and he never even saw the field. Why should anyone care about him?"

We walked over to the fence to watch the half-time shows. Riverton's band was now on the field. They were small and sounded like a room full of injured birds, but one of their majorettes lit her baton on fire and the crowd roared. "That looks dangerous," I said.

"It's not," Becca assured me. "You just can't wear pantyhose or hairspray."

"How do you even know that?"

"My sister was head majorette, so I tried out freshman year."

"No you didn't."

She gave me a playful shove and said, "What, you don't think I could pull off sequins?"

I held up my hands in surrender, and it occurred to me I didn't know much about Becca pre-senior year. Or post-senior year for that matter. I tried to remedy the latter.

"So, do you have some muscle-headed boyfriend who'll break my nose when he sees us talking?"

Becca smiled and said, "No, no boyfriend, muscle-headed or otherwise. You'll see this isn't a great town for singles, though it's fun to swipe through Tinder sometimes to see who's cheating on their wives. What about you? Is there a lucky lady waiting for you back in the islands? Or do you just date groupies these days?"

"No," I said. "No lucky lady. Or groupies, for that matter."

Rome's Marching Legion wrapped up their halftime show, and both teams returned to the field, and Becca said, "I'd better get back to my seat. God forbid I let Mom and Dad's hotdogs get cold. We can make room for you though. Come sit with us."

"That's okay," I said. "I need to get home and check on Mom." This wasn't true, but the last time I'd seen Becca's parents it had been, well, awkward to say the least, and I didn't relish the thought of sitting next to them for the next ninety minutes.

"Oh, of course," she said, grabbing my hand. "But hey, next week's game is at Hornby, so if you're free, maybe we can have dinner and catch up?"

"Yeah," I said, "I'd love that."

Then I walked home, smiling like the fool I was.

"The fear, when a songwriter spills this much blood, is they've none left to spill."

—*Pitchfork*, 10.0 review of *Dear Brutus* by Dear Brutus, November 23, 1997

Chapter Seven

"You guys coming to Macedonia tomorrow night?" Jackson asked Silas and me as we played *Bill Walsh College Football '95* in Silas's parents' garage. I was losing, 35-7 in the second quarter, because Silas was already tinkering with the hurry-up no-huddle vertical passing game he'd one day perfect. Silas and I looked at each other, then at Jackson, and shook our heads no in unison.

There is an image, often propagated by film and television, of entire towns following their high school team's bus past the city limit sign and down some winding country road toward a distant foe, but that image is a lie. Sure, some Rome fans went to road games, and fans from other towns came to Rome, but unless the game was between close rival schools, visiting crowds were typically sparse and composed mostly of parents and girl-friends.

"Fine," Jackson said, knocking the controller from Silas's hand and allowing me to cut his lead to three touchdowns, "it's not like I visited you in Children's Hospital after you were diagnosed."

"Yeah, because my nurses were off the hook," Silas said, flipping Jackson off.

"That's true," Jackson said then turned to me and asked, "You're not going either?"

I shrugged and said, "I don't even know where Macedonia is."

"It's near Glencoe."

"That doesn't help."

"Fine," Jackson said, grabbing an iron from Silas's dad's golf bag and making practice swings, "but I plan to pick off another pass tomorrow night, and this time, I'm definitely going to high-step, and you'll both miss it."

"We'll see it on SportsCenter," Silas said, and Jackson knocked the controller out of his hand again, but this time, I couldn't take advantage.

"What the hell are you two going to do if you don't go to the game?" Jackson asked.

"We could go to Main Street," I said to Silas, who shook his head and said, "No one goes on Friday nights."

"My sister heard they're shutting Main Street down," Jackson said.

"Bullshit," Silas said. "That rumor starts every fall."

Jackson shrugged and Silas said, "I can't speak for Brinks, though I assume he has an evening of masturbatory delight planned, but my folks are taking me to tour Newberry College."

"Newberry College?" Jackson barked.

"Yeah, it's in South Carolina," Silas said.

"I don't care where it is," Jackson said. "We're supposed to go to Alabama together."

"Calm down, Beavis," Silas said. "We're still going to Alabama. Mom and Dad met at Newberry, and they've always wanted me to see it, that's all. It's no big deal."

"Fine," Jackson said, "are you visiting a college too, Brinks?"

"No," I said. Truth was I hadn't given much thought to college. My mom was an accountant, she went to Auburn on scholarship, and up until sophomore year, she'd pushed me hard in school. But the whole Dad leaving for his secretary thing messed her up, and she no longer excelled at the finer points of parenting. I knew I wanted to go to college, preferably one far away from here, but how that would actually happen I did not know.

"Then why can't you go to Macedonia?" Jackson asked, and

it took me a moment to realize he was still talking about his stupid football game.

"I'm going to hang out with Mom," I said. "She's been acting weird lately, because of the divorce I think." I knew Jackson wouldn't give me shit about wanting to spend time with my upset mother, and he didn't.

"Yeah, that's fine," Jackson said, like I needed his permission not to drive to Macedonia and watch him ride the bench, then he knocked the controller from Silas's hand again, but this time, I somehow gave up a touchdown in the process.

~ ~ ~

"I don't feel like cooking tonight. Where do you want to eat?"

It was Friday evening, and I'd been lying on my bed in boxer shorts playing Mortal Kombat II since school let out three hours earlier.

"I don't know," I said to my mom, who hadn't cooked since we'd moved to Rome in July but apparently did want to eat, which I took as an improvement. "Taco Bell?"

"Marcus, when someone asks where you want to eat, they're assuming you won't suggest Taco Bell," Mom said then looked on in horror as Kung Lao used his hat to slice Johnny Cage in two. I put down the controller and said, "Fine, you pick a place."

"I will," she said. "We're leaving in ten minutes. Oh, and put on some pants. The nicer places around here require pants."

She picked Morrison's, a cafeteria-style restaurant in the Riverton Mall, where we were the youngest customers by at least sixty years. I ordered meatloaf, the first green vegetables I'd eaten in over a month, and a plate of jiggling blue Jell-O. Mom paid and I found a table and we ate in silence for a few minutes until she asked, "How's school going?"

I'd just finished my tenth day at Rome, and this was the first time she'd bothered to ask how things were going.

"Fine," I said, because that's all I ever said when she asked questions like that, which might explain why she rarely bothered to ask them.

"Just fine?" she asked.

"Yeah. I mean, everyone is football crazy, but no one is picking on me or anything." This was a lie, but the last thing I needed was her calling the school to narc on Deacon Cassburn for occasionally shoving me in the hallway.

"They were football obsessed when I went there too," Mom said. "Is Mrs. Sulla still teaching?"

"No, I don't think so."

"Mr. Ruga?"

"No. No Mr. Ruga."

My mom graduated from Rome twenty-six years ago, and odds were none of the teachers who taught her were still around, but she listed seven or eight more anyway. Then she delved into a story about her and some friends throwing eggs at houses one Halloween and how a policeman pulled them over, found ten dozen eggs in the trunk, but let them go because the mayor's son was driving the car. I'd stopped listening to her halfway through though, because that's when I noticed Becca Walsh and her parents having dinner across the room.

My mom laughed. "It was so stupid. We could have gone to jail for—Marcus, who are you looking at?" She turned and looked behind her, and before I could beg her to stop, Becca looked up from her plate and saw us both staring her way. "Shit," I said, and my mom slapped my hand. Then to my horror, Becca said something to her parents and walked our way while I prayed for an extinction-level asteroid.

"She's coming this way, Mom, so be cool. Okay? Please."

My mom winked in a decidedly uncool fashion just as Becca reached our table and said, "Hello, Marcus."

"Hey Becca," I said, and Mom coughed until I added, "This is my mom, Beverly Brinks. Mom, this is Becca Walsh. She's in my class at Rome."

"Nice to meet you, Mrs. Brinks," Becca said. "Your son is my Friday night boyfriend."

Mom raised an eyebrow and said, "Well, what are you doing here with me, Marcus? Shouldn't you two be on a date?"

I gave Mom my best please-shut-up look then turned to Becca who, much to my surprise, said, "Yes, we should be. You can pick me up at that table in five minutes. I drove separately, so I can take you home later. Nice to meet you, Mrs. Brinks. See you in five minutes, Marcus."

After Becca left the table, Mom looked at me and asked, "Why didn't you tell me you had a girlfriend?"

"Because it's a joke, Mom. She dates the quarterback, and he's busy on Friday nights, winning football games and stuff."

"Well," Mom said, less than discreetly looking back at Becca's table, "I think she likes you."

"Yeah, well, you thought Milli Vanilli were good singers."

Mom laughed and handed me a ten-dollar bill and said, "Have fun on your fake date."

~ ~ ~

"Relax your eyes."

"I'm trying!"

Becca and I left Morrison's, and we stopped at Riverton Art to stare at their display of 3D posters. Becca swore she saw all sorts of things in the images. I did not believe her.

"You have to look through the poster."

"You keep saying that, but what does it even mean?"

"Pretend you're looking at something behind the poster, something in the distance."

"That's what I'm doing. I think."

"And you don't see the waterfall? It's right there."

"You're lying," I said.

"You're hopeless," she said.

We walked on, wading through hordes of pre-teen guys at the mall for a baseball card show, and Becca said, "How cool are we, by the way, eating dinner with our parents on a Friday night."

"The coolest," I said, following her into Camelot Music. Becca took a pair of headphones off the new release tower and listened to a band called Toadies. She bobbed her head a little then said too loud, "This is really good, listen," but instead of

65

handing me the headphones, she just pulled one side off her face and had me lean in close enough to hear.

"Wait, is this about vampires?" I asked.

"I kind of hope so," she said. "If not, it's a little disturbing."

She smelled incredible, and I closed my eyes, not so much to enjoy Toadies, who were good, but because I might never be that close to Becca Walsh again, and I wanted to relish every second. However, by the time Toadies were asking if I wanted to die for the third time, I lost balance and stumbled backward into a CD rack, all but ruining the moment.

I used half my ten bucks to buy us both an Orange Julius, and we sipped them on our way to Aladdin's Castle, the mall's arcade, where I spent the rest of my money trying and failing to win Becca a stuffed cow from the claw machine.

"It's the thought that counts," Becca said, as the useless claw lifted the cow six inches before dropping it for the last time.

Later, after we spent ten minutes in the bookstore finding Waldo, we stopped to see one of her friends who worked at Hibbett Sporting Goods then sat on a bench under a ficus tree near the center fountain and people watched.

"Why didn't you go to Macedonia?" I asked her.

"Because there's nothing in the world I hate more than watching football," she said.

"But you're dating the quarterback."

"Not tonight," Becca said and leaned her head on my shoulder. I knew then I was going to get myself killed.

She kept her head on my shoulder and said, "I tell Deacon my parents won't let me drive that far, and I tell my parents I want to spend time with them. Deacon is none the wiser, plus I score some points with Mom and Dad. Besides, I'll see him later tonight, and he'll tell me all about the game in excruciating detail. Then he'll tell me all about it again on Saturday, then on Sunday, and Monday."

The mall closed at nine, but we stayed on the bench because Becca wanted to see if they'd lock us inside. A security guard walked over and begged us to leave though, so we did. Becca's red, two-door Saturn waited outside Morrison's, and we left the mall, driving aimlessly through Riverton, passing street after street of beautiful old homes.

"I'd love to live in an old house like that one day," Becca said.

"In Riverton?"

"No, not in Riverton. Other cities have old houses too, you know."

"They're so big though. They'd take forever to clean. And can you imagine the upkeep?"

"Keep your practicality out of my dreams, Marcus."

We crossed Main Street, which was empty as promised, before winding our way up the mountain toward something called Winona Falls.

"Have you ever been here?" Becca asked as we parked.

I shook my head no, and she explained, "Legend has it, a Cherokee girl named Winona wanted to marry a boy from another tribe, but her father, the chief, wouldn't allow it, so in overly dramatic teenage fashion, she jumped off the falls to her death."

"That's terrible," I said.

"I'm pretty sure it didn't happen," Becca said as we walked through the entrance toward the falls, where a larger-than-life statue of a Native American woman stood, forever frozen mid-leap, "but it makes a nice tourist attraction."

We crossed the bridge over the creek and sat on a bench listening to water rush over the hundred-foot falls. "So," Becca asked after a moment, "how do you like Rome so far?"

"It's okay, I guess."

"Yeah, it sucks," Becca said, and I laughed.

"This is nice though," I said, motioning toward the falls but hoping Becca knew I meant the night in general.

"This has been nice," she said. "If it were always this nice, I wouldn't be in such a hurry to leave for college."

"Where are you going?" I asked.

"I don't know," Becca said. "My stupid sister went to Jacksonville State and lived at home. Of course, Mom and Dad worship the ground she walks on, so I can see why she didn't want to leave. I'm going somewhere far away though."

"Silas is visiting some Lutheran college in South Carolina this weekend," I told her.

"Way farther away than South Carolina," Becca said, and I got the feeling she didn't think of college so much as further education but education farther away.

"What about you?" she asked.

"I don't know," I said, "but far away doesn't sound bad."

Becca glanced at her watch, and I glanced at mine. It was a quarter past ten. "Well, Friday Night Boyfriend," she said, "I'd better get you home. Deacon expects me at the field house when the bus gets back. God, I hope they won. If not, he'll be in a shit mood."

I hadn't thought about Deacon in a while, and hearing his name reminded me I was not out with my girlfriend, but someone else's, and my mood darkened. Then I shouldn't have but asked, "Why do you date him? He's kind of a dick."

Becca looked at me for what felt like a full minute before finally smiling and saying, "He can be kind of a dick. And Rome kind of sucks. But he does worship me, and socially speaking, there are some benefits to dating the starting quarterback. I sort of figure, if I'm going to live in this hell hole, I might as well be the queen. Does that make me a terrible person?"

"Yes," I said, and she stuck her tongue out at me, and when I smiled, she touched my arm and said, "Thanks for a lovely evening, Friday Night Boyfriend," then she kissed my cheek.

We drove home, blasting Green Day and singing along, and she even walked me to my door. But there was no second kiss, just a hug and a promise to talk to me on Monday.

A promise she broke.

Chapter Eight

"Son, I do appreciate the gesture, but you don't have to wear cologne for my benefit."

My mother looked like a child in the king-sized bed she'd slept in mostly alone for the last twenty-three years. She was sixty-seven, not old, but she wouldn't see her sixty-eighth birthday next summer. Her doctor told me privately not to count on Christmas.

"Wait, can you smell my cologne?" I asked Mom, straightening my tie in her dresser mirror. "It's not too strong, is it?"

"Not as strong as middle school, when you'd take baths in Drakkar Noir," Mom said and coughed out a laugh. "Marcus, do you have a date?"

"I might," I said, and with considerable effort, she sat up to scrutinize my clothes.

"You could lose the tie," she said. "And you really might want to dab off some of that cologne."

I pulled off the tie and tried to soak up some of the cologne with a damp washcloth from her bathroom. "It's been a while," I said. "This is my first date in … wow, three years I think."

"Jim Morrison never had trouble finding women," my mother teased.

"Yeah," I said, "and he died at twenty-seven."

Mom shrugged, and I asked how she felt.

"Never better," she lied. "If your date has a brother, maybe we could double."

"A sister," I said. "But seriously, you're feeling okay? You don't mind if I'm out for a few hours?"

"Marcus James Brinks, are you asking if I think I might die while you're out gallivanting around town?"

"What? No. I—"

"Marcus, stop lying; you're terrible at it. Of course that's what you're asking, and if you'd like an honest answer, I feel shitty. But I've felt shitty for months now, so I've no reason to believe the next three shitty hours will do me in."

Rita Bell, a former classmate of mine at Rome, and one of my mother's hospice nurses, entered the room, and Mom added, "But if I do, I'll make sure Rita doesn't call and ruin your dinner."

"If you do what, Mrs. Brinks?" Rita asked, setting down a tray of food for my mother to ignore.

"Shuffle off this mortal coil," my mother said, and Rita laughed.

"Don't worry, Marcus," Rita said. "I'll keep her alive till curfew."

"Curfew?" I said. "What if things go well and this girl invites me back to her place?"

Mother put her fingers in her ears and said, "Take me now, Jesus."

"Oh, I get it," I said, checking my hair in the mirror. "You're free to make me uncomfortable, but I can't return the favor."

"Yes, Marcus, because morphine and making people uncomfortable are the only perks of dying. When you're dying, you can make people uncomfortable too. It's the circle of life."

"Fair enough," I said and re-did my tie because the shirt didn't look right without one.

Rita fluffed my mom's pillows and cleaned the nightstand and asked, "So who is this hot date with anyway?"

I mumbled something, and Mom and Rita looked up in unison.

"Who?" Mom asked.

"Becca Walsh," I said, and Rita, who by now must have known all our family secrets, raised an eyebrow and turned on one heel to leave the room.

"Marcus, never mind everything I told you," Mom said. "I'm going to die in the next hour or so. You'd better cancel your date. You'll want to be here to listen to my deathbed confessions."

"Very funny," I said.

"Seriously, I plan to tell you where I buried my treasure and how to contact your long-lost sister in New Mexico."

"Mom."

"Her name is Traci. You'll like her."

"Mom."

"I'm not joking, Marcus. I can see the Reaper. He's standing right behind you, choking on your cologne."

"Mom, we are the only two single people our age in Rome."

"That hasn't slowed her down."

I sighed. "What does that—never mind. I don't want to know. It's dinner, Mom. Just dinner."

I kissed my mother on the forehead and said, "Don't wait up."

"I'll have Rita call you when I die."

I stopped in the doorway and said, "I'm turning off my phone."

"Don't forget your curfew."

"I already have."

"Traci never treated me this way."

"Yeah, yeah."

~ ~ ~

Becca lived in a two-bedroom cottage on Eagle Court, a couple blocks from Rome High School. A tall oak with a tire swing hung from its thickest branch shaded her front yard, and oleanders were growing outside her door. I parked on the street and, walking to her porch, felt the immediate effects of gastro-intestinal Lepidoptera, more commonly known as butterflies in your stomach. Despite what I told my dear mother, this was a date, and I hadn't been on a date in some time, which was reason enough for nerves. But this wasn't just any date. This was a date with Becca Walsh, the girl who'd, since I met her half a lifetime ago, owned considerable real estate in my mind. My stomach churned accordingly.

After a deep breath, then six more, I knocked on the front door and heard footsteps, the turn of a lock, then saw Becca hopping on one foot while slipping a shoe onto the other. She wore a low-cut summer dress, and eventually my eyes drifted up to her smiling face, and she asked, "A tie, just for me?" before inviting me inside. "Make yourself at home," she said, disappearing around the corner. "I need two minutes, maybe three."

I snooped around Becca's living room while she finished doing whatever it is women do when they look ready to go but are apparently not. There were half a dozen paintings of London in her living room. One of Big Ben, another of Trafalgar Square, a big one of Tower Bridge over the couch adorned with Union Jack pillows. "You must love London," I said to her through the wall.

She ducked her head out of the bathroom door and said, "I do. Every time T.J. Maxx has a sale on home goods, I can't help myself."

"It's wonderful, isn't it?" I asked, then added, "London," in case she thought I was talking about T.J. Maxx.

"I've never been," she said through the wall, "but God I want to."

"We spent a few days there after our show at the Royal Albert Hall, but I never made it back."

"I'm going one day," Becca said, "maybe after I retire. You know I can retire from Rome in six years."

"No you can't. Wait, for real?"

"I'm forty, Marcus, and I started teaching at Rome when

72

I was twenty-two. Six more years makes twenty-four, and I've banked enough sick leave to retire a year early."

On a bookcase in the corner was a copy of our album on vinyl, and while I wondered if she'd set it out for me to see, I noticed her Rome yearbooks stacked neatly on the bottom shelf. I picked up the one from senior year—I never received my copy—and flipped through the pages until I found prom.

"Wait, the prom song was "Love Me Tomorrow" by Chicago? That song was old even then."

Becca walked out of the bathroom, ready to leave. She was every bit as stunning as she was senior year, and I felt sorry for the pubescent boys in her class who were expected to focus on social studies in the presence of this woman.

"I know," she said, holding up her hands to show her innocence. "It came down to either Chicago, or that Mazzy Star song, "Fade Into You." Mazzy lost."

I laughed and opened her door, and we stepped outside into the pink August sunset. As we walked under the oak toward my car, I asked, "Who'd you go to prom with senior year?" even though I thought I knew.

"Chase Malone," she said. "No wait, that was the Christmas dance. Prom was Brent Holdbrooks."

"You went to the Christmas dance with Chase Malone?" I asked. "The drum major?"

"Yeah," Becca said as I opened the car door for her. "We started dating right after the state championship game. I think we actually broke up at the Christmas dance or maybe the next week. Gosh, it's hard to remember."

This was a lot to process in the time it took to walk around my car. The math didn't add up, but maybe Becca remembered things wrong. I made a mental note to bring it up again, without being too weird about school dances two decades ago, and as I climbed into my car, I asked, "Does Trevi's sound good?"

Trevi's was a BBQ joint on the Coosa River, and along with Pantheon Pizza and the WigWam (a Native American themed burger joint that flew in the face of our town's ancient Rome mo-tif), was one of three restaurants in Rome without a drive-thru and playground. She said it sounded delicious, and twenty min-utes later, after a waitress brought our fried pickle appetizer, Bec-ca asked, "So, what's it like sleeping in your old bedroom again?"

"Really weird," I said. "Mom never changed a thing. Like, nothing. My Hakeem Olajuwon and Weezer posters are still on the walls, my Warren Moon toys are still on the dresser, my old acoustic guitar is in the corner right where I left it. I checked, just out of curiosity I promise, and even my *Playboys* were still under the mattress."

Becca slapped my hand and said, "You left your *Playboys*? Wow, you really were in a hurry to get out of Rome."

I smiled. "So what did people think when I left?"

"Rumor was your dad offered to pay for college and buy you a new truck."

I shook my head. "No. He did pay for college. One year at least. But no new truck. Mom and I just had some drama … so I moved back in with Dad."

Becca flashed a sad smile and asked, "How is your mother?"

"Not great," I said. "She still has her sense of humor, but her doctor doesn't think she'll make it to Christmas."

"Oh, Marcus, I'm so sorry. She's too young."

"Thanks," I said, and after we ordered our barbecue, I asked, "How are your parents?"

"Same as always," Becca said. "My sister married a surgeon, and they've got a picket fence and a minivan and three perfect kids, so by comparison, I'm just as big a failure as I've always been. But Mom did stop asking when I'd get remarried about five years ago, and we've actually gotten along better since then."

Thanks to my mother, I knew Becca married a guy she met at Troy, and they moved to Huntsville after college. My mother also told me all the reasons she'd heard for their divorce five years later, but in the pantheon of Roman rumors, I ranked them all high in imagination and low in accuracy.

"How'd you never get married?" Becca asked after a moment.

"I thought I'd marry the girl I dated in college," I lied, "but it all sort of fell apart."

"*The* girl?" Becca asked. "The one that inspired it all?"

"Yeah," I lied again.

"Where was she from?"

"Hell, I think."

Becca laughed, and I said, "After her, things got weird. I can't even remember my last real date before this."

Becca frowned. "Wait, Marcus, did you think this was a real date?"

Evander Holyfield could not have punched me harder in the stomach, but before I could answer, Becca laughed and grabbed my hand and said, "This is my first date in a while too, Marcus. I'm glad it's with you."

Barbecue and second beers arrived, and I asked Becca what I'd missed in the last twenty years.

"Not much," she said. "Coach P finally retired in 2010, and the team struggled and the town sort of lost its way for a while. Then Jackson moved back, and, well, it's silly, an entire town getting so much of its identity from a game played by kids, but what else is there in Rome?"

"Do you ever talk to Jackson?"

I'm not sure why I asked this. I didn't want to talk about Jackson, and if she did talk to him, I didn't want to know.

"Rarely. He's so busy. His oldest boy is in my class, so I see his wife a lot. They are such sweet people."

"Deacon doesn't seem to think much of him," I said.

"Well," Becca whispered, "Deacon is an asshole."

I laughed and she said, "Seriously though, Deacon and Fletcher and all those guys, they're pathetic. If they ran Jackson off and hired some loser who couldn't win two games a year but let them watch practice, they'd think they'd done the town a service. You should stay as far away from those guys as you can. Their bitterness is contagious."

After dinner, we sat on the boardwalk bench behind Trevi's, watching pontoon boats float down the Kusa. My phone buzzed with a text. It was from Rita and said, "Your mother wanted me to tell you she died and that she is leaving all her earthly belongings to someone named Traci."

I laughed to myself and noticed Becca had left her hand on the bench between us. It took me a minute to read the sign and another five to convince the more apprehensive parts of my brain that it was a good idea, but eventually, I reached out and took her hand in mine.

"You know," I said after a moment, "it's really beautiful here. Why were we ever in such a hurry to leave?"

"Because hating your hometown is like teenage angst 101," Becca said. "But it's not a bad place. Better now that a certain someone came back."

I smiled and squeezed her hand, then the speakers at Trevi's back patio, which were always turned to 100.3 FM, '90s Hitz & More, played "Fade into You." I stood up, held out my hand, and said, "Becca Walsh, will you go to prom with me?"

Becca took my hand, and we slow danced on the boardwalk, while above, enough people from Rome watched to assure we'd be the topic of Monday's grapevine.

"People will talk," I said, as Becca put her head on my shoulder and insisted on dancing to the Boyz II Men song that followed Mazzy Star.

"Let 'em," she said, and we danced until the DJ played that weird Crash Test Dummies song and ruined the mood.

"Following the members of Dear Brutus around Manhattan the week of their network television debut, their camaraderie is apparent. But perhaps more obvious is that this is Marcus Brinks's band. 'Oh yeah, this is his thing,' said drummer Porter Clayton. 'All that pain was in Marcus's head; we just helped him get it out.'"

—*NME*, "Masters of Their Fate,"
February 15, 1998

Chapter Nine

Despite her promise, Becca didn't talk to me the Monday after our night at Winona Falls. In Mr. Galba's world history class, she strolled right past me in her sunflower babydoll dress, taking the seat behind her asshole boyfriend. The scene repeated itself on Tuesday, and Jackson, the only person I'd told about the previous Friday night, gave me knowing looks both times.

"I swear, we really hung out," I said to him at lunch that day.

"I don't care," he said, channeling his best Tommy Lee Jones.

On Wednesday, Becca ignored me again, but Jackson didn't take notice. No one took much notice of anything that day. The school buzzed with peculiar excitement. An unspoken anticipation, shared only by those with Y chromosomes, while the girls of Rome looked on with open disgust.

During homeroom, I asked Jackson what was going on, and his eyes widened, and he shook his head to discourage any follow-ups. I wasn't about to ask some random jock for fear of them stuffing me into a locker. And I couldn't ask some random girl that day either, for fear of the same. But I cornered Jackson after homeroom, and he whispered, "Dude, just meet me at my truck after school."

~ ~ ~

"Now can you tell me what the hell is going on?" I asked Jackson as we drove into Riverton, blasting Oasis through speakers that rattled your fillings.

"Nope," he shouted and turned the music up even louder, "you'll see soon enough."

I'd never seen Main Street during the day when the shops were open, and Jackson parked in front of a place called Alverson's Sundries.

"What are sundries?" I asked.

"I don't know," Jackson said, "but you need to stay in the truck. It'll look suspicious if we go in together."

"Wait, are you about to rob Alverson of his sundries? Jackson, I don't want any part of this."

"Just stay in the truck," Jackson repeated and ducked into the store.

While waiting outside, I saw two guys I recognized from school walk inside and another walk out holding a brown paper sack. Minutes later, Jackson jumped into the truck and tossed his own brown paper sack into my lap.

"What's this?" I asked.

"Sundries," Jackson said. "Open it."

Jackson backed out of his parking space, letting another car full of guys from Rome pull in, and I opened the sack, pulling out a glossy magazine with a Tanqueray Gin advertisement on the back. I flipped the magazine over, and on the cover smiled a topless woman, boobs in hands, with bunny ears atop her bleached blonde head.

"*Playboy?*" I asked.

"Yes!" Jackson said, with an enthusiasm he typically reserved for describing his interception against Pinkerton.

"You're joking, right?" I asked, holding up the magazine then quickly putting it down because the woman in the car next to us at the red light noticed and shook her head disapprovingly. "This is what everyone was so weird about today?" I asked. "A *Playboy*? Jackson, I've got three issues of *Playboy* at home." In fact, everyone I knew had at least three issues of *Playboy* at home, hidden under a mattress, or at the bottom of a box of baseball cards, or buried in the backyard if their mothers were particularly nosy. Some guys stole them from their father's closet, others had older brothers, who charged interest rates similar to those of banks in third-world countries, make their purchases, and some guys randomly stumbled over discarded issues in the woods, like smut grew on vines in the wild. But most towns had a store whose proprietor played fast and loose with local minimum age of purchase and possession laws, and young men with wispy mustaches could purchase copies for themselves. Alverson's Sundries was apparently that store in Riverton.

"Freaking out over a damn *Playboy*," I said. "If I'd known everyone in Rome was so repressed, I'd have shared my copies with you. You guys do know channel 99 sometimes shows scrambled boobs, don't you?"

"It's not just any *Playboy*, dick-ear," Jackson said, pointing at the cover. "Look."

I looked, and next to the boob-holding rabbit-eared woman were the words, "Girls of the SEC."

Jackson stopped in the back of the Walmart parking lot and grabbed the magazine from me. He flipped through the pages like a speed-reader, and as I watched the blur of skin and advertisements go by, he mumbled to himself, "Alabama, Auburn, Georgia, Kentucky, there! Mississippi State!" Jackson held the magazine for me to see, and there, wearing a pair of maroon Mississippi State socks and nothing else, was a pretty blonde studying in the library.

"Don't you worry," I asked, "that this is going to warp your sense of the female form … and college libraries?"

Jackson shook his head in disappointment and held the magazine where I could no longer see it.

"What?" I asked. "I mean, she's hot and she's naked, and that's great and all, but like I told you, I've got three copies of *Playboy* at home."

"She," Jackson said, holding up the magazine again and pointing to the girl in socks, "went to Rome."

"Wait, for real?"

81

"Yeah, for real. Her name is Tiffany Thompson. She was a senior when we were freshmen, and now she's a junior at Mississippi State."

"And now she's naked," I said, finally understanding the day's unspoken excitement.

"And now she's naked," Jackson repeated, looking at the picture again.

"Wait, how'd everyone know she'd be in this issue?"

You've got to remember this was the early days of the internet—AOL had only just begun sending free trial CDs in the mail. I'm not sure how anyone found out about anything in those days, and Jackson didn't seem like the sort of guy who'd have insight into the underground pornography pipeline, but perhaps I had him all wrong.

"Her sister Tabatha is a sophomore," Jackson said, "and Tiffany told her, and she told some people, and now everyone knows."

Jackson carefully slid the magazine back into the paper sack and placed it under his seat, explaining if a cop pulled us over, he could arrest us for child pornography.

"How do you figure?" I asked.

"We're children, with pornography," Jackson said.

"I don't think that's—yeah, better safe than sorry I guess."

We drove to Silas's house, and Jackson stuffed the *Playboy* down the back of his pants before we rung the bell. Silas's mother answered the door, and Jackson and I sweated through small talk until she told us Silas was in his room.

"Who's there?" Silas asked when we knocked on his door.

"A Roman," Jackson answered, and minutes later, behind a door we'd checked the lock on six times, we opened the magazine again to bask in Tiffany Thompson's glory.

"You know," Silas said, after a minute or ten of silent appreciation, "she was in my study hall freshman year. She was so hot."

We waited for the rest of the story, but confirming Tiffany

Thompson's hotness was apparently the point, so we gazed upon her a little longer before turning the page and ogling the rest of the Girls of the SEC who, at one point, were seniors in other freshman study halls and, in theory, someone's daughter.

"Dinner at the WigWam?" I asked, after we'd learned Ms. October's hobbies (shopping and tanning) and laughed at some comics that none of us got. "My mom has a date tonight with some guy named Steve Pitts, so I'm on my own for food."

My two friends exchanged a look, and Jackson said, "Can't tonight. I've got Ignite."

"Ignite?"

"Yeah, that's the name of our youth group at Rome First Baptist," Jackson said. "You should come with me. Or you can go with Silas to his cult meeting."

"Lutherans are not a cult, asshole," Silas said and swung a crutch at Jackson's head. "But you should go with Jackson," he conceded. "His church has more hot chicks."

"Sure," I said, "why not?"

And that's how a guy I spent the afternoon looking at naked girls with invited me to church.

~ ~ ~

My dad was Catholic, and Mom grew up Baptist, and when they were still married, they compromised by sleeping in on Sundays. I'd been to church just enough to know I thought it was boring, but Jackson and almost everyone else from Rome, apart from half a dozen Methodists, a couple Presbyterians, Silas the Lutheran, and Darryl the school's only confessing atheist, regularly attended Rome First Baptist.

Jackson picked me up at six, and we parked at the church but didn't go inside because Ignite met across the street in an abandoned warehouse the church purchased and converted into a space where the student ministry could make all the noise they wanted. The warehouse was massive, with graffiti-covered brick walls and exposed ductwork high above. Threadbare couches and recliners covered the floor, along with a ping-pong table, a pool table, an arcade-style Miss Pac-Man, and a disco ball, which was odd because these Baptists strongly discouraged dancing.

"It doubles as the star of Bethlehem in the nativity play," Jackson said, when I inquired about the glittery orb.

There was even a basketball goal inside, and you could lower the rim to eight feet and dunk like Shawn Kemp. After five minutes, I realized why Ignite was so popular. This was, without doubt, the greatest room in Rome.

I followed Jackson to the back of the room where some guys I recognized from school huddled conspiratorially around the world's ugliest couch.

"Yeah," I heard one guy whisper as we approached, "but didn't you think her boobs looked funny? I mean, at least compared to the other girl from Mississippi State—"

Not sure if we were friend or foe, the guy shut up as we approached, but after seeing it was us, he asked Jackson, "Did you get a copy?"

Jackson nodded in the affirmative, and the guy asked, "What'd you think? About her boobs, I mean."

Jackson shrugged, and the guy asked me, "What about you, new guy? Didn't you think her boobs looked weird?"

"They look better in person," I said, eliciting a quick roar of laughter and an even quicker silence as we noticed the girls across the room glaring at us.

We continued to discuss Tiffany Thompson's anatomy in reverent tones for a minute or two until a long-haired man in his late twenties entered the room and everyone found seats on various couches and chairs. We sat segregated, boys in the back, girls up front, and I wondered if this was a Baptist thing or if the girls were just mad at us.

The long-haired man, they called him Brother Shawn, grabbed a microphone and made some announcements, most concerning a youth retreat to Gatlinburg between Christmas and New Year's, then he pulled out an acoustic guitar and played while the girls up front swooned.

I'd never heard these songs, but everyone else knew them by heart, along with the accompanying hand motions. I stared at Jackson while he made a heart with his hands and waved it over his head, and when he noticed me looking, he shrugged and continued. After the last song, which was slower and involved lots of hand raising, Brother Shawn moved the podium that held his sheet music, picked up his Bible said, "I know you expected part three of our six-week series on the book of Revelation, but God has laid something heavy on my heart today. Something even more pressing than the end times, which I assure you, are close at hand."

"Wait, how close?" I whispered to Jackson. "Because if I die a virgin—"

Jackson shushed me, and Brother Shawn said, "Tonight, I want to talk to you about sexual immorality."

He knew. I don't know if one of the girls told him, or if he was the one with insight into the underground pornography pipeline, but he knew. And though he never mentioned *Playboy*, or Tiffany Thompson, or her boobs, by the time he wrapped up his forty-five-minute sermon, there was no doubt he knew how every guy in the room had spent their afternoon.

After the sermon, which involved one slippery-slope argument suggesting the viewing of pornography led directly to mass murder, Brother Shawn grabbed his guitar again and played an old hymn even I recognized. During the second verse, I watched in confusion as, one by one, the guys I'd discussed Tiffany Thompson with earlier made their way to the front of the room where they fell upon their knees to beg either Brother Shawn or God or the girls in the room for forgiveness. Jackson wouldn't look at me when he came back to the couch, red-eyed from tearful repentance, but he made us hang around after the service. All the guys hung around afterwards, and Brother Shawn knew why.

"Back here in thirty," he said, and the room nodded. Half an hour later, we were back behind the Ignite warehouse, and one at a time, the guys tossed their October 1994 issue of *Playboy* into a steel trash can that Brother Shawn subsequently set on fire. There were no songs, or hand motions, or prayers, and as the fire died down, Brother Shawn said he'd see us all on Sunday, and the crowd dispersed.

The ritual, while impromptu, felt staged. Liked they'd done it many times before and would do it again. I learned later, from Silas, that they had done it before, with explicit lyric albums, cans of Copenhagen, and a dozen VHS recordings of a recent porno film called *Forrest Hump*. It seemed Brother Shawn always knew when his sheep had strayed, and they strayed a lot. A month later, I accompanied Jackson to Alverson's Sundries, where he purchased a copy of *Playboy* featuring Pamela Anderson, then later that night watched him burn it while I hummed "Circle of Life," but the joke went over his head.

Chapter Ten

Rome's high school and middle school were conjoined by a lunchroom, and on Mondays, Wednesdays, and Fridays, if I hurried, I could catch Becca before she walked her students back to class. I always hurried.

"Hello, Mr. Brinks," she said with a wink when I saw her on Wednesday.

"Hello, Ms. Walsh," I said. "What's on the menu today?"

"Something brown they are calling fish," she said, "soggy tater tots, and a decent fruit cocktail."

Ignoring the unwritten rules of dating, which up until this point in life hadn't done me any good anyway, I called Becca the day after our date and, throughout our hour-long conversation, told her I enjoyed our dinner at least a dozen times. Hard to get, I was not.

I made a face and said, "Ugh, I think I'll try the salad."

"I'm pretty sure it's yesterday's grass clippings," she said, "but knock yourself out—Tyler, stop running!"

Having only been a teacher for two weeks, it was still jarring to have the person you were talking to break off mid-sentence to scream at a student, but this time I managed not to flinch.

"You should go," I said, motioning toward the students waiting for her by the door, underneath the too-detailed-to-look-at-while-eating mural of a Roman gladiator holding the head of a decapitated foe. "But I'm looking forward to Saturday."

"You've told me that six times already," Becca said, snapping her fingers at two boys shoving each other near the wall. Then she smiled and said, "But I'm looking forward to it too. Oh, and I meant to ask, do you want to go hear Jackson speak tonight at Rome First Baptist?"

No. Most certainly not. Under no circumstances. Absolutely not. By no means. Not at all. Never. Not Really. Negative. Nope. Not on your life. Nah. No way, José. Nay.

"Sure," I lied. "What time should I pick you up?"

~ ~ ~

Norma Porter, mother of Methy Mark, cornered me as Becca and I entered the church that night. When I was in college, my mother rejoined Rome First Baptist. She'd faithfully attended for the last twenty years, and now Norma, who from what I gathered was her Sunday school teacher, wanted to know how Mom felt and if she could do anything, to comfort her I assume, not cure her cancer.

"Marcus, you let that dear mother of yours know this entire church is praying for her healing."

"I will, Mrs. Porter."

"You've got to have faith, Marcus. If your faith is strong enough, God will make your mama whole again."

"I'm trying, Mrs. Porter."

"I'm sure you've heard about Mark," she said. "Sometimes God lets us hit bottom, but he always has a plan for us."

"I know, Mrs. Porter."

"You know," she added, "God never closes a door without opening a window."

"Wait, does God have OCD?" I asked, and Norma's face melted into confusion. "I'm sorry," I said. "That was a dumb joke. I'll be sure to tell Mom you asked about her," and when Norma offered a tearful embrace, I realized no one really knows what to say in situations like this, but some people are there to hug your neck, and maybe that's what counts.

I only remembered Norma Porter because she caught me first, but after having similar conversations with two dozen others, I stopped keeping track and conceded that my mother would have to trust me when I said everyone at church asked about her.

This was only the third time I'd been inside the sanctuary at Rome First Baptist—the previous two times were for my grandparents' funerals—and things hadn't changed much. The carpet was still a deep red, and sitting on a pew near the back, I whispered to Becca, "Doesn't this carpet make you feel like you're at church in hell?"

"Everyone always says that. When we replaced the old carpet a few years ago, the church voted on blue. But the red carpet was so much cheaper, we saved enough money to buy the projector."

A large video screen now covered the pipes to the old organ, which was either no longer in use or sounded quite muffled when it was, and on it a projector mounted high above us displayed an advertisement for Elevate, the youth ministry formerly known as Ignite, which still met on Wednesday nights across the street in the converted warehouse. From what I could tell, Elevate was not meeting this night, because every student from Rome was in the sanctuary, along with most of the town's adults. At seven, the lights dimmed, and a band consisting of three guitarists, a bassist, a drummer, a keyboardist, and six singers all brandishing microphones kicked off the service with a song that, by my count, lasted twelve minutes. When the song mercifully ended, a bald man wearing a Madonna-style microphone took the stage and said, "Good evening, I'm Pastor Shawn, and I'd like to welcome you all to Rome First Baptist."

"Wait," I whispered to Becca, "is that the same guy who was the youth minister when we were in school?"

"Yeah," she said. "He came back to serve as lead pastor six years ago."

"Shame about his hair," I said, and Becca punched my arm.

"This is a special night in the life of our church," Pastor Shawn said. "Rome's favorite son, Coach Jackson Crowder, is here to share what God is doing in his life."

The crowd applauded at the mere mention of Jackson's name, and once they'd stopped, Pastor Shawn said, "Now, I don't have to tell you all what Coach Crowder has done for our town, so I won't. But let me just say I hope Coach has no intentions of leaving football for the ministry, because judging by the size of tonight's crowd, I'd soon be out of a job." The crowd laughed, and some shouted amen, and Pastor Shawn said, "So, without further ado, Coach Crowder, come bring us a fresh word from the Lord."

Jackson was on the front row, next to a blonde I presumed to be his wife, and a couple kids I presumed they procreated, and as he stood, the crowd stood with him, showering him with enough praise to drown a mere mortal. I stood too; it would have been awkward not to, but when Jackson finally raised his hands to signal to his believers that he felt adequately exalted, I quickly sat.

"I've received many great honors in my life," Jackson began, "but the opportunity to stand here, before my home church, and tell you my story, well, this might be the greatest honor of all." The crowd cheered again, but Jackson silenced them quicker this time. "I grew up in this church," he said. "My mom and dad, they brought me here every time the doors opened. Later, as a teenager, I was across the street every Wednesday night for Elevate. We called it Ignite back then, when dinosaurs roamed the Earth and Pastor Shawn had hair." The crowd howled with laughter. They were putty in Jackson's hands.

"I met Jesus in this church," Jackson said, turning serious, "one Wednesday night in ninth grade. He changed my life. He put me on a path. A path that led away from alcohol and drugs and pornography."

This didn't exactly jive with my memories of Jackson, which postdated his ninth-grade run-in with the Son of God, but that was twenty-something years ago, and I forget my email password once a month, so maybe I was the one with the faulty memory.

"It was tough then for a teenager," Jackson said, "but students today, they have it far worse. There are so many more temptations facing our kids today. They walk into school and they're confronted with drugs. They turn on their computers and they're confronted with pornography. That's why football … that's why football is more important now than ever."

The crowd roared their approval, and I set a new world record for hardest eye roll.

"I understand my responsibility," Jackson said when the applause died out. "It is a crown that weighs heavy on my head but one I wear with honor. I am humbled you've entrusted your children to me, and when I can't sleep at night, it's not because I'm worried about next week's game. What keeps me up is the fear I'm not doing all I can to mold these young men and women into citizens that Rome will be proud of. What helps me sleep is accepting I cannot do it, not alone. That's why we preach Jesus to these kids. Only Jesus can reach them, like he reached me all those years ago. You won't read about this in the papers, because they'd never print a good story like this, but on the last day of summer practice, we filled up the Quarterback Club's old dunking booth, and we baptized every member of the Rome football team."

The crowd was on their feet again, and as Jackson let them go on for some time, I realized football coaches had stolen religious opportunism from the politicians' playbook.

"I think of our team as an extension of this church," Jackson said, "another ministry. Perhaps the most important ministry, because we're shaping the lives of young people, and they are the future of Rome. Look, wins are important. I know that. I know what another state championship would mean to this town. But I hope you understand whatever happens on the field on any given Friday is secondary to my primary goal of winning young people for the Lord."

Another round of applause, and if you listened carefully, you could hear parents around the sanctuary telling their children they would play football next year whether they wanted to or not.

Jackson walked out from behind the pulpit and sat on the top step of the altar. "Some of you may not know this," he said, in a softer voice, "but Amy had a miscarriage last year, just before the playoffs began. It was tough, and then we lost to Mytilene, and our sorrow doubled. But we made it through. Because of our faith, we made it through. And when these young people leave Rome, I want them to have a faith that will get them through the tough times as well. So, in closing, I want to ask, if you're comfortable doing this, that you come to this altar and pray for our team. Pray that we will practice hard and that we will play hard, and play fair, and compete to the best of our ability to bring glory to God. And I ask that you pray for me that these young people will see Jesus in me and that lives will change. If you will, come."

Everyone with functioning legs was at the altar in a matter of seconds. Even Becca went, only leaving the five oldest people in Rome and me in our pews, while perhaps four hundred people prayed down front. The old people obviously did not approve of my not praying for their team, so I went to the bathroom to avoid their stink eye and returned after the band played its closing song, another interminable ditty that made *Stairway to Heaven* seem brief by comparison. Jackson remained up front after his talk—a line had formed to kiss his ass. I found Becca off to the side talking to an older woman she introduced as Fletcher Morgan's mother.

"This is Marcus Brinks. He was in the band Dear Brutus," Becca said, and Fletcher's mother said she'd never heard of me.

"That happens a lot," I said to Becca after Fletcher's mother walked away.

"Marcus?" a voice said from behind, and I turned around to see a pretty blonde I didn't know.

"Yes," I said, and Becca grabbed my hand.

"I'm Amy Crowder, Jackson's wife."

"Oh, hi," I said. "Nice to meet you."

"You too," she said, smiling. "Jackson wanted to talk to you, but he'll be shaking hands for half an hour. So he wanted me to ask if you'd like to have dinner with us on Sunday night. It's the one night I won't let him study film."

"Uh, yeah, sure," I said, though there weren't many things I'd rather not do.

"Great," she said, "we live at 2226 Amherst, in Coach Pumphrey's old house. Does seven o'clock work?"

"Uh, sure."

"We'll see you then," she said. "I know Jackson is excited."

~ ~ ~

"Please come with me Sunday," I said to Becca later that evening on her front porch swing.

"I don't think I'm invited," she said. "Besides, I teach their son, and he's not doing well. It would be awkward."

"That's no excuse," I said. "It's already going to be awkward."

"What makes you say that? You and Jackson were best friends."

"We were only friends because Rome is so small. If we'd gone to a bigger school, we'd have been friends with people we actually liked instead."

"I don't buy that for one second," Becca said. "Now tell me what happened between you two."

"He ... nothing. He wouldn't even know he did something to upset me."

"Oh my god," Becca said. "So you've just held a grudge for twenty-three years. You're such a guy."

I laughed. "I guess, but even so, he's so full of shit now."

Becca stared at me for a moment before asking, "How so?"

"You heard him tonight? All that, 'Jesus kept me away from porn' crap. I was here for what, four months, and all he ever wanted to do was look at porn. I went with him to Alverson's once a month to buy the new *Playboy*. And for him to say Jesus kept him away from alcohol? That's such bullshit. I once saw him so drunk he pissed on my neighbor's Dachshund. He only said that crap tonight because it's what the people in this town want to hear, you know?"

Becca had let go of my hand by now, and she was silent for a long time then said, "What I know is you've been away a long time, and people can change a lot in two decades, and I don't want to be judged on the things I did when I was seventeen. And I suppose you don't either, Marcus. Am I right?"

I sighed and said, "You're right."

"Of course I am," Becca said, then she kissed me on the head and said goodnight.

"The son of divorced parents, you could easily mistake Marcus Brinks for just some guy in your freshman history class. He's affable and a bit shy, yet when asked about his lyrics, particularly allusions to Lois Lowry's YA novel *The Giver*, in songs like "Without Colour, Pain, or Past, Pt. 1," or "My Fiona," a song rumored to be about the girl who broke his heart freshman year of college, Brinks grows frustrated. 'Look, my job is to write this shit and sing it, not explain it to you.'"

—*Blender*, "Et tu, Brute?"
May 28, 1998

Chapter Eleven

Friday marked the one-week anniversary of my faux date with Becca, and one week since she'd spoken to me. Not a hi, or a hello, or a how are you as we passed in the hall. Not a wink, or a smile, or even a subtle nod when she walked by my desk. Inside the halls of Rome High School, Becca gave no indication we'd spent what I thought was a lovely evening at Winona Falls or that she even remembered my name. And maybe we hadn't, and maybe she didn't. I occasionally took Albuterol for my asthma, and in rare instances, it can cause vivid dreams. Of course, Silas and Jackson didn't believe me and gave me hell every time Becca walked by without acknowledging my existence, though never within earshot of anyone else, because we all knew, if Deacon found out I'd even dreamed I hung out with Becca, he'd kill me, and Silas and Jackson would likely receive supplemental ass whippings just for being my friend.

"The lead singer is this big dude with crazy sideburns, and he always wears a vest full of harmonicas and, like, a fedora or something." Jackson was telling me about Blues Traveler, a band his sister Julia introduced him to over the weekend, while we waited on Mr. Galba's world history class to begin.

"Does the album have explicit lyrics?" I asked. "Because if it does, can you just give it to me before Brother Shawn makes you burn it?"

Jackson flipped his middle finger my way, then his eyes widened, and I felt the slightest brush on my shoulder as Becca Walsh dropped a note on my desk.

I looked at the folded paper then at Jackson, who motioned for me to open it, but Deacon walked in, so I closed my fist around the paper until he'd passed. Once Deacon made his way to the back of the room, I unfolded the note, and on the center of the page, in curly cursive, Becca wrote, 'Stay in your desk after class.' Against my better judgment, I glanced back at Becca, but she was talking to Deacon and took no notice, so I refolded the note and said to Jackson, "I need to stay here for a few minutes after class." He nodded conspiratorially, and after what had to be the longest hour of my life, the bell rang and everyone packed their books and began to leave. Jackson took his time until I glared at him and he hurried along, and then Deacon and Becca left together, and I wondered if this was a prank to see how long I'd sit there waiting. But a minute later, Becca ducked back into the room and smiled.

I stood to meet her, and after she looked behind her to make sure we were alone, she asked, "Can you tell your mom you're going to the game tonight and that you're spending the night with Silas afterward?"

"Uh … yeah. I'll need to check with Silas and make sure it's okay with his—"

"No, you don't. Just tell your mom where you'll be and meet me in the mall parking lot at 4:30 outside the food court."

"Yeah, I can do that," I said, because there was nothing she could ask of me that I wouldn't say yes to.

"See you then, FNB," she said and kissed two fingers before touching them to my cheek and walking away. But then she stopped in the doorway, turned around, and whispered, "Oh, and Marcus, bring all the money you can get your hands on."

~ ~ ~

Becca was ten minutes late to the mall, which gave me ten minutes to invent nightmare scenarios to explain her mysterious invitation, most involving Deacon Cassburn et al. jumping me, taking all the money I could get my hands on to buy themselves a keg, and tossing my broken body into the lake behind the mall. But Deacon was at the school with the rest of his team, waiting to board the bus that would carry them to destroy another hapless foe, this week the Wilson High Wildcats.

"You know," Jackson said to me at lunch, after I told him about the note and mysterious rendezvous, "if Deacon does murder you, that should be enough to get him kicked off the team." I laughed then, but here, alone in the mall parking lot, it didn't seem as funny.

"Shit!" I yelled when Becca appeared out of nowhere and knocked on my window.

"Are you okay?" she asked when I opened my door.

"I thought you were your boyfriend," I said.

"Ooo-kay," she said. "Well, sorry I'm late. *Saved by the Bell* was on. So how much money did you bring?"

"I had sixty bucks saved and found another twenty in my mom's purse."

"It'll have to do," she said. "Do you have any gas?"

"Uh … no."

"We'll take my car then," she said, grabbing me by the wrist and pulling me from my car, "but you're driving."

Becca and I climbed into her Saturn, and I shifted into reverse and asked, "Wait, where are we going?"

"Atlanta."

I put the car back in park.

"The one in Georgia? Just the two of us? We can't do that. Can we?"

Becca looked around the parking lot and said, "I don't see anyone here to stop us."

"But my mom—"

"Will never know. And neither will my parents. Or anyone else."

"Okay," I said, "but you've at least got to tell me why we're going to Atlanta."

Becca smiled and said, "We're going to see Weezer."

Weezer was in the middle of their first headlining tour. They'd played The Nick in Birmingham the night before, the concert Jackson suggested we go to on my first day at Rome, and it crushed me they were only an hour from my house and there was no way my mom would even consider letting me go see them. I knew they had a show in Atlanta tonight, at a place called The Point—they were my favorite band, I knew pretty much everything about them. But not once after Becca asked me to meet her at the mall did I allow myself to dream the hottest girl in school wanted to take me to see my favorite band. Some things are too absurd even to dream about.

I smiled back and said, "Okay, yeah, we're going to see Weezer. But wait, do you know how to get there?"

MapQuest wouldn't be a thing for another two years. Google Maps another nine. I don't know how anyone got anywhere back then.

"I called The Point," Becca said, then reading from a slip of paper said, "It's on 420 Moreland Avenue NE."

"Okay, but I still don't know where that is. I don't know where anything in Atlanta is."

"Shouldn't be a problem," Becca said. "When we get to Atlanta, we'll stop at a gas station and ask for directions."

This was a terrible idea, but I wasn't not going to go just because we didn't know where we were going, so we left the mall and headed east, singing along to the *Blue Album* at full volume.

"I wouldn't have pegged you as a Weezer fan," I said somewhere near the state line.

"And why not?" Becca asked.

"Because it's like nerd rock," I said, "and you're not particularly nerdy."

"I'm the nerdiest person you know," Becca said.

"You date the quarterback. You're practically a cheerleader."

Becca flipped me double birds, and I said, "Okay, since you're so nerdy, what's your favorite book?"

"*The Giver*," she said, "have you read it?"

I said no and she said, "Well, it's dystopian and totally nerdy. My copy is in the back seat. You can borrow it."

"Fine, but naming a nerdy book is easy. What's your favorite Star Wars action figure?"

"Hammerhead," Becca said, without hesitation.

"Shit. I stand corrected," I said, and she gave me one of those winks usually reserved for Deacon. I almost wrecked.

We lost an hour crossing time zones and arrived on the outskirts of Atlanta around seven. By then, the interstate had mutated from four lanes to eight, and I was more than happy to exit and ask for directions, if for no other reason than to let my hands stop shaking. We stopped at a Chevron with bars on the window, and the man behind the counter, who was likely still cashing royalty checks from his role in *Deliverance*, shook his head no when Becca asked if he knew how to get to a placed called The Point.

"It's on Moreland Avenue," I said, and the man glared at me and asked, "You gonna buy something or not?"

Becca placed a pack of gum and a dollar bill on the counter, and after he tossed her change into his tip jar, the man said, "Stay on twenty. You'll see an exit for Moreland in five or six miles."

Out of curiosity, I mapped this the other day, and in theory, we could have driven from Riverton to The Point in no more than four turns, but in reality, it took significantly more, including one U-turn of debatable legality. And this was just to find Moreland Avenue. We needed to ask directions twice more to find the club, which was in a part of town called Little Five Points. We finally made it though, sometime after nine, and parked between a vegetarian restaurant and a liquor store.

"How much do I owe you for our tickets?" I asked Becca as we walked down the sidewalk toward The Point.

"It's a free show," she said. "You just need a 99X Freeloader card to get in."

"Oh, that's awesome," I said, as we joined the back of the

line outside The Point. "Where'd you get those?"

She didn't respond, and after a while, I said, "Because they're going to want us to have one." Then noticing the "No persons under 21 allowed" sign, I added, "And they're going to want us to be four years older."

The line crept forward toward the three-hundred-pound man checking IDs and, I suppose, breaking the necks of anyone without one, and Becca said, "Give me your money. I've got this figured out." I handed her my eighty dollars, and she combined it with whatever cash she brought before counting out fifty bucks and pocketing the rest. My heart pounded as the line inched toward the man who would soon kill us, and I whispered, "This is dumb. Let's just go back home. I don't want to get into trouble."

"Marcus, shut up," Becca said, so I did, and when we reached the door, she tucked fifty dollars into the bouncer's front pocket. He looked us over, then the slightest trace of a smile flashed across his face.

~ ~ ~

Weezer opened with "No One Else" and played every song off the *Blue Album*, except "My Name is Jonas." They even played three songs from their unreleased second album, closing the show with "Only in Dreams" and "Tired of Sex." Jake Dawson, in his *Atlanta Music Monthly* review said, "Rivers Cuomo and pals treated fans to ninety minutes of geeky teenage insecurity wrapped in face-melting guitar riffs that no one in attendance will ever forget."

I know this because the setlist for every single Weezer concert is available online, along with the archives of *Atlanta Music Monthly*, a newspaper that went under in 2003. I do not know it from experience because the bouncer, after pocketing our fifty dollars, kicked us out of the line and threatened to have us arrested for bribing an officer of the law, which in retrospect, I don't believe he was, but we were seventeen and easily scared.

Defeated, we sulked back to Becca's car and saw three tow trucks clearing out the lot between the vegetarian restaurant and the liquor store. One of the tow trucks was backing up to Becca's Saturn, and we took off running and shouting and jumped in the car just before they attached the hook or whatever it is tow trucks use. The driver climbed out from his cab and shouted something at us, but I floored it, and we squealed out of the parking lot, smashing through a small row of shrubs and onto Moreland Avenue, hearts racing, and laughing hysterically.

"I'm sorry I lost our money," Becca said an hour later, as we drowned our sorrows in chili dogs from The Varsity.

"It's okay," I said between bites. "All things considered, it's been a fun evening."

"It has been fun, FNB."

I took a sip of my milkshake and asked, "So why didn't you talk to me all week?"

"Why do you think?" Becca asked.

"Deacon?"

Becca nodded. "Last year, he wanted to fight my cousin Doug after he saw us talking in the lunchroom. If we didn't have the same last name, I think Deacon would have killed him."

"Oh great," I said, and Becca reached across the table, squeezed my hand, and said, "I'm not going to tell him about this. I'm not going to tell anyone. So if you don't either, Deacon will never know."

We made it back to Rome around three in the morning, and that's when I noticed a gaping hole in Becca's plan, namely that it was three in the morning and we had nowhere to go.

"I've prepared for this," Becca said, and I followed her directions to the park at the top of Oppian Road. We parked and Becca pulled a blanket from her trunk and set it under a tree. From the park, we had a spectacular view of Rome. Well, spectacular is a stretch, but it was a nice view, and I said, "I wonder if the team won."

"I don't," Becca said.

"Yeah, me neither," I said, and she laughed.

We laid back and looked up at the stars, and after a while,

Becca asked, "Have you heard of Big Star?"

"I don't think so," I said.

"They're old," she said, "but you'd like them. I accidentally ordered their album from Columbia House in one of those eight-CDs-for-a-penny deals, but it's amazing."

She pulled out her Discman and introduced me to Big Star's *#1 Record* through shared headphones.

"I've decided," Becca said after we listened to "Thirteen," the song she called her favorite in the whole wide world, "I'm dumping him next week."

I sat up and said, "No shit? Why?"

"Because there are a lot better guys out there than Deacon," Becca said.

She was about as subtle as Marshall Ford speaking at a pep rally, but if she wanted me to kiss her, and looking back she totally wanted me to kiss her, I didn't take the hint. Or maybe I took it but didn't think it worth the risk of Deacon Cassburn retroactively kicking my ass, pending breakup or not. So, I just laid back down next to her and said, "Yeah, there are a lot better guys out there," and Becca scooted close and put her head on my shoulder.

We slept that way until sunrise.

Chapter Twelve

In the mid-1980s, when Coach Pumphrey built his house on the Coosa River, it was the only house in Palatine Bend. An oasis from the stresses of coaching a small Alabama high school football team. Now double-mortgaged McMansions cover the area, many built on swampland kids from Rome used to ride four-wheelers through. I stood on Jackson's porch and looked out on a sea of Honda Odysseys and adjustable height basketball goals, imagining them under murky brown water the next time the river left its banks, then I rang the bell.

Becca advised me not to bring a bottle of wine, because Amy Crowder was, as she put it, "Jesus's second cousin or something." I argued that Jesus turned water into wine, but Becca said, "Not in Amy Crowder's house," so I waited at the door empty-handed.

A boy who looked remarkably like Jackson the day I first met him answered the door, and he stared at me for a moment before shouting, "Mom, Dad, some man is at the door."

Amy Crowder appeared in the foyer and said, "J. J., this is our guest, Mr. Brinks. Say hello."

"Hello, Mr. Brinks," J. J. said.

"Hello, J. J.," I replied.

"Some man is at the door," Amy repeated and laughed. "My apologies for our less than welcoming welcome committee. We're glad you could make it, Marcus. How are you?"

"Good," I said, stepping inside. "Thanks again for having me."

"Of course. Jackson is out back grilling steaks. J. J., show Mr. Brinks outside while I finish up in the kitchen."

I followed the boy through the living room and onto the stone deck, where water flowed from an elevated hot tub into a custom pool. Below us, an immaculate lawn sloped toward the Coosa River and a boathouse where Jackson's boat lived in luxury. Jackson stood in the corner, facing the river, next to his Big Green Egg, and J. J. said, "Hey Dad, your friend is here."

Jackson turned around and said, "Brinks! My man. Come here." We met halfway, and Jackson gave me one of those firm handshakes that morph into a half-hug with three or four fist pounds to the back, then he stepped away and said, "Brinks, you haven't changed a bit."

"You either," I said, "except, you're all ripped."

"It's one of the perks of having a weight room outside your office."

He looked at me again and shook his head. "My God. I remember watching you on MTV back in college. Y'all had that video where you were making out with the girl from *Dawson's Creek*."

"Yeah, but she hated me. That wasn't nearly as fun as it looked."

Jackson shook his head. "That was wild. We were all like, 'How the hell did someone from Rome end up on MTV?'" Jackson flinched after saying "hell" then said to J. J., "Son, don't tell your mama," but the boy never looked up from his phone.

"What a dream though," Jackson said to me. "Make millions and spend the rest of your life in the Caribbean, living off royalties."

I shrugged. "That's not exactly—"

"I get it," Jackson said, "but I don't think I could do it, you know? Just lying in a hammock sipping fruity drinks all day. I'd be bored after a week."

"Well, I fish a lot, and sometimes I—"

"You know I worked in Manhattan for a while, don't you?"

"Yeah, I heard."

That Jackson gave up a lucrative position with a New York City investment bank to coach high school football in Alabama was considered, in Rome at least, a sacrifice on par with Abraham and Isaac.

"Miserable city. I hated it, Amy hated it, and I burned out pretty quick. But God, I'd already made more money than our great-grandchildren will ever spend. I suppose I could have bought an island then and lived the rest of my life in a hammock, but I'm like a shark. I've got to keep moving or I'll die. So I took some time off and realized what I missed most was football. I knew Rome had fallen on hard times, so I called up Principal Trajan and told him I wanted to come back as head coach."

"Well, I know everyone is happy to have you back in Rome," I lied.

"Most everyone," Jackson said. "But I learned a long time ago you can't please everyone. How do you like your steak, Brinks?"

I told him medium rare, and after a few minutes of Jackson extolling the grilling prowess of his Big Green Egg, he put the steaks on a plate, and I followed him inside. "Have a seat," he said, motioning toward the den, and I sat on the big leather sectional with J. J., leaving the La-Z-Boy for Jackson.

"Did you watch much football in Jamaica?" Jackson asked when he returned to the den. The Cowboys and Giants were playing on NBC, and I said, "Not much. I think Flow TV had an NFL package, but I didn't pay for it. Jamaicans are more into track, and cricket, and soccer."

"I love the Premier League," J. J. said.

"No you don't," Jackson scolded. "Now go wash up, and tell your sister it's time to eat."

J. J. ran upstairs, and I followed Jackson into the dining room, which had a panoramic view of the river. "Your home is beautiful," I said to Amy, as she set dish after dish on the table.

Amy thanked me, and Jackson said, "It ought to be after all the money we've spent on it."

Jackson's self-aggrandizement was tolerable when we were kids. That he thought so much of his lowly spot on the Rome depth chart, or the used truck his parents had probably bought for five hundred dollars, or that Maggie Duncan had let him get to second base once in ninth grade was somehow endearing. Back then, when Jackson would start to gloat, Silas and I would always exchange a quick smile and just tune him out. But now that Jackson was truly wealthy and successful, I found his boasts particularly grating.

"Never renovate an old home," he continued. "We'd been better off knocking this one to the ground and starting over. I'm not sure what Coach P was thinking when he built this place. The kitchen, the bathrooms, we had to redo them all to get them up to our standards."

"Hi, I'm Madison, and I'm eight," said a little girl I hadn't noticed standing next to me. She extended her hand, so I shook it and said, "Hi Madison, I'm Marcus, and I'm forty."

"I know. My mother said you are lost, and we should pray for you."

"Madison," Jackson said with wide eyes, but I laughed and waved him off. "I am a little lost," I said. "So, thank you."

Jackson shook his head, and Madison and J. J. took their seats as their mother brought out the last plate of food. We passed around mashed potatoes and gravy, fried okra, green beans, and cornbread, and just as I shoveled the first forkful into my mouth, Amy said, "Madison, will you please say grace?"

The Crowders extended their hands; I held Jackson's and Madison's, and as we all bowed our heads, I quickly swallowed my potatoes. "God is great, God is good. Let us thank him for our food," Madison prayed, and though I wanted to point out that *good* and *food* do not rhyme, I said amen instead.

We dug in, and when my mouth was full of okra, Madison said, "My mother said you were exclusive."

"Madison!" Jackson and Amy said in unison.

I swallowed a laugh and said, "Exclusive?"

"I'm sorry," Amy said. "I told her you were reclusive."

I laughed again and said, "I was reclusive, Madison, but not anymore."

"What does that even mean?" Madison asked.

"It means I was famous but didn't want to be."

"Were you as famous as my daddy?"

"Not even close," I said, and the little girl beamed. "I'm not even famous enough to be a recluse anymore. If anything, I'd be a hermit."

"We have a hermit crab at school," Madison said, and I smiled.

"Marcus," Amy asked, as I cut into my steak, "did you attend church often in Jamaica?"

"Not often," I said. "I dated a Rastafarian woman, and she used to take me with her to church, but it was just a bunch of people smoking pot and chanting over bongo drums in the community center." None of this was true, but Amy already thought I was lost, so why not exaggerate my depravity?

"Oh," Amy said, frowning at either the mention of dating or smoking pot or bongo drums, I wasn't sure which. I took a bite of my steak, which, thanks to Jackson's less than deft touch with the grill, looked like it had reentered Earth's atmosphere at 28,000 miles per hour, and Amy asked, "Do Rastafarians believe in Jesus?"

"Oh sure," I said, swallowing my steak with considerable effort. "They believe he was a black African and that he was emperor of Ethiopia for most of the last century, but they believe in him."

"My mother said you were in a band," Madison said.

"Yes, I was in a band," I said, happy to change the subject, "a long time ago."

"Can I listen to your songs?"

"No," I said, "probably not."

"Why? Are they about Harry Potter?"

I laughed then realized I shouldn't have and said, "No, no wizards."

I took another bite of steak, and while Madison waited for me to chew it, she asked her mother, "Have you heard Mr. Brinks's songs?"

"A long time ago," Amy said. "I remember one of the videos being particularly gratuitous."

"I didn't have anything to do with the videos," I mumbled through a full mouth, but I'm not sure Amy Crowder believed me.

~ ~ ~

After dinner, Jackson and I walked to his boathouse, which had a second story that served as his man cave. There was comfortable leather seating for six, but the walls were bare apart from a seventy-inch television, and I suspected Jackson rarely brought people up here, if ever. "Is this where you watch film?" I asked, pointing at the television.

"This is where I get away from watching film," Jackson said then added, "and everything else."

He opened the fridge in the corner of the room, and after moving some boxes around, pulled out two Heinekens. "Amy doesn't approve of having alcohol in the house with kids around," Jackson said, handing me one of the beers.

"It's nice you have this place then," I said, taking the beer.

"She doesn't approve of alcohol in here either, but what she doesn't know won't hurt her. Cheers."

We walked out onto the balcony, and I sat in one of the rocking chairs and looked out on the river while Jackson turned on some music. The drum intro of Oasis's "Live Forever" came through the speakers as Jackson sat next to me and said, "Amy doesn't care for secular music either, so I have to listen to this out here. Man, I loved this album."

I looked at Jackson tapping his state championship ring to the beat and smiled. He was different up here. He was the old Jackson, not a colossus straddling the world, but a man so scared of his wife he hides his beer and music.

"Didn't you hate Oasis?" he asked.

"No, I liked them," I said. "Not as much as you, but I liked them."

"I saw them in college," Jackson said. "In Atlanta, with Amy actually. She wasn't always so …"

"Religious?"

"Yeah," Jackson said. "I mean, we're all Christian around here, but she's drifting toward the fringes. Last year, she got really into Levitical law, all that 'if a man eats an ostrich, the community must stone him to death' stuff. Dream interpretation is her latest thing, and she's freaked out because one night she dreamt blood was pouring from my statue at the Colosseum."

"That is kind of freaky," I said.

"I suppose it is," Jackson said, then he looked me over and shook his head and said, "Marcus Brinks, I never thought I'd see you in Rome again. Would you have ever come back if your mama hadn't got sick?"

"No," I said. "I'd settled into a pretty deep rut. But maybe things happen for a reason. I've had a couple dates with Becca Walsh."

Jackson stared at me for a long second and said, "Becca Walsh…I forgot how obsessed you were with her when you first moved here."

"I was not, but I—"

"You were too. But good for you, Brinks. After all this time, you finally asked her out. Becca is a sweet girl. J.J. adores her. So do you think anything might come of these dates? Are you back in Rome permanently?"

"I don't know. I'd be lying if I said it hadn't crossed my mind. We're both forty and single, but I …"

"Don't want to scare her off?"

"Yeah. I mean we've only had three dates, and one was to hear you speak."

Jackson shook his head. "Shawn has begged me to do that since we moved back. I finally ran out of excuses."

"You were good," I said. "You should've been a preacher."

"Shit," Jackson said, and I laughed.

We were quiet for a moment, and I said, "Thanks for having me over."

Jackson waved me off, and I said, "No seriously, I've only seen you from a distance since I got back, and you're larger than life around here. I didn't know if I'd be able to talk to you anymore."

"It's all an act, Brinks. The spectacle gets us more press, and more families move to Rome, and more kids play football. It's just part of the game now, but I don't think the Quarterback Club realizes it."

"I've gathered they're not your biggest fans," I said.

"You, my friend, are a master of understatement. I'm not scared of those guys though. They're dumber now than they were in high school. But if one of them did scare me, it's Deacon. He's not a happy person, Brinks. I don't think he watches TV or listens to music or anything. He just sits and thinks of ways to bring me down, and guys like that are dangerous. I wish he were fat and stupid like the rest of them, but even so, he doesn't scare me. That bunch, they'll get on board when we win state, and even if they don't, no one will care what they say anyway."

"It's funny, they probably thought they'd be running this town forever. If we hadn't—"

Jackson grabbed my shoulder and said, "Brinks, we don't talk about that. Ever."

He was different again, scary almost, and I said, "Yeah, that's cool."

He let go of my shoulder and said, "You're right, though. I doubt in high school those miserable bastards ever envisioned the ebb and flow of life placing me on such a high tide. It's my time now, Brinks, and I plan to take full advantage of it."

We finished our beers, and Jackson tossed them in a garbage bag then put that bag under some other bags in the can so his wife would never see. It was pathetic and endearing all at once because, beneath all the swagger and bravado, he was still the same guy who asked if I liked Weezer on my first day at Rome.

I didn't like him necessarily; we'd grown too far apart to be friends again, but I liked his family, well, his kids at least. And I had no desire to hurt them just so Deacon Cassburn could watch practice again.

"Come see me in the field house during your off period one day," Jackson said as I climbed into my car. "Our snack machine has twice the selection of the teacher's lounge."

I told him I would then stopped by Becca's on the way home to tell her she was right.

"Dear Brutus lead singer Marcus Brinks abruptly walked off stage last night, halfway through his band's set before a sellout crowd at Amsterdam Arena. Citing both mental and physical exhaustion, keyboardist Piper Van Pelt told reporters, 'Marcus received an IV at the hospital last night and is feeling much better. Of course he feels like s— for letting down the fans, and we're working to schedule a makeup show as soon as possible.'"

—*The Guardian*,
October 3, 1998

Chapter Thirteen

The night after Becca and I drove to Atlanta, didn't see Weezer, and slept in a park, Riverton closed Main Street for good. There was no formal announcement. No ceremonial last night of low-speed flirting. When legions of teens descended upon downtown Riverton Saturday night, they encountered half a dozen police checkpoints, and the sad realization that one of the few fun things to do in town had died with a whimper.

"Each time you passed the checkpoint, a cop recorded your tag number," Jackson told me in homeroom on Monday, "and if you passed by three times in one night, they wrote you a ticket."

"They can do that?"

"They're the cops; they can do anything."

"Shit. Did you get a ticket?" I asked him.

"No, but a few people did, and after that, everyone left. A truck full of guys told us everyone was going to cruise the Walmart parking lot, but when Silas and I got there, it was just those dudes, so we played Sega in his garage the rest of the night."

I suspect this theory might not stand up to intense historical analysis, but I'll always believe a bored Riverton teen drove home and invented meth that night.

~ ~ ~

A week of school came and went, and by now, I knew better than to expect even the slightest acknowledgment from Becca, which was good because, as usual, she ignored me completely. With Main Street closed and nothing promising on the horizon for Saturday night fun, I went to the football game on Friday night. Rome played J. P. Hornby, and won, by Rome standards, a close game, 35-14. I sat with Silas and listened with disinterest as he explained the superiority of the no-huddle offense and why Eazy-E was a punk-ass bitch. And late in the fourth quarter, when I assumed she'd forgotten about me, Becca came and sat between us.

"Did my Friday Night Boyfriend tell you what we did last weekend?" Becca asked Silas.

"No, he did not," Silas said.

"That's because he is a gentleman," Becca said.

"Wait, did you two go to Vegas?" Silas asked. "Are you secretly married? Congratulations! I wish I'd known. I'd have sent a gift."

Becca laughed and, much to my horror, said, "No, we drove to Atlanta and tried to sneak into a Weezer concert then spent the night together in Oppian Park."

This time Silas laughed, I guess because he thought Becca was joking in an oddly specific way, but when neither Becca nor I laughed with him, he asked, "Wait, did you really?"

"Yeah," I said then added, "but I didn't think we were telling anyone about it."

"Silas isn't just anyone," Becca said and pinched his cheek. Then she tousled my hair and stood and said, "All right, FNB, I'll see you next week." But before she left, Becca turned around and asked, "Did you hear about the party?"

Silas said he had, and Becca said maybe she'd see us there, and when she was gone, he looked at me with wide eyes and said, "Brinks, holy hell man, are you trying to get yourself killed?"

My heart was racing now, because if Becca told Silas, there was no telling who else she'd told, and in a school the size of Rome, it was only a matter of time until Deacon Cassburn heard and broke me into a thousand little pieces.

"It was her idea," I said a little too defensively. "What could I do?"

"Say no," Silas said. "You could tell her no and live to lose your virginity."

"Shut up. Besides, she said she's going to dump Deacon, and then none of this will matter."

"Yeah, Brinks, keep telling yourself that."

~ ~ ~

On Saturday, my mom made me do two months of neglected yard work then help her clean out the garage, but late in the afternoon, to my shock, she said, "Steve's taking me to dinner and a movie tonight, so you're on your own for food. If you want to eat Taco Bell with your friends, knock yourself out, but normal curfew rules apply."

I called Jackson, who was all depressed about not getting to play a single snap against Hornby, and he said he and Silas were going to the Riverton Mall and that I could tag along, but I had to drive. We ate Chinese food in the food court, and Jackson spit out his Coke when Silas told him about my previous weekend's adventure.

"So that's what her note was about? You told me she just wanted to borrow your world history notes. And you two slept in the park together? Did anything happen?"

"No. Nothing happened. We just fell asleep. I mean, we slept close because it was kind of chilly, but nothing happened."

"Doesn't matter. As far as Deacon is concerned, talking to her and sexing her are the same thing. Brinks, he's going to murder you so hard."

"He's not going to find out if people will stop talking about it," I said, staring at Silas, who raised his hands and said, "Your Friday night girlfriend told me. There's no telling who else she's told."

I sighed and Jackson said, "I guess you weren't lying about hanging out with her at Winona Falls a couple weeks ago."

"Why would I lie about that?"

"We've only known you a month," Jackson said. "You may lie about everything."

I flipped a middle finger in his direction, and he laughed and said, "So what's your endgame here, Brinks?"

"Besides death by Cassburn," Silas said.

"Do you like her?" Jackson asked.

"What? No. I mean, she's cool and all, but we were just hanging out. It didn't mean anything. We're friends."

Of course I liked her. She was pretty much all I thought about. But I couldn't admit it to Jackson for two reasons: (1) she was out of my league, and I didn't care to have him remind me of this, and (2) Deacon Cassburn was an existential threat, and I hoped if I never actually admitted to liking Becca, my execution would at least be mercifully swift.

"Yeah, she's cool," Jackson said, "but if you don't like her, you might want to stop risking your life to hang out with her."

After dinner—my fortune cookie told me I was the master of my fate (in bed)—we walked to Aladdin's Castle, and I held Silas's crutches while he spent five bucks playing *Cruis'n USA*, a car game he was terrible at.

"Remind me never to get in a car with you," I said.

"Remind me to beat you with my crutches when I run out of quarters," he replied.

Jackson walked over and said, "Hey, I just talked to Meghan-Jennifer."

"There's a girl at school named MeghanJennifer?" I asked.

"Two girls," Jackson said, "but they are always together and usually wearing the same thing. Anyway, they're going to the raceway tonight. Maybe we should go."

Silas wrecked his convertible in spectacular fashion, cursed loudly, and said, "MeghanJennifer is going?"

"That's what they said."

"Yeah, maybe we should go."

"Go where?" I asked them.

"There's a party at the old Riverton Raceway tonight," Jackson said, "but we didn't think it was our sort of crowd."

"But MeghanJennifer is cool, or is it are cool?" Silas said, "And if they're going, maybe it won't be the jackass convention we'd envisioned."

"Then let's go," I said.

The Rivertown Raceway was a 3/8-mile dirt track that closed sometime in the late eighties. The infield was grown up with pine trees and kudzu, but the dirt oval remained mostly visible, thanks to the rednecks who'd, on occasion, conduct their own drunken races late on Saturday nights. Every town had a spot like this where kids went to party in relative seclusion. Macedonia had a place called Heaven, an abandoned restaurant high on Taurus Mountain you needed four-wheel drive to reach. Kids from Hornby partied in Paradise, the dead-end of a street in a subdivision that was never built. And Carthage students hung out deep in the maze of fire roads running through a local timber farm. Of course I only heard of these places; no one from Rome ever went. Unlike Main Street, which was neutral territory, showing up uninvited to another school's secret hang out—and you were never invited—was a foolproof way of acquiring a kicked ass.

"That has to be it," Jackson said, pointing toward what looked to me like no more than a muddy spot between some trees.

There was no official entrance to the raceway anymore, just a muddy driveway you had to pass three or four times before you noticed. Once we found it, my Mazda struggled back to the track, where we spotted a bonfire and a few dozen cars and trucks parked on a bare spot in the infield.

Two kegs sat on someone's tailgate next to a stack of Solo cups, and Silas and I helped ourselves, while Jackson declined, saying, "I could get kicked off the team."

"Dude," Silas said, "everyone on the team is here, and everyone here is drinking."

"Then I guess I'll start on offense and defense next week," Jackson said.

I followed them into the crowd, and we passed Deacon, Marshall, and Fletcher sitting on the hood of a truck. Marshall, who was a very happy drunk, fell off the truck when we walked by and, stumbling to his feet, embraced the three of us in a giant bear hug. Weezer's "Undone—The Sweater Song" blasted through someone's speakers, and Deacon said, "This band's my favorite, man." Then pointing to me said, "Don't you love 'em, new guy?"

For some reason, hearing this dickhead say he liked my favorite band pissed me off more than the dozens of times he'd shoved me in the hallway. I wanted to fight him. Okay, that's not true, but I wanted to hurt him somehow. I wanted to tell him I took his girlfriend to Atlanta and slept with her in a park just to see the reaction on his stupid face. But of course that would likely be the last thing I ever saw, so instead I mumbled, "Yeah."

The air hung heavy with cigarette smoke and car exhaust, and as we walked from group to group, Jackson and Silas occasionally stopped to say hello to people I didn't know. I recognized a few kids from school, but a lot of people there looked old, like they'd graduated from Rome years ago, particularly a man everyone called Skeeter, who appeared to be in his mid-forties. Skeeter probably explained the kegs.

Three beers and an hour later, I was talking to MeghanJennifer, who were wearing matching plaid skirts with vests, when Becca Walsh stumbled into me and shouted, "Marcus!" She was very drunk, or a little drunk and acting very drunk, and she spoke way too loud. "This sucks so much," she said. "Doesn't this suck? Who wants to take me home? I want to go somewhere else. I'm so hungry and bored."

One of Becca's friends grabbed her by the arm and pulled her away. "Don't you leave me, Friday Night Boyfriend," she shouted. "I am hungry and bored!"

Silas walked over, and we exchanged a look. He whispered, "You wanna bounce?"

"We'd better. There is no telling what she's already—whoa! What the hell?"

120

Some idiot had their Camaro on the dilapidated track now, doing high speed laps, and the crowd roared every time it passed. Jackson walked up and said, "This isn't going to end well," and no sooner had he said it, we heard a loud crash through the trees. A group of guys ran to investigate, and Silas said to Jackson, "We're about to leave."

"That's cool. This sucks," Jackson said.

We'd started toward my car just as a guy returned from the scene of the accident and shouted, "He's okay, but his car is upside down. Does anyone have a wench on their truck?"

About twenty yards away, near the kegs, there was a commotion I thought involved a truck wench but soon realized was something else entirely.

"You did what?!"

The shouting was so loud and so angry, all normal conversation screeched to a halt, and as people backed away from the noise, I saw Deacon grabbing Becca hard by the arm and screaming, "You bitch. You lying bitch. I can't believe you. Is he still here? Where is he? I'm going to kill him."

"Uh, Brinks, we might want to leave now," Silas said with understated urgency.

I didn't reply. I didn't do anything, though a part of me wanted to charge Deacon and rescue Becca, while the rest of me wanted to run deep into the woods. I felt like a spectator. Like I was standing next to myself, watching the scene unfold, and had no control over what my body did or did not do.

"There he is," Fletcher Morgan shouted, pointing toward us.

"You little fuck," Deacon screamed and threw Becca to the ground before charging me with ill intent.

There is a trope, popular in country and folk music, of large, violent men who, after making unwanted advances toward a married woman, are humbled by much smaller men. Think "Bad, Bad Leroy Brown" or "The Coward of the County." The trope doesn't exactly apply here though, because I, the much smaller man, had made advances, however passive, toward the woman of the large, violent man, and now I was going to get my ass beat. This would not be a popular country song.

Deacon ran hard in our direction. I think I saw steam pouring from his ears, and Silas and Jackson both stepped aside, something I cannot and will not blame them for. The quarterback leapt in an attempt to remove my head from the rest of my body, but I ducked just in time, and his thighs hit my shoulder, flipping him over my head. The crowd cheered, assuming I'd taken the first point in our contest, but I knew I'd only delayed the inevitable. Deacon came back, this time aiming lower, and form-tackled me to the ground, where he proceeded to pummel me with an indeterminable amount of punches to the stomach and face.

To their credit, both Silas and Jackson tried to intervene on my behalf, but Fletcher and Marshall held them back. And I suppose Deacon would have continued punching me until he was late for school on Monday, but Becca, screaming and half-mad, kneed him hard in the side of the head. Deacon reared back and, for a moment, looked like he was about to punch his girlfriend, but instead he kicked me in the side before jumping into his Jeep and leaving at high speed.

"Brinks, are you okay, man?"

"Yeah, I think so," I said, looking up at Silas and Jackson through swollen eyes. "Where is Becca? Did he hurt her?"

"She's fine," Silas said. "She just left with her friends."

They helped me to my feet and I asked, "Did I win?"

"You didn't die," Jackson said.

"And I think he improved your face a little," Silas added.

I tried to laugh, but it hurt so I stopped and said, "We'll call it a draw then. Plus, I was right."

"About what?" Silas asked as they helped me into the back seat of my Mazda.

"She's totally breaking up with him."

Chapter Fourteen

In days of yore, the Rome Quarterback Club met in the smoky backroom of Pantheon Pizza. I never attended one of these meetings, but it is not difficult to envision three dozen men shooting the shit for a couple hours over greasy pizza and un-filtered Pall Malls. The back room at Pantheon Pizza had three long, Last Supper-style tables, and I always pictured Coach P sitting in the center of one, with his disciples on each side, asking him to explain a parable about the spring fundraiser. Rumor was the Quarterback Club spent most of each meeting discussing the social lives of every member of the team, and if a player drank too much or spent too much time in the backseat of a car with a cheerleader at Oppian Park, Chief Evans, head of the Rome Police Department and Quarterback Club treasurer, would have one of his men pull over the offending party and scare them straight. Grades were never discussed. Grades were easily changed.

Now that they were gone, it was obvious the Rome Quar-terback Club never wielded any actual power or made any im-portant decisions. This, I suppose, caused the members some level of embarrassment, since for years they'd taken most of the credit for everything the football team accomplished. However, I suspect what angered them most was the loss of an excuse to leave their families and get a little drunk every Thursday night.

Even though the Rome Quarterback Club no longer officially existed, a few of them still met in secret at members' homes. This seemed like overkill to me. I can't fathom anyone in town noticing or caring if they still went to Pantheon Pizza. But I think the members got off on all this cloak-and-dagger shit. The meeting I went to, late that September, was at Deacon Cassburn's house, high on Aventine Hill overlooking Rome.

I arrived late, but was still the first one there, and parked in the driveway behind Deacon's black Cadillac Escalade. His home was a brick and stone monstrosity that looked like the love child of a McMansion and Buckingham Palace. It even had corner towers, from where I suppose Deacon could defend his family from an invading horde. I knocked on a massive door that took six or seven trees to make, and as I wondered why Deacon didn't splurge and have a moat installed, he opened the door.

"Brinks, come in," Deacon said, slapping me on the back. "I'm glad you could make it out tonight. Here, have a beer." Deacon shoved a cold Budweiser into my hand, and I took a sip and said, "You have a beautiful home."

"If you like this, you should see our lake house," Deacon said, and I wondered where he got his money, but I didn't wonder long because he immediately told me. "Ain't it crazy to think a guy like me could have a house like this? I was just out of college when I opened my first Cassburn's Check Cashing. I've got ten of 'em now, and I even bought that seedy no-tell motel in East Riverton, but you want to know where I made my real money?"

No, I thought. "Sure," I said.

"I've got this group of meth-heads who work for me. Well, they don't actually work for me, but I sort of pay their rent. What I do is, I buy a house in a nice neighborhood in Riverton or Hornby or Gaul, those gated communities work best, then I move my crew in. After a week or so, they start doing what meth-heads do—robbing neighbors, shitting in the yard, running naked through the streets—then I swoop in and make all the neighbors offers on their homes. They're always more than eager to sell, so I snatch up their houses at a bargain, then I move my meth-heads across town and resell all the homes I just bought at market price. Rinse and repeat, Brinks."

It's hard to imagine a chain of high-interest payday loan stores as the ethical apex of someone's business portfolio, but here we were. I didn't know what to say to this that wasn't insulting, so I didn't say anything and walked through the den, pretending to admire Deacon's gaudy furniture.

"What do you think of that view?" Deacon asked as I walked over to the floor-to-ceiling sliding glass doors leading out to his backyard.

"It's beau—holy shit, Deacon, there's a wolf on your back porch!"

I jumped back from the glass, and Deacon roared with laughter. "What are you scared of, Brinks? That's just Diana."

"Diana—wait, you have a pet wolf?"

"Got her as a puppy six years ago."

"What? Why? Why the hell would you adopt a wolf?"

Deacon sighed and said, "Okay, you know how Georgia keeps that ugly wrinkled dog on their sideline?"

"Yeah," I said.

"And Auburn flies that big-ass hawk around the stadium right before kickoff every Saturday?"

"I think it's an eagle but yeah."

"Well, I thought it would be awesome if Rome had a live mascot too."

"So you bought a wolf?"

"Yep. I heard about this old man at the Sparta flea market who had a litter of wolf puppies for sale, and I went and bought one. Bought her a cage too. A nice one you could pull behind a truck like LSU hauls their tiger around in. I wasn't planning on letting her run around the field before the game or anything. I'm not an idiot. But when I talked to Principal Trajan about it, he pussed out. Kept going on and on about lawyers and liability and how much trouble the school would get in if Diana got loose and ate a cheerleader. You want to pet her?"

"What? God no."

"Ain't nothing to be scared of," Deacon said. "Sit, Diana." The wolf sat on command while I looked at it and Deacon in disbelief. "Best damn dog I've ever had," he said, and Diana rolled over at the motion of his hand. "That old man in Carthage told me, if I were to spray another wolf's piss on someone, Diana would tear them to pieces, but I don't believe it. She's a sweetie. Might lick you to death, that's all."

Fletcher Morgan walked through the door without knocking, and Diana stood and bared her teeth. "Evening men, Diana," Fletcher said, helping himself to a beer in the fridge before walking over to us.

"We heard you had dinner with the great Jackson Crowder last night," Deacon said to me as we moved from the window back into the living room.

"Who told you that?"

"I did," Fletcher said, swigging his beer. "I live down the street from him. Saw you goin' in."

"Jackson have anything to say about us?" Deacon asked.

"Yeah, actually. He said he had to shut down the Quarterback Club because of some racist email Fletcher forwarded everyone."

Fletcher laughed and Deacon said, "That's some bullshit right there. That email Fletch sent wasn't even that racist."

"Nope," Fletcher said, "besides, I've got black friends."

One by one, the rest of the Underground Quarterback Club arrived. There were only about eight of them now, including Marshall Ford and a couple of men whose names I recognized from my first stint in Rome. All of them spoke to me, asked about my mother, and said they were happy to see me and hoped I could help the Quarterback Club in their struggle against the great Jackson Crowder. We drank beers and watched South Florida and Temple play football on Deacon's seventy-five-inch

Samsung, while Diana looked on and dreamed of eating us all.

"Okay, let's get this started," Deacon said, turning off the television. "I've been reading a lot of history lately." The men laughed because they thought this was a joke. "I'm serious," Deacon said. "I've been reading a lot of history, and there was this man named Marcus Aurelius who used to rule Rome. The big one, in Italy," he added for clarification, lest his compatriots think he meant a former mayor of their town.

"I know that name," one of the men said. "He's the guy who wanted Russell Crowe to rule Rome, but his dickhead son murdered him."

"None of that is true," Deacon said.

"No shit."

"Listen," Deacon said, "what I'm trying to tell you is Marcus Aurelius, the most powerful man in the world, hired a man to walk behind him all day long whispering, 'You are only a man.'"

The room considered this for a moment, and Marshall Ford said, "We should hire someone to walk behind Jackson all day whispering, 'You are only a dipshit,'" and the room roared with laughter that slowly morphed into hacking coughs.

"Y'all laugh," Deacon said, "but we need to remind the great Jackson Crowder he's just a man, and we gotta do it now, before he goes and wins the damn state championship and becomes untouchable. Melvin, how are things going at the school?"

Melvin, the high school janitor, said, "I spoke to six teachers this week, and ain't none of 'em wanting to go on record about changing grades. One of 'em told me they all want to help us, that Jackson had blackmailed 'em all, but if they came forward, they'd be implicating themselves, and that's the sort of thing they can lose tenure over. Lot of 'em are close to retirement, and that would ruin 'em, you know."

"We could pay 'em off," Fletcher suggested.

"It would take a hell of a lot of money for someone to risk losing their pension," Deacon said. "More than I'm willing to cough up, especially since we'd have no guarantee anything

127

would come of it. Hell, wouldn't surprise me if Jackson has the county school board in his pocket by now."

A man in a tie who looked like he came to the meeting straight from his desk job said, "What about a young teacher, one who doesn't have tenure yet? They might be willing to risk it for, say, a new car. Or maybe some help with their student loans."

"That's a thought, Bill," Deacon said.

"What about Brinks?" asked Darryl Loder, the only confessing atheist in Rome and now editor of the *Riverton Times*. "He doesn't have tenure, and he doesn't even need the money."

"I haven't changed any grades for—"

"Now Darryl, Brinks is our guest tonight," Deacon said, coming to my rescue, "and we're not gonna ask him to do anything he's uncomfortable with."

"Look," Marshall Ford said, "I know we've talked about this before, but I still don't see no point in taking down Jackson if we don't go after Silas too. If he gets the job, things won't be no better for us."

"Hell, things'll probably get worse," said Melvin the janitor. "Coach Carver is the brains of that bunch; without Crowder holding him back, they's no telling what he could do."

"But that's my point," Deacon said. "Silas's crippled ass would fall outta his wheelchair laughing if we took down Jackson. He'd be so appreciative of us, things would be back to normal in no time. Now Fletcher, where are things with your plan, what's it called … Operation Triple X?"

For some reason, Fletcher Morgan stood to address the crowd and said, "I'm calling it the eXXXtravaganza now. With three X's."

"Whatever," Deacon said, "where are you with it?"

"Well, I made myself fake Facebook, Snapchat, and Tweeter accounts, and I've friended a lot of the kids from Rome, but I'll be honest, Deacon, half the time I don't even know what they're talking about. They don't even use the alphabet, just those little ouijas."

"Emojis?" Deacon asked.

"Yeah, emojis, or whatever the hell they call 'em. I need the damn Poinsettia Stone to translate that shit."

Deacon sighed and rubbed his temples. "Well, keep at it, Fletch. I know it's only September, but this stuff takes time. What else was there … Zane, you were gonna look into Jackson's financials for us?"

Zane, a short man who'd been smoking an e-cigarette all night, stood, pulled a sheet of paper from his pocket, and read, "Jackson bought 2226 Amherst in June 2014, for $349,000. In August 2014, he sold 237 Virginia Avenue in Birmingham for $503,000. He also owns seven more acres on the Coosa River a few miles south of Rome, but I couldn't figure out how much he paid for 'em or when he bought 'em."

"That all?" Deacon asked.

Zane flipped his paper over a couple times and said, "Yeah, I guess so. I mean, I can't just call the bank and ask how much money he's got."

"Bill, you work at the bank. Can you—"

"No, Deacon, I can't do that."

"Okay, okay, I had to ask. Darryl, your girlfriend found out anything about Amy's miscarriage?"

Darryl, who wore a fedora and a T-shirt featuring Jesus riding a dinosaur, said, "I asked her if she could look in Amy's file for me, but she said that was illegal, and I was an asshole for even asking her."

Some of the others laughed, and Darryl said, "I don't understand why we can't get Jackson fired on some sort of moral clause. Everyone knows he's screwing what's her name."

"Now Darryl, that's libelous," Deacon said, "unless you've got any proof you want to share?"

Darryl shook his head no, and Deacon said, "What about the rest of you? Any of y'alls wives know anything about Amy?"

Around the room, men shook their heads no, and Deacon cursed and said, "Well, I'd bet my house Jackson made up that miscarriage story to cover his ass on the Mytilene loss, but I can't prove it if y'all don't help me out." He hit his hand on the coffee table and took a deep breath and said, "Okay, well, I feel like we've taken a step back here. We're gonna need to double our efforts. We all know the great Jackson Crowder is as crooked as the day is long, but if the rest of Rome don't figure it out soon, he'll be untouchable. Now, is there any official club business?"

"Mr. President," Marshall said, rising to his feet.

"You have the floor, Marshall."

"I propose we carry on with the Cow Patty Party as planned this spring."

"Wait," I said, "y'all still do that?"

"Now, Brinks," Deacon said, "Marshall has the floor. They'll be time for questions in a moment."

"Sorry," I mumbled.

The Cow Patty Party was, and apparently still is, a fundraiser where the Quarterback Club draws a 100x100-foot grid on the football field and sells each square on the grid for $100. Then, on a Saturday morning in the spring, they release a cow onto the field and everyone in town watches and prays the cow will shit in their square, earning them half the $10,000 pot. If the cow shits on the line, they split the money, obviously.

"Anyway," Marshall said, "I think it'll show the community the important role we play, and—"

"The community don't give a shit about us; if they did, we'd—"

"Sit, Zane. You're out of order," Deacon barked. "Marshall, you were saying."

"Well, I just think it would earn us a lot of good will, and it would let Jackson know we're still here."

Marshall sat and Deacon said, "We have a motion to conduct the Cow Patty Party as planned, any questions?" No one said anything, and Deacon said, "Okay, all in favor?" A few people mumbled ayes. "All opposed?" Zane offered a feeble "nay." "The ayes have it," Deacon said. "The Cow Patty Party will go on as planned."

They went on like this, observing Robert's Rules of Order, for the better part of the next hour, until the group ratified a motion to "Go on home and get the hell to bed."

Deacon held me by the shoulder as the other men left, and when we were alone again, he said, "Brinks, I know Rome means as much to you as it does to the rest of us. And I ain't asking you to do something you might be uncomfortable with, but I just want to know if …"

At that moment, I almost felt sorry for Deacon. He was once the King of Rome, and now he was just the leader of the biggest collection of kooks in Rubicon County. Hell, he kept a wolf in his backyard; he probably was the biggest kook of all. But even if I did feel a twinge of pity, and even if Jackson and I would never truly be friends again, Deacon was still an asshole, and I wasn't about to join his ranks.

"… if we can count on you to help us get rid of Jackson?"

"No," I said, "you can't," and walked to my car while Diana howled at the moon.

Rolling Stone: Can you talk about what led to the cancellation of the European leg of your tour?

Marcus Brinks: Talk about it? You mean with words?

Rolling Stone: Well yeah, preferably with words.

Marcus Brinks: No.

—*Rolling Stone,* "Interview with Marcus Brinks,"
January 11, 1999

Chapter Fifteen

During the tenth month of the year of our Lord nineteen hundred and ninety-four, as foretold in the book of Garth, the gods unleashed a plague upon Rome. Not a plague of frogs, or lice, or locusts—those would've been fine. The Coosa River did not run red with blood—that would've been okay too. No, the gods were not messing around that October, and they blighted our fair town with a pestilence of heel, toe, do-se-dos that seemingly afflicted everyone in school but Jackson and me. Like a zit, Dixie Dancehall & Taxidermy materialized overnight, filling the void of Main Street cruising with, perhaps, the worst recreational activity in the history of human recreation: Country. Line. Dancing.

"Should we check out Dixie Dancehall?" Silas asked Jackson and me through a mouthful of French fries.

It was Saturday night, and we were eating dinner on a picnic table outside the WigWam, two weeks after what I'm loosely calling my fight with Deacon at the raceway. My mom grounded me that night, mostly for coming home with alcohol on my breath, but also for refusing to discuss the origins of my swollen black eyes. I missed the Riverton game, a 63-7 shellacking (yes, Jackson gave up the only touchdown), and the succeeding Saturday night, in which Silas and Jackson spent six straight hours playing *NBA Jam* in the garage.

"Hell no," Jackson said. He was in a pissy mood because Rome played a close game the night before, a 17-7 win over Koch, and he never saw the field after warmups.

"Well, I'm open to suggestions if you've got better plans," Silas said, "but I'm not spending another Saturday night in the garage beating y'alls asses at Sega. Brinks, you up for some country line dancing?"

I took a sip of my grape milkshake (it tastes better than it sounds) and said, "Sounds bitchin'." But when Silas didn't laugh in reply, I said, "No, wait, for real?"

"Everyone from school will be there tonight," Silas said. "A lot of people went last weekend and said it was fun."

"Country line dancing?" I asked. "The only one of those three words that sounds fun is 'line.'"

"Like I said," Silas said, "I'm open to suggestions."

Jackson and I looked at each other then back at Silas, who shrugged and said, "Dixie Dancehall it is."

Dixie Dancehall & Taxidermy was in an old tire warehouse on the outskirts of Riverton. Most people just called it Dixie Dancehall, but Monday through Friday, they'd gladly stuff any dead animal you brought in. Silas told me it's now a CrossFit gym. That night, the parking lot was full, so we parked next door at a carpet factory and joined the short line at the door, where a man in overalls took our five dollars and said, if he caught us with alcohol or "tobaccy" on the premises, he'd never let us come back.

"You promise?" Jackson asked, but the overalled man just glared at us, so we quickly went inside.

Dixie Dancehall was a bit Spartan in decor. A few deer heads hung from the walls but not much else. A mismatched collection of folding chairs was distributed randomly along the edges of the room, and the concession stand consisted solely of a woman in the corner selling canned Cokes from a cooler. Overhead, at Dixie Dancehall, was low. We each bought a Coke and gravitated toward the chairs against the wall and watched a few hundred kids kick left, kick right, kick left, heel shift, stomp, stomp, and kick ball change. I wanted to throw up.

"Should I worry that my ears are bleeding?" I shouted to Silas and Jackson over a particularly twangy number from Messrs. Brooks and Dunn.

"Yeah, this sucks," Jackson said.

"You suck, and you suck," Silas said, and after hitting us both in the shins with his crutches, he was on the dance floor, boot-stomping with the rest of Rome.

"To be on crutches and not know what he's doing," I said to Jackson, "he's not half bad."

"He could always dance," Jackson replied with what sounded like a hint of envy. I know I was jealous, because within literal seconds of hitting the dance floor, a half-dozen girls surrounded Silas, helping him learn the moves. But one song wore him out, and by the merciful end of "Cotton-Eyed Joe," Silas sat between us again.

"I called Warren G and Nate Dogg while you were out there doing whatever the hell you were just doing. They said they're coming to regulate you."

"It's not my favorite music," Silas said, still catching his breath. "But I know N-A-T-E and The Warren to the G wouldn't begrudge a brotha' for mackin' skirts by any means necessary."

"Maybe not," I said, "but they're under legal obligation to cap your ass for calling yourself a brotha', in general, and while country line dancing at Dixie Dancehall, in particular."

Silas shrugged and said, "Yeah, that's fair."

We sat there, sipping our Cokes and watching our classmates dance themselves whiter, and after three or four more songs, Jackson said, "Can we go anywhere else?"

"Where?" Silas asked.

"Let's go to Winona Mountain and see if we can hear the ghost baby cry on the haunted bridge."

"You're supposed to take girls up there so you can hold them when they get freaked out. I'm not going with you two."

"He's scared," Jackson said to me, and I laughed.

"You guys aren't leaving, are you?"

It was Becca Walsh, wearing boots, painted-on Wranglers, and a red and black checkered button-down shirt tied above her midriff. She somehow looked amazing and ridiculous all at once.

"Yeah, this blows," Jackson said.

"It's fun," Becca said, hitting Jackson on the arm. "Have you guys even tried it?"

"I did," Silas said.

"Marcus," she said, reaching out her hand, "try this next dance with me. It's super easy. I promise."

We hadn't really spoken since the fight. She said hello to me at school now, and I said hello back, but that was the extent of our post-ass-beating relationship. She did dump Deacon. Rumor was her breakup talk culminated in a swift knee to his balls, but this is unverified, and Deacon still strutted around school with the cockiness of a starting quarterback, not the shuffling limp of a dude with bruised testicles. I didn't care either way. Not about Deacon's balls. I never cared about Deacon's balls. I didn't care about Becca. Silas warned me she was a hall of fame tease, but I ignored him. I ignored him because, even though a girl this hot had never liked me before, I thought Becca and I had a connection—something special she couldn't find with the other guys at Rome, and I followed her siren song into the rocky shore where her boyfriend beat the shit out of me. Becca was a careless person, and I didn't care to do whatever it was we were doing any more.

"No," I said, looking up so she could see my still-black eyes, "we're leaving."

"Oh, okay," she said as I stood and walked past her. "You guys have fun. I'll see you Monday."

Jackson and Silas may have said bye to her, but I'm not sure. I kept walking, out of Dixie Dancehall and to my car, where I blasted Soundgarden in a futile attempt to wash the Garth Brooks from my ears.

"Okay, now what?" Silas said as we left Dixie Dancehall, heading back toward Rome. Jackson and I knew Saturday night protocol required us to find something else fun to do, since we'd made the call to leave.

"Big Bertha's?" Jackson asked.

"Where?"

"Big Bertha's," Jackson repeated without explanation, leaving me to envision a strip club I really did not want to go to.

"Okay," Silas said, "but you are paying for my balls."

This did not clear things up.

Big Bertha's, thank god, was a dairy farm and converted driving range near Carthage. Bertha, an entrepreneurial farmer's wife, bought ten thousand golf balls, set up some flood lights, and now people paid her six bucks to hit a hundred golf balls at the rusted tractors, dilapidated cars, and wooden cow cutouts doubling as yard markers in the pasture. The dairy farm's real cows mooed at golfers behind a gigantic net over three hundred yards away, and though Marshall Ford swears he hit one once, Bertha says no one has ever come close.

"That was terrible," Jackson said, teeing up a ball and slicing it into the net that kept errant shots from hitting passing cars on Highway 9.

"You're a terrible golfer," Silas said. "What did you expect?"

"I'm talking about the line dancing place."

"There were a lot of hot chicks there," Silas said. "I mean, the music sucked, and the dancing really sucked, but if you haven't noticed, we're now alone in a cow pasture on a Saturday night."

"We've got Bertha," I said, motioning toward the cigar-smoking woman sitting outside the little shed where she sold buckets of golf balls.

Silas laughed, and propping himself up with his left crutch, proceeded to hit a one-armed, high, fading seven-iron off the rear bumper of an Oldsmobile that doubled as the 150-yard marker.

"We'll always have Bertha," Silas said then proceeded to hit the car twice more.

Jackson teed up another ball and, overcompensating for his slice, hooked it deep into the woods, drawing an evil glare from Bertha. He cursed and said, "Okay, this sucks too, and there are considerably fewer hot girls in tight jeans here, but Brinks didn't want to line dance either."

I'd just teed up a ball of my own and said, "True, but hitting golf balls in a cow pasture was not my suggestion." I swung at the ball, missed it entirely, and felt pain in every bone and muscle Deacon had punched, kicked, or stomped a fortnight ago. "Shit!" I shouted.

"No cursing, asshole!" Bertha screamed from her shed.

"Sorry," I mumbled, and Jackson asked, "Are you okay?"

"I'm fine," I said, wincing. "It's just my bones and organs and stuff still aren't quite right from a couple weeks ago."

"See?" Jackson said after shanking a wedge that almost hit Silas, "We've got to take that dickhead down."

"Not this shit again," Silas said and walked off toward Bertha's shed.

"You in, Brinks?" Jackson asked.

"I don't know."

"Seriously man, what do you have to lose at this point?"

"Feeling in my extremities. Functioning kidneys. Some of my favorite teeth."

"But he'll never know it was us," Jackson said.

"Are you gonna go all Tonya Harding and hire someone to whack his knee?" Silas asked, coming back with two beers and handing me one.

"What the hell? Bertha sold you beer?" Jackson asked.

"She's selling alcohol out of a shed on her farm without a liquor license," Silas said. "Shockingly, she didn't bother to check my ID."

Silas and I opened our beers, and Jackson shook his head and said, "No, I'm not planning to hurt him. But think about it; if we can get him thrown off the team, he loses all his power. Football is his Kryptonite."

"That analogy makes no sense at all."

"Shut up. You both know what I mean. We've just got to think of a way to get him thrown off the team."

Silas set down his beer and dinged another seven-iron off the rusted Oldsmobile before turning to us and saying, "If you do this, you've gotta keep it on the down-low. No one can ever find out it was you."

"Us," Jackson corrected.

"No, you," Silas said. "Because if he gets kicked off the team, Rome isn't winning state, and if the school finds out you cost Rome a state championship, they'll crucify you."

"No one will know it was us," Jackson said.

"You," Silas corrected.

"So what are you thinking?" I asked. "Like, slipping a laxative into his Gatorade before kickoff?"

"No, Brinks. I want him off the team for good, not missing the first half with the shits."

"You could put a dead hooker in his trunk and call the cops," Silas offered, and Jackson flipped him off.

"You're right," Silas said. "The Rome Police Department wouldn't even arrest him for that."

"Okay," Jackson said, "now you're thinking. It's got to be legal trouble, but something outside of Rome, because we know the Rome police won't do shit to him."

"Dude," Silas said, "it's October. We've got eight months of Deacon left, then we'll never see him again."

"Pussy," Jackson said, and Silas nearly decapitated him with a swinging crutch.

"Brinks, can I count on you?" Jackson asked.

"Probably not," I said and tried to hit a ball one-handed, thinking that would hurt less. It didn't, but I did make contact and sent the ball rolling toward Bertha, who was not amused.

"You didn't say no," Jackson said. "I'll put you down as maybe."

~ ~ ~

Mom's boyfriend Steve was at our house when I got home, two minutes before curfew. He'd been there a lot the past few weeks, which wasn't great because he, how can I put this delicately, sucked donkey balls.

"I'm home," I said, walking through the den, where Mom and Steve sat on the couch, watching some Tom Cruise movie they'd rented from Blockbuster.

"Yeah, we can see that," Steve said, and I glared at him before turning to go upstairs to my room.

"Hold up there, son," Steve said, jumping off the couch. "I need to make sure you didn't get your ass beat again."

He was in my face, making a show of examining me with an imaginary magnifying glass, and said, "Nope, all these bruises look old."

"Steve, leave him alone," my mom said.

"What?" Steve asked, rejoining her on the couch. "That's why boys should play football. It toughens them up."

I turned to go upstairs again, and Steve said, "Hold up, son. I'm not done talking to you."

"I'm not your son, Steve," I said, and he started to get off the couch, but Mom put a hand on his shoulder, and he sat back down. Was he going to fight me too? What the hell was wrong with people in this town?

"Good night, Marcus," my mom said, and I went up to my room and hated Rome until I fell asleep.

Chapter Sixteen

"You gave Darryl Loder an interview?"

Alabama offers no guarantees of crisp, fall weather. October temperatures in the nineties are not unheard of, and though I cannot prove it, I suspect slutty Halloween costumes originated here to combat the autumn swelter. Rome's default setting is hot and muggy, calendar be damned, but mercifully, we were in the middle of a cool snap that October, and the weather had my mother feeling well enough to venture from her bedroom. She was in the kitchen that morning, sipping coffee and ignoring the plate of eggs Rita had scrambled.

"Well, good morning to you too," she said as I sat across the table.

I held up the Friday edition of the *Riverton Times* and asked again, "You gave Darryl Loder an interview?"

"Of course not," she said, moving her eggs around with a fork. "He called, and we had a little chat, but it wasn't an interview. No one would want to interview me, Marcus."

"He's the editor of the newspaper, Mom. Of course, it was an interview."

My mother reached for the paper, but I pulled it away, pointed at the front-page article, and said, "You told him I didn't speak to you for ten years?"

"You didn't speak to me for ten years."

"Yeah, but you didn't have to tell the world."

I walked to the counter and poured myself a cup of coffee, and my mother said, "You know, Darryl is an atheist."

"Yeah, Mom, I know. We were in school together."

"Marcus, are you mad?" she asked as I sat back across from her.

I took a sip of coffee, sighed, and said, "No … I'm not mad. But this article makes me look awful, and I wish my own mother wasn't one of the primary sources." I held up the paper and read aloud, "Every mother dreams of their son winning a Gramy, but not at the expense of their relation with the child."

"That's true," my mother said.

"No, it's not," I said, louder than I meant to. "First, he misspelled "Grammy." Second, we didn't win a Grammy; we were nominated for Best New Artist but lost to Paula Cole. And third, my band had nothing to do with what happened between us."

"I told him that was all my fault," Mom said. "Did he leave that part out?"

"He left it out," I said and handed her the paper.

"That's not a flattering picture of you," she said, pointing to the article about the Rome Fire Department's new Dalmatian mascot.

I couldn't help but laugh, and she said, "Marcus, I am sorry if I embarrassed you."

"That's okay," I said and kissed her on the head. "Yours is the least embarrassing part of the article. Love you, Mom. I'll see you after school."

~ ~ ~

I hadn't given an interview since an admittedly bizarre 1999 Q&A with *Rolling Stone* after the cancellation of our first and only headlining tour. But unlike some other reclusive celebrities, I quickly faded from the public consciousness, and no sooner was I out of sight, I was out of mind. Which was fine with me. I had all the money I needed, or at least I thought I did, and I'd grown tired of answering the same questions with the same lies ad nauseam.

But then I pissed off Deacon by not joining his little coup, so he had Darryl, local atheist and editor of the *Riverton Times*, do a little digging and write a mostly libelous hit piece on yours truly. Suddenly, I was news again, but I took some solace in the fact that no one reads the *Riverton Times*. Most days, Rita threw my mother's copy away still in the wrapper. And if a sixty-seven-year-old woman doesn't read the paper, I thought there was no way the teenagers in my first-period class had seen the article. I was wrong.

After the tardy bell rang and Kyler walked in late, I took a bite of my breakfast apple and said, "Okay, *Julius Caesar*, act two, scene one, who wants to read for us?"

The mousy-looking girl on the front row raised her hand, and when I called on her, she said, "Mr. Brinks, you were in the paper today."

"Yes, I was," I said, sitting on my desk. "But so was Kyler," I said, pointing toward the young quarterback already napping at his desk, "so that's not much of an accomplishment." Kyler looked up, confused, and some of the class dared to laugh at their quarterback.

"Did you really live in a hotel in Jamaica for sixteen years?" asked the short blonde sitting next to the air conditioner.

"No ... well, yes," I said, "but it was a nice, all-inclusive place. I wasn't like Rick Majerus living in the Salt Lake City Marriott."

"Who?"

"There was this man who coached basketball in Utah, and he—you know what, it's not important. *Julius Caesar*, who wants to—"

"Wait, you were a basketball coach?" asked the guy in glasses sitting against the far wall. "I thought you were in a band."

"What? No, I—"

"No, dumbass," the guy behind him said. "Castro won't let them play basketball in Jamaica."

"That's not—"

"Why did you live in a hotel that long?" asked the curly-haired girl near the door.

"Because they had nice hammocks," I said, "and alcohol was included, and I was trying to drink myself to death."

"Oh."

"I'm joking. Sort of," I said, walking over to look out the window. "But I didn't check in thinking I'd stay there sixteen years. When we were on tour in Europe, our record label kept asking to hear material for a second album, but I hadn't written the first song."

"That's some hall-of-fame-level procrastination," said the mousy-looking girl on the front row.

I smiled and said, "It's not that I was putting it off. I literally couldn't write another song. The part of my brain responsible for lyrics and melodies was empty. The stress finally got to me, so I walked off stage one night in Amsterdam, spent a few months in New York keeping the tabloids busy, then went back to college."

"Your Wikipedia page says you dated Sarah Michelle Gellar," said the short blonde by the air conditioner.

"For real?" I asked, and when she nodded, I said, "No, I didn't, but please don't edit it."

"It says you dated Kate Hudson too," said the curly-haired girl by the door. "There's a picture of you two at a club."

"Our publicists set that up," I said. "She was dating the lead singer of The Black Crowes then. I never dated anyone famous."

My classroom mumbled their collective disappointment, and I said, "I finished college, tried writing again, but after a week with no progress, I went on a month-long bender culminating with me punching a police horse in Central Park. My friends were all worried, and they wanted me to go to this super-exclusive resort in Jamaica to relax, but when I got down there, it was booked solid, so I checked into the Sandals next door. I liked it so much I called my accountant and asked if I had enough money to stay a little longer, and he told me I could stay there for fifty years if I wanted to. Of course, he couldn't have predicted the housing market bubble and that I'd actually go broke in sixteen years, but what can you do?"

"Hey, Brinks," Kyler said, raising his hand with a smirk, "what will Ms. Walsh think about you nailing all those tourists?"

His classmates giggled, and I rubbed my eyes and said, "It's Mr. Brinks, Kyler, and—"

"Don't be embarrassed, Mr. Brinks. I'm proud of you."

Somehow, Darryl got in touch with David, a former bartender at the Sandals resort where I lived, and he told the *Riverton Times*, "Whenever a group of women arrived at the resort for a girlfriends' weekend, and new groups arrived every day, Mr. Brinks made sure I pointed them toward the famous rock star sitting alone across the bar. It's hard to say how many women, but he kept pace with Wilt Chamberlain for a while."

Wilt Chamberlain was a famous basketball player, who once claimed he slept with twenty thousand women. The math on this works out to around five hundred women a year, and I promise you, I was never anywhere close to that pace. Did I take advantage of my fame and fortune and a seemingly unending supply of uninhibited women? Maybe. But sex with strangers loses its novelty after a year or two or six. That, and eventually, the women had never heard of me, and after googling me on their phones probably decided they could do better.

"Okay, look," I said, "there are things in that article I'm not particularly proud of. But I went from young and heartbroken to young and rich and famous way too fast, and, well, it took me a little longer than normal to grow up."

"I hear you, Mr. Brinks," Kyler said, "but Ms. Walsh is gonna be pissed, ain't she?"

I stared at him for a moment and said, "Yeah, probably. Now, *Julius Caesar*, who is reading for us?"

~ ~ ~

I didn't see Becca in the lunchroom and could only assume she was pissed off and cut her students' lunch short to avoid me.

I called her when school let out for the day, but my call went to voicemail, so I waited ten minutes and called again with the same result.

I tried texting her.

—Hey, do you want to rent a movie or something tonight?

We had plans for tomorrow night but not tonight, and I suspect she saw through this thinly veiled attempt to find out if she was mad. Her reply came five minutes later.

—Dinner with my parents.

Shit. No emojis from someone who typically used three per text. She was so pissed she didn't even use a verb.

—Cool. By the way, did you see the article about me in the paper?

This time, she made me wait ten minutes.

—Yes.

Shit. Shit. Shit. She was making me ask, so I asked.

—So, are you pissed?

Thirty minutes later.

—I'll see you tomorrow night, Marcus.

Shit.

~ ~ ~

On Saturday, one night after our alma mater defeated Koch

35-0 to run its 2017 record to 7-0, the Rome High School Class of 1994 held it's twenty-three-year reunion. That we reunited in a year not divisible by five was partially my fault but mostly Chase Malone's, our senior class president who joined the army and now lived in South Korea. A few weeks ago, Becca and I were on her couch, flipping through an old yearbook, and I asked her who at our twenty-year reunion was now fat and/or bald.

"Oh shit," she said. "We never had a twenty-year reunion. With Chase in Korea, everyone sort of forgot."

Seconds later, despite my protests, she was one the phone, talking to classmates and reserving the Palatine Bend clubhouse for an evening of alcohol-fueled reminiscing.

With Becca in charge of the reunion, I didn't see her that afternoon, and this only added to my anxiety over the previous day's article, which the *Huffington Post* had picked up overnight. Around three p.m., I gave up and texted to see if she needed any help. Her reply was brief.

—No.

The reunion began at six p.m., and I fought the urge to show up early so I could talk to Becca. When I did arrive, at a quarter after, I skipped the small talk gauntlet in the clubhouse and found Silas parked by a poolside table out back.

"Brinks, you pimp," he said as I sat next to him. "I never thought you had it in you."

I forced a laugh and said, "Thanks, have you seen Becca?"

"Yeah, she was showing the guy from Trevi's where to put the food when I got here."

"I think she's pissed off … about the article."

"Why would she be pissed that you slept with a bunch of groupies twenty years ago? Wait, are you two a thing now?"

"No … yes … I mean, sort of. We were, at least."

"Huh," Silas said then started to add something but put his hand to his mouth and reconsidered.

147

"What?" I asked. "Were you going to warn me about her again?"

Silas smiled and said, "No, you'd never listen to me anyway. Now go get us some beers."

I walked inside and saw Becca, but she was talking to a group of people in the corner of the room, so I grabbed two beers and went back outside with Silas.

"Nice win last night," I said, handing him his beer.

"I guess," he said. "We had thirty-five points midway through the second quarter, and Jackson shut down my offense. I swear, Brinks, we'd own every record in state history if he'd let me run my damn offense." He took a sip of his beer and said, "I know this sounds paranoid, but I'm starting to think he's holding me back because he doesn't want to lose me. It's not unheard of for colleges to hire high school coaches these days. Hugh Freeze. Art Briles."

"Yeah, and those ended well," I said.

Silas laughed and said, "Look, here comes our fearless leader now."

Jackson and his wife made the short drive from their house in a golf cart, and when I walked inside a few minutes later to grab another beer, a small line had already formed to kiss his ass. I skipped the line but went back outside through the wrong door and found myself on a patio with Fletcher Morgan, who was smoking a joint.

"Doctor subscribed this," Fletcher said. "It's metamucinal."

I held my hands up to show him I didn't care then turned to go back inside and he said, "Hell of an article about you in yesterday's paper."

"Yeah," I said.

"You know, you probably ought to help him out, 'cause one way or another, Deacon always gets what he wants."

I stared at Fletcher for a moment then pointed to his state championship ring and said, "He didn't get one of those," before walking back inside.

As the reunion wore on, the Class of 1994 slowly broke off into old cliques, and as the cliques drifted toward the edges of the room, we all realized we didn't care much for each other's company; otherwise, we wouldn't have forgotten our twenty-year reunion. I sat poolside with Silas while the evening wound down, and as he concluded an exhaustive lecture on the history of the word "shorty" in hip-hop, Becca came outside and walked toward us.

"Good luck, Brinks," Silas said and nearly drove his wheel-chair into the pool because he'd downed at least six beers that I'd seen, and then Becca and I were alone.

We sat silent for a moment, then when she let out a long sigh, I blurted out, "It wasn't that many women. David, the bartender, he's the biggest liar on the island. He used to tell people he beat Usain Bolt in the 100-meter dash while wearing a pair of wingtips."

"I'm not mad about that," Becca said.

"Plus, I still owe David money, so he's probably mad and just trying to … oh, you're not mad about that?"

"No. You were in a rock band, Marcus. It sort of goes with the territory. I won't lie and say I enjoyed reading it, but I don't suppose you'd enjoy reading about the guys I slept with in college either."

"Not particularly," I said and stuck my fingers in my ears in case she began listing them off. We were quiet for another moment, then I said, "If it's the stuff about not talking to my mom, I can explain. She—"

"She told me everything about that," Becca said.

"Wait, she did?"

"She did. She called me after school yesterday and explained everything."

"Then what … I don't understand why—"

"Marcus, I'm not mad at you. I'm disappointed because you're a talented musician. That album you wrote … it meant so much to so many people … and even though your band broke

149

up, and you hadn't released a new song in decades, I always liked to think you were in the islands somewhere, slaving away on your next masterpiece, not drinking yourself numb in a hammock for nearly two decades."

"I stopped doing that when I turned twenty-eight," I said.

"Your mother told me that too."

"Did she tell you I took up paddle boarding? It's not like I didn't do anything."

"She told me, Marcus."

I suppose I could have confessed to her then why I hadn't written anything in twenty years, but it seemed easier to apologize, so I said, "Becca, I'm sorry."

Becca sighed. "You don't have to apologize to me."

We sat in silence, and after a long while, I asked, "What do I have to do then?"

She stood up, kissed me on the head, and said, "You're going to have to figure that out on your own."

Then she left me sitting by the pool alone.

"After rocking the 41stst Annual Grammy Awards with an impromptu solo performance, Dear Brutus lead singer Marcus Brinks reportedly commandeered The Backstreet Boys tour bus, picked up two dozen fans waiting outside Shrine Auditorium, and went on an ill-fated joyride that caused over $100,000 in damage to the University of Southern California campus.

—*The Los Angeles Times*, "Grammy News & Notes," February 25, 1999

Chapter Seventeen

"It's not like prom, Brinks. You don't need a date to go."

It was Friday afternoon, homecoming week, and Silas was trying, and failing, to persuade me to attend the homecoming dance after that night's game.

"Yeah," I said, "but you have a date."

"Look at me, Brinks. Of course I have a date. But I'm telling you, lots of people won't. It's no biggie."

Jackson shook his head to indicate my lack of a date was a biggie.

"Fine," Silas said. "Go with Crowder to Jesus Prom, but understand you don't have a date to that either."

"He doesn't need a date to the Fifth Quarter," Jackson said.

"But you have a date," I said.

Jackson, who was in the middle of one of his short-lived religious phases, was skipping the homecoming dance to attend a Fifth Quarter at Rome First Baptist, and though he claimed this was a better option for someone without a date, he was taking Meghan (of MeghanJennifer), and Silas asked Mandy Duke to the homecoming dance, but I didn't find out any of this until Wednesday, at which point it was too late to secure a date of my own to either event.

"It's not a real date," Jackson said. "Besides, there won't be any music or dancing or anything."

"See," Silas said, "Jesus Prom sucks."

"Stop calling it that," Jackson snapped, and Silas grinned at me.

"He's right though," I said to Jackson. "It doesn't sound like much fun."

"Oh, and watching other people dance does?" he said.

"I'm not going to the homecoming dance either," I said.

"Yes, you are," Silas said. "I'm telling you, Brinks, half the people there won't have dates. There will be plenty of skirts there to dance with."

They argued back and forth for the better part of our lunch period until I finally snapped and said, "Oh my god, both of you shut up. Can't I go to both for a little while?"

"I guess so," Silas said.

"Yeah, I don't see why not," Jackson agreed.

~ ~ ~

Silas was by himself when I arrived at the game that night, and when he motioned for me to join him, I asked, "Where's Mandy? I don't want to be the third wheel when she gets back."

"At home," he said. "She's meeting me at the dance. It might rain later, and apparently, she's styled her hair in such a physics-defying way that a single drop of water will cause it and the rest of the universe to collapse into a black hole."

"Oh," I said. "I'm glad she stayed home then."

Rome led 49-0 at halftime, and as the teams headed to their locker rooms, four trucks pulled the four class homecoming floats onto the field. Mr. Gaba, our world history teacher with the Barry White voice, handled public address duties, and he announced the places in the float contest. "In last place," he said, "a float depicting a Roman gladiator disemboweling a Weepel Warthog, the senior class." I'm not sure about first, second, or third place, because I couldn't hear Mr. Gaba over the angry protests of the senior class, protests I joined in on, even though I'd contributed exactly 0.0 man-hours to the creation of our float.

Next, the Marching Legion took the field for their home-coming show, featuring songs from the film *Aladdin*, and as they played "A Whole New World," golf carts made to look like flying carpets carried members of the homecoming court onto the field. Becca was up for homecoming queen, but I voted for Jennifer (of MeghanJennifer) to spite her. After a dramatic pause though, Mr. Gaba called out Becca's name to loud cheers, and after they placed a crown on her head, her golf cart drove around the field so she could wave to the admiring crowd.

"So, that Steve guy dating my mom is kind of the worst," I said to Silas sometime during the fourth quarter, a quarter that saw Jackson make two tackles and give up a long touchdown pass.

"Yeah," Silas said. "We didn't want to say anything, but his son was in our class until he went to live with his mom in Horn-by a few years ago. Steve helped coach our little league team in sixth grade, and dude is a world-class bag of dicks. He fought with parents, shoved kids at practice, and showed up to games drunk. Eventually, the league suspended him."

"Oh. Great," I deadpanned.

"I wouldn't worry about it," Silas said. "Your mom won't date that dude long."

"I hope not, because—" I started to say but fell silent as Queen Becca and her entourage passed by. She looked our way and flashed a sad smile, but I only managed a head nod in return.

"I voted for Jennifer," Silas said, "out of solidarity."

We bumped fists and I said, "Thanks."

"So you're going to the dance, right?"

"Yeah, I guess. But I don't plan to enjoy it."

"That's the spirit, Brinks."

Mercifully, the game ended with Rome only defeating Wee-pel 70-7, and Silas and I made the short walk from the Colosse-um to the Ronald J. Pumphrey Gymnasium for the homecoming dance.

Silas was right when he told me homecoming wasn't a big deal. Unlike prom, all students from the high school and middle school could attend. You just needed two bucks to enter and a desire to hear "Tootsee Roll," "Whoomp! (There It Is)," and the lesser known "Whoot, There It Is," on repeat until your ears bled. Once inside, we tossed our shoes into an ever-growing pile, lest we scuff the basketball court with our gyrations, then we sat on the bleachers with everyone else except a handful of idiot sixth graders who hadn't reached the age of self-awareness and could therefore dance like no one was watching.

"Where's Mandy?" I asked Silas as the DJ played a Lisa Loeb song.

"On her way, I guess."

"Wait, is that the homecoming song?" I asked, pointing toward the stage curtain behind the far basketball goal, where someone had spelled out in three-foot glittery letters, "Don't Know What You Got (Till It's Gone)".

"I guess," Silas said.

"Holy shit, man. It's 1994, and our homecoming song is a glam-metal power ballad?"

Silas shrugged and said, "I didn't choose it. Besides, all guitar music sounds the same."

I glared at him until he finally smiled, and I said, "You can go to hell. And when you get there, I hope the DJ only plays Cinderella."

Mandy arrived a few minutes later, wearing a short dress, and with her hair, as promised, defying the laws of physics. Silas was in jeans and a Michael Jordan jersey, and as they said hello, I suspect they both realized they'd misread each other's intentions entirely.

"Marcus, who is your date?" Mandy asked, and when I told her I did not have one, she just said, "Oh. I'm sorry."

"Silas told me homecoming dates aren't a big deal," I said,

because I was mad at him for talking me into coming. He looked at me with wide eyes then said to Mandy, who was on the verge of tears, "Let's dance," even though the DJ was spinning a Tori Amos song no one in human history had ever attempted to dance to.

Then I was alone, watching the handful of Romans who'd managed to shake off their inhibitions dance, while most watched from the bleachers with me. During the next undanceable song, this one by the Cranberries, I heard some commotion by the door and saw the group of girls Becca usually hung out with entering the gym. They tossed their shoes into the pile then performed a Navy Seal-esque surgical strike on the homecoming dance. A few girls began dancing immediately, others pulled shy guys from the bleachers, and three more approached the DJ, pleading with him until a record scratch brought the dance to a halt, and Van Morrison's "Brown Eyed Girl" pulled everyone except me onto the dance floor.

The DJ followed up with "Celebration" by Kool & The Gang, "You Shook Me All Night Long" by AC/DC, "I Want You Back" by The Jackson Five, and a dozen more songs that no one can resist.

Confession time: I hate dancing. Not slow dancing so much, even though I'm terrible at it and spend most of my energy avoiding my partner's toes. But regular, fast dancing, I just can't. Within seconds of hitting the dance floor, I convince myself the people around me dancing and having fun are in fact watching me, and laughing at me in their heads, and wishing I'd go away so they could mock me with their competent dancing friends. Laugh if you want, but chorophobia (fear of dancing) is a real thing, and I'd appreciate your sympathy.

I wanted Silas to tire out and come back and keep me company, but he was still going strong on the dance floor, likely out of guilt, so I stood to leave just as Becca Walsh sat next to me.

"This DJ works at the Ford dealership in Riverton," Becca said. "He calls himself DJ Push-a-Button, and he's the undisputed worst DJ in history, yet for some reason, Rome hires him every year."

"It's like he brought a mix-tape of the least danceable songs of the last decade," I said, "but I hate dancing, so I can't really complain."

Becca smiled and said, "Yeah, I hate dancing too."

"No shit? I didn't think girls could hate dancing."

"It's 1994, Marcus. Girls can do whatever they want."

I smiled and apologized and after a moment said, "I read that book you let me borrow."

"And?" she asked.

"It was good," I said. "I liked how they live in a place where you can never be hurt."

"Marcus, I think you missed the point entirely," Becca said through laughter.

I shrugged and we sat there, watching our classmates bust moves to Young MC's aptly titled, "Bust a Move," and Becca finally said, "Marcus, I really am sorry about the night at the Raceway. I was drunk and didn't mean to—"

"It's okay," I said, cutting her off. "Don't worry about it."

"Thanks," she said, and more silence followed until DJ Push-a-Button, having danced our classmates to near exhaustion, slowed things down by saying, "And now let's slow things down." Boyz II Men came through the speakers, and on the dance floor couples paired up, while those left alone walked sullenly back to the bleachers. I glanced over at Becca, looking at her for the first time since she'd sat down. She was still wearing her homecoming crown and her green dress, and she saw me looking and smiled, and I cursed in my head because she was so pretty I couldn't help myself. My mouth, in complete violation of the peace treaty between my brain and my bruised ribs, asked Becca, "Would you like to dance?"

"Of course," she said, and I took her hand and led her onto the dance floor.

"I'm not very good at this," I said as she wrapped her arms around my neck, and I placed mine around her waist. "There's a significant chance I'll crush your pretty toenails."

"I'll risk it," Becca said, and she put her head on my shoulder, and we swayed to the music.

"Congratulations," I said after a moment, "on your crown and all."

"Yeah, Rome homecoming queen," Becca said, "just like my sister. Not that my parents even care. They're in Birmingham tonight, celebrating some lame promotion she got at work."

"Sorry," I mumbled, and she held me tighter. As the song ended, I remember praying that DJ Push-a-Button would find it in his heart to play another slow song because I wanted to stand there holding her forever, and he followed up Boyz II Men with a slow Bon Jovi song I usually couldn't turn off fast enough, but hearing it was a small price to pay for six more minutes with Becca's head on my shoulder.

At some point during that second song, I realized the football team had arrived. Most wore jeans and white T-shirts, and their hair was still wet from post-game showers. I didn't care about them though, because Becca was running her fingers through the back of my hair. I closed my eyes and held her tighter until the record scratched to a halt again, and Deacon Cassburn's voice echoed through DJ Push-a-Button's microphone.

"Is Becca still here?" Deacon said, and she let go of me as a few classmates pointed our way.

"Babe," Deacon said, "I'm sorry. I didn't mean to hurt you, and it'll never happen again. I swear. Just give me another chance. I love you, babe."

There was an audible, "Awwww" from the crowd, and Deacon turned to the DJ who played All-4-One's "I Swear," which was apparently Deacon and Becca's song, and Becca turned to me and said, "I'm...I'm sorry, Marcus," and she went to Deacon, leaving me alone on the dance floor.

~ ~ ~

By the time I arrived at the Fifth Quarter, all the girls had gone home, and Jackson and a few other guys were dunking on the nine-foot basketball goal.

"Nice dunk, Baby Jordan," I said, walking over to Jackson.

"In middle school, Silas and I used to record ourselves dunking on this goal so we could watch the replays in slow motion. Remind me and I'll show you the video one day."

"No thanks," I said, and he tossed a mini basketball my way.

"How was homecoming?" he asked.

I shot an airball, gave him a thumbs down, and asked, "How was Fifth Quarter?"

"You're looking at it," he said. "The girls went home once we broke out the basketballs."

I poured myself a glass of punch and sat on one of the nasty couches, and soon Jackson joined me while the rest of the guys continued to dunk.

"Shit. I'm sorry, man," Jackson said after I told him about Becca and Deacon. "Why the hell were you dancing with her anyway? I thought you were done with her?"

"I am … I mean, I was … I mean, I don't know. She does weird things to me, man. I can't explain it."

"So do you know if they got back together?" Jackson asked.

"I'm not sure, but she left me to go talk to him. It doesn't matter though. I don't care what they do. That's all over, for real this time."

"Good call," Jackson said.

"But I do want to help you bring Deacon's ass down," I whispered, and Jackson nodded. "I want him to pay for what he did at the raceway and for every other shitty thing he's ever done. I want him off the team and kicked out of school and deported."

"Well, he's an American citizen," Jackson said, "so I'm not sure if—"

"We're taking him down," I said. "And I think I have a plan."

ACT III

Chapter Eighteen

"As you can see, Brutus is torn. Caesar is his friend. He loves Caesar. But he also loves Rome and cannot stand by while any man, even his best friend, rises in power and becomes a dictator. So, Brutus and his fellow conspirators form a boy band, and they churn out hit song after hit song, until Cassius Longinus leaves the group to pursue a solo career."

I'd say stuff like this on occasion, when I felt like my classroom wasn't paying attention, just to see if anyone would notice. They never did, although the kid wearing glasses who sat by the wall once answered the test question, "What three-word phrase is Julius Caesar most famous for?" with "Pimpin' ain't easy." In the end, I had to give him credit, since technically, I'd said this in class when I thought no one was listening.

"Brutus's bandmates used his love of country to their advantage," I continued. "They played on his honor and convinced him Caesar's death would benefit Rome. That, in the end, is why Brutus joined the conspiracy to assassinate Caesar."

"That doesn't make any sense," said the mousy-looking girl on the front row.

"Well, they didn't really form a boy band, I was just—"

"No, it doesn't make sense that he would stab his best friend because he thought that was best for Rome."

I left my chair to sit on my desk and asked, "Why doesn't that make sense?"

The girl shrugged, because any time an actual classroom conversation was about to take place, my students reversed course and stared at me like I was an idiot.

"Okay," I said, "So Brutus—"

"She's right," said the curly-haired girl by the door. "Think about it. All these dudes, these senators and whatnot, why would they care if Caesar becomes king? They're all his friends, right? It's not like, if he becomes king, their lives will be worse. They'd be best friends with the freaking king. Who wouldn't want that?"

"So you think dictators are cool as long as you're friends with them?" asked the short blonde by the air conditioner.

"No," said the curly-haired girl by the door. "I'm just saying these guys didn't kill Caesar out of goodwill for their common man. They hated their common man. Look at how they talked to those carpenters and cobblers in the opening scene."

"Okay," I said, "then why do we think the conspirators wanted to kill Caesar?"

"Power," said the curly-haired girl by the door. "They didn't so much hate the idea of someone being dictator as they hated the idea of that someone not being them."

"But Brutus didn't want to be dictator," the mousy-looking girl up front said.

"Of course he did," said the curly-haired girl by the door. "He stabbed his best friend."

"For real," said the kid in glasses by the wall. "He could have talked to Caesar and been like, 'Hey man, you're being a real dictator,' but instead he stabbed him. Unless you want someone dead, stabbing shouldn't be your first option."

"All right," I said, "so despite Shakespeare telling us repeatedly that Brutus acted on noble motives, none of you buy it?" The handful of students paying attention shook their heads no, and I said, "It does say here in my notes that, in Dante's *Inferno*,

Brutus is one of only three people bad enough to be chewed in Satan's mouth for eternity, so maybe you guys are on to something. But after the assassination, Brutus doesn't make a grab for power, so does anyone else have a theory on why he joined the conspirators? Kyler, why don't you enlighten us with your thoughts?"

Kyler looked up from his nap, and after I repeated the question, he said, "Yeah, I think he killed Caesar over some chick. Cleopatra maybe."

"Wrong play, Kyler. Cleopatra's not in this one."

"Whatever, Mr. Brinks," Kyler said. "It's always about some chick."

~ ~ ~

"And as the teams head to their locker rooms, Rome leads Sparta, here at the half, 13-10. Bubba and I will be right back with the halftime stats, and the crowning of our homecoming queen, right after this message from our longtime sponsor, Trevi's BBQ."

"Close game," I said, walking into my mother's bedroom.

My mother turned down her radio and said, "Shouldn't be. I don't know why that Silas Carver insists on running the most conservative plays sometimes. Third and five from midfield and he runs the damn fullback. Then on fourth and one from the ten, we kick a field goal. It should be 31-10, and I should be going to bed, but no, they're gonna make me stay up and listen to the whole—" Mom began to cough, and by the time she stopped, she'd lost her train of thought.

"Silas told me Jackson meddles with the offense; otherwise, they'd set every record in the state."

My mother huffed and said, "So sayeth every offensive coordinator in the history of football. Silas is just mad Jackson won't let him run more than one trick play a game."

"He does have some good trick plays," I said, and Mother smiled and said, "He sure does. Now, tell me again why you are home on a Friday night."

"I wanted to spend time with my dear mother."

"Hogwash."

I shrugged. "Becca wasn't going to the game, and I didn't want to go by myself."

"She's still mad at you, isn't she?"

"We haven't spoken much this week, but yeah, I think so. She told me you called her after the article came out."

"I did," my mother said.

"Well, that was very nice of you."

"It was not. I just didn't want to go to my grave thinking she was mad at you for my sake. But if she's mad at you for some other reason, there's not much I can do about it."

"She's mad because she thinks I wasted my life, or at least the last half of it."

"Well, she's not wrong, is she?"

"Yes … no … I don't know. Sometimes I think that album came too easy. I had these songs in my head, and I felt like, if I didn't get them out, they'd kill me. There was no process. I wasn't really an active participant. I just opened a faucet and they poured out, and when it was all over, I couldn't even say what happened."

My mother grinned. "Oh, my poor baby boy. I'm sorry life's been so cruel to you."

I stuck my tongue out at her and said, "You try being called a genius at twenty-one. Unless your last name is Lennon or McCartney, there's only one direction your career can go from there."

"So why do anything if people might criticize it?"

"That's the thing, Mom, I tried. I tried to write songs while we toured. I tried when we got home. I tried for months and nothing. And I don't mean I wrote a bunch of songs but they didn't live up to the first album so what was the use. I mean I never wrote another single lyric. I had nothing left to say. Whatever part of me music came from was empty."

"And lying in a hammock for twenty years didn't fill it up?" my mother asked with a sly grin.

168

"Okay, maybe I wasted some of my life, but people do still talk about our band. If we'd followed up with a bunch of shitty albums, no one would care anymore. But we didn't, and they do. Not doing anything for the last twenty years wasn't the worst career move."

"I don't believe that, and neither do you," Mother said and turned the game back on, and we heard Mr. Gaba say, "Your 2017 Rome homecoming queen is ... Portia Kerr." We could hear the crowd cheering through the radio, and my mother said, "You know, I've heard you playing your guitar at night this week."

"I'm sorry," I said. "I tried to keep it down."

"You haven't bothered me," Mom said, "but I didn't recognize the song."

She already knew, but she made me say it anyway. "Yeah, I'm writing a new one ... for Becca."

"Of course you are," Mom said and squeezed my hand before turning the game back on. She fell asleep during the fourth quarter of what turned out to be a 35-17 win, and when it was over, I turned off the radio, kissed her on the head, and went back to my room to finish my first new song in two decades.

~ ~ ~

I can't say for certain when the homecoming dance at Rome became a big deal, but it was no longer the informal after-the-football-game affair I remembered. It was still in the gymnasium, because the gymnasium was free, and the Rome Student Government Association didn't have enough money to rent the Riverton Museum of Art for both homecoming and prom. But the homecoming dance was now on Saturday night, and all the girls now wore dresses, not just the ones on the homecoming court or who mistakenly thought Silas Carver was totally into them. The guys dressed up too. They didn't rent tuxedos like for prom, but most at least put on a tie—a marked improvement from white T-shirts and wet hair from a post-game shower.

I volunteered to chaperone because the school paid chaperones two hundred bucks and, as sad as it sounds, I could use the cash. Becca volunteered to chaperone too because chaperones could not bring dates, and this way we could go together, but this was before the newspaper article and our fight. I picked her up an hour before the dance, and she didn't say much on the drive over, and once inside the gym, she left to talk to another middle school teacher, leaving me alone to watch the band set up.

A few students were putting the finishing touches on the decorations, and the crazy girl who took selfies with me every day stopped for a photo, then the SGA President, a girl I couldn't name but recognized from school assemblies, walked by and I asked, "What happened to DJ Push-a-Button?"

"Who?" she asked.

"When I went to Rome, there was a car salesman from Riverton who DJ'd all the dances. He kinda sucked."

The girl shrugged and said, "I'm not sure. These guys have played homecoming the last four years. They're an eighties cover band. They kinda suck too."

I went over to talk to the guys in the band, because Becca continued to ignore me, and I felt self-conscious sitting on the bleachers alone.

"Hearing Impaired Leppard," a man in spandex pants and what I hope was a wig said, when I asked him the name of his band. I laughed and he asked, "Are you a chaperone?" I nodded, and he said, "We all went to Sparta. Rome absolutely destroyed us my senior year. I'm Elliott by the way."

I shook his hand and said, "Marcus. Marcus Brinks."

"Marcus Brinks," he said, "like the lead singer of Dear Brutus."

"I was the lead singer of Dear Brutus," I said.

"Ha," he said, but after a double-take, added, "Holy shit, you were, weren't you?"

Elliott called the other members of Hearing Impaired Leppard over to meet me—the drummer had both arms but played with one tucked in his sleeve—and after taking some selfies with them, I asked, "By the way, could you guys do me a favor tonight?"

~ ~ ~

Ten minutes before the doors opened and the dance began, Principal Trajan gathered the chaperones for final instructions. "I need eyes on the punch bowl at all times," he barked like a general going into combat, "and we must halt any dancing that exceeds a PG-13 rating. A child may be conceived tonight but not in this gymnasium." Mrs. Nero asked how we'd know if dancing exceeded PG-13, and Principal Trajan said, "You'll know it when you see it. Now good luck men and stay safe."

The doors opened, the students flooded in, and the dance began, with the lads from Hearing Impaired Leppard working through the same catalog of eighties hits DJ Push-a-Button played two decades ago. Becca kept her distance, leaving me to spend the first hour of the dance standing next to the biology teacher, Mr. Severus, who droned on about frogs while I watched the punch bowl. The homecoming song was "When I'm with You," a power ballad released by the Canadian band Sheriff in 1983. I wasn't sure if the senior class selected this song ironically, or if kids from Rome always have and always will love eighties power ballads, but either way, the boys from Hearing Impaired Leppard performed it admirably before taking their last break of the evening. Then I was on.

The students shuffled off the dance floor toward the food and punch, and no one noticed me plug my acoustic guitar into the amp. I bumped my chin into the microphone, steadied myself, and said, "This is an old song I learned to play a long time ago," then I shut my eyes, began to strum, and sang.

My voice was shaky. It was always a little shaky but felt extra so after years of neglect, and as I sang the final line of Big Star's "Thirteen," I wondered if I could get through another song, but I continued playing, eyes shut, and sang, "Rebecca please, believe me when I say …"

I fumbled through the new song, sang one verse twice, left another out entirely, and pulled a muscle in my back belting out the last "Rebecca, pleeeeease." But I made it through, and when the song was over, I mumbled into the microphone, "And that was a new song," but I couldn't open my eyes, because no one was clapping. Not even politely. But the Earth refused to open up and swallow me whole, so after a moment, I dared to look and saw every student in the school recording me on their cell phones, and standing in front of me, alone on the dance floor, was Becca.

She was smiling through her tears.

"Friends of the eccentric rocker expressed concern last month after learning Brinks, during a red-eye flight from Los Angeles to New York, downed four bottles of wine, stripped to his boxers, and threatened to throw a fellow passenger's guide dog out the emergency door somewhere over Kansas."

—*People*, "The Rise and Fall of Marcus Brinks," July 25, 1999

Chapter Nineteen

"It's got to be at your house, Brinks. My parents never go anywhere. They haven't even seen a movie in the theatre since *Top Gun.*"

"Well, my mom stays at Steve's some nights, but it always seems spur of the moment. There's no way I could plan for it."

"Does she keep a planner in her purse? Maybe she writes it in there."

Silas sat between Jackson and me and asked, "What we talking about?" But when neither of us answered, he said, "Dammit, I refuse to waste another lunch period listening to you two plot the demise of Deacon Cassburn."

"Can we talk about those then?" Jackson asked, pointing toward Silas's new cowboy boots. The previous Saturday, the night after Rome defeated Sparta to run its record to 9-0, Silas went line dancing without us. By now, everyone in school, minus Jackson and me, went every Saturday night. Some kids were even wearing cowboy hats and chaps to school. And sure, this is Alabama, but I can promise you kids in the nineties didn't typically go around dressed for a rodeo. It was like going to school at the Grand Ole Opry, and it somehow made Rome suck even worse.

"We can talk about how jealous you are of them," Silas said.

Jackson ignored this and asked, "Do your parents ever go anywhere on weekends?"

"No, but even if they did, I'm not helping you with whatever it is you've schemed up," Silas said then leaned in and whispered,

"He's the starting quarterback of what may be the first unde-feated team in school history. Do you have any idea how much everyone in school would hate you if you ruined that?"

"No one will ever find out it was—" I started to say but stopped mid-sentence when Becca Walsh placed a note in front of me and walked away. As I opened it, Jackson said, "Careful, the last time she gave you a note, it led directly to an ass-kicking."

"I don't think they got back together," Silas said. "They're not sitting by each other in every class at least. What's it say?"

"To call her after school," I said, and they both shook their heads with what I think was pity.

~ ~ ~

Back in the day, when you wanted to communicate with a member of the opposite sex, or anyone for that matter, you had to call them on a landline telephone. This involved punching seven consecutive numbers into the phone, each one giving you ample opportunity to panic and hang up. Becca's number was 315-0044—I still remember it and all my friend's parent's land-line numbers twenty years later, yet forget my ATM PIN on a weekly basis—and it took me three tries to hit that last four. And this was calling a girl who asked me to call her; you can imagine the sheer terror of cold-calling a girl. I finally punched that last four though, and the phone rang twice before Becca answered.

"Can you come over tonight around six?" Becca asked. I was there at 6:01.

Becca's parents lived on Aventine Hill in a two-story brick house on South Eagleville Road, and when she opened the door wearing her Lisa Loeb glasses, I could tell she'd been crying.

"Are you okay?" I asked as she grabbed my hand and walked me through the house. The lights in the kitchen and den were off, and I was pretty sure her parents weren't home as she led me into her bedroom and handed me a CD.

"It came out today," she said, and I looked at the case—it was Nirvana's *MTV Unplugged in New York*.

Becca pressed play on her CD player, and "About a Girl"

came through the speakers, and she sat on her bed and said, "I … I didn't know how much I missed him until I listened to this. I've cried all afternoon."

Kurt Cobain died over seven months ago, and MTV had aired Nirvana's Unplugged special almost exclusively ever since, but I suppose you can't fault the way other people grieve. I sat next to Becca on her bed and said, "It's a great album."

"It's beautiful," she said. "He was beautiful." Then, over the opening bass riff of "Come as You Are," she said, "Deacon and I are seeing other people."

"Okay," I said. "What does that mean?"

"I don't know," she said. "Like, we're together, but we can see other people I guess."

Her hand was on mine now, and I knew if I looked at her we'd kiss. I mean, I didn't want to be co-boyfriends with Deacon but figured we could work all that out later. I turned to tell her something I'd read about Dave Grohl, but before I could, we kissed. We kissed through "Come as You Are" then fell back on her bed and made out through the David Bowie song, and "Dumb," and "On a Plain," and then the three Meat Puppets' songs, even the weird one about birds. And it wasn't until forty-five minutes later, during "Where Did You Sleep Last Night," that we noticed her parents standing in the doorway.

~ ~ ~

"That's all he said?"

"Yeah, he was freakishly calm, which honestly made him scarier. We both stood up, and Becca buttoned a couple buttons on her shirt, and her dad was like, 'Please, leave this home,' so I left as fast as I could."

Silas bent over laughing and said, "Oh god, I wish I could have been there to see it. The parents walking in part, not the making out part, obviously."

"Maybe next time," I said.

"Next time," Silas repeated. "Dammit, Brinks, I warned you about that chick on day one, and I hereby absolve myself of any guilt regarding your pending heartbreak."

"She's not going to break my heart. I told you she and Deacon are seeing other people."

"And girls like that pick guys like you over Ken-doll quarterbacks all the time?"

"Yes … well, no … but I saw a flyer for the school talent show in December, and if I—"

Silas covered his ears and said, "I can't listen to this; it's too sad."

"Ten bucks says, by Christmas, she's seeing me exclusively."

"Keep your money, Brinks. You'll need it for therapy."

"Whatever, just promise me you won't tell Jackson about any of this."

"Why not? He'd tell you the exact same thing I told you."

"I know," I said, "but for some reason, it pisses me off more when he says it."

Silas smiled and shook his head, "Fair enough, now hold the umbrella still. I'm getting soaked."

We were in Carthage for the last game of the regular season, and God was reneging on his promise not to destroy the Earth by flood again. The skies opened just after the pep rally that afternoon, and it had rained, sometimes sideways, ever since. Of course, no one in Rome would complain if God wiped Carthage High School off the map. I'd only been here a few months, could not care less if Rome ever won another game, and I wanted to crush Carthage so bad that night I was willing to put on shoulder pads myself, fake heart condition be damned.

You'd see them, cruising Main Street, or at the Riverton Mall, or line dancing, I suppose. Kids from Carthage, driving late model BMWs and dressed head to toe in Tommy Hilfiger, because that was the most expensive store in the mall. Carthage was affluent, at least by Rubicon County standards. The doctors and lawyers of Riverton lived in Carthage, in stately homes on the river, and they only came to Rome to watch their sports teams beat ours and to eat BBQ at Trevi's, because the BBQ joint in Carthage sucked and they knew it.

Carthage High School was bigger than Rome. We had three hundred students; they had over twice that. This wasn't an area game; it had no effect on the play-offs, and going into the 1994 season, Carthage had defeated Rome thirteen straight times.

No doubt the rain helped Rome that night. At halftime, neither team had threatened to score, and at one point, they alternated fumbles on four consecutive plays. The bands did not perform at halftime in a hopeless effort to preserve the playing surface, but it didn't matter. The teams played the second half in a mud pit that rivaled Woodstock.

The Rome students roared all game, taunting Carthage fans with chants of, "We've got molars, yes we do, we've got molars, how 'bout you," a reference to an unlicensed "luxury dentist" who practiced in Carthage for five years before being arrested, leaving a generation of Carthage students with missing permanent teeth that the con man pulled to collect insurance money. But despite our efforts, our team couldn't string together consecutive positive plays, and late in the fourth quarter, Carthage broke off a long run that led to a short field goal attempt.

"No way he makes this," I said to Silas. "Not in all this wind and mud. This game's been too weird. It's our night, man."

"It's been a weird game," Silas agreed, "but that doesn't mean we're going to win," and as the kick split the uprights, he turned to me and added, "I've been around too long to get my hopes up. We're never going to beat them, Brinks."

After the kickoff, Deacon threw two incompletions, fumbled the snap, and lost ten yards on third down, and as the clock went under ten seconds to play, Coach Pumphrey called timeout. It was over, and some Rome fans began the sad walk to their cars while Carthage fans taunted, "Is there a fire drill?"

On fourth down, Carthage only rushed three defenders and placed some defensive backs as far as fifty yards from the line of scrimmage. From shotgun, Deacon took the snap, rolled to his right, and pulled up to throw the ball as far as he could but reconsidered and took off downfield. Rome fans cheered because

Deacon was running in open field, but he was still sixty yards from the end zone, with eight defenders and only a few blockers in front of him.

"What's he doing?" I asked.

"Idiot," Silas said and sat down.

But Deacon made a tackler miss then slipped from the grip of another and reversed field toward the far sideline.

"Holy shit," Silas said, standing up again, and Deacon cut back once more, hurdled a tackler, and caught a couple blocks as he turned the corner.

He was at the thirty, the twenty-five, the twenty, and it was about then my mind calculated all possible outcomes of Deacon actually pulling this off, and a foreboding dread replaced any excitement I felt about possibly beating Carthage.

Two defenders slipped and fell in the mud when Deacon cut back one last time. He was at the fifteen, the ten, and the noise from both sides was deafening as a final defender hit Deacon high, wrapped his arms around the quarterback, and was dragged the final seven yards to the Carthage goal line, where Deacon collapsed forward into the end zone.

Final Score: Rome 6, Carthage 3.

Rome students poured from the bleachers, over the fence, and onto the muddy field. Silas was with them, though I can't for the life of me figure out how he scaled the fence with his crutches. I alone remained in the bleachers, soaking wet and dumbfounded, and watched as Rome students taunted Carthage fans with middle fingers and ass slaps. Then the Marching Legion struck up the fight song, and Romans sang at full voice while the players lifted Deacon onto their shoulders. The quarterback raised both hands in victory, and when the students started to chant his stupid name, I wanted to throw up.

I assumed Becca was at the game, but it rained so hard she never came to talk to me, and I didn't see her until she pushed through the crowd to Deacon. The players lowered him, and she wrapped her arms around him and kissed him like a world war had just ended. A photographer snapped a shot of the kiss, and it was on the front page of *the Riverton Times* the next day below the headline, "The Fall of Carthage."

The Carthage public address announcer asked the Rome students politely, then impolitely, then demanded they leave the playing surface, but they remained, celebrating with the greatest mud fight of all time. The grounds crew turned on the sprinkler system, thinking this might run them off, but they'd been standing in the rain for hours, and a person can only get so wet, so they continued to throw mud and ruin Carthage's field until some taser-toting Carthage police officers entered the gate, and everyone ran for the parking lot and returned to Rome, where most of the town celebrated at Pantheon Pizza until the sun rose on Saturday.

I went home to play my guitar.

~ ~ ~

I was up by seven the next morning, playing my guitar and hating life, when Steve barged in without a knock. He'd spent the night, I guess, and I figured he was about to scream at me for waking him up, but he didn't say anything, so I kept strumming while he walked around my room, looking at my posters and flipping through an issue of *Spin* on my desk.

"Not bad," Steve said, after I finished the song I'd been playing.

"Thanks," I mumbled, and he continued to walk about the room. "Can I ... uh ... help you find anything?" I asked after a moment.

"No," Steve said, shuffling through my stack of Sega games before picking up my Warren Moon Starting Lineup figure, taking off his helmet, and setting him back on my dresser.

"Hell of a game last night, huh?"

"Yeah," I said.

"We beat Carthage twice when I was in school. They were just another shit town on the river back then. Did you know," he asked, sitting on my desk chair, "me and your mama used to date in high school?"

I shook my head no.

"We did," Steve said. "All senior year. She broke up with me that summer, right before she moved to Auburn."

Good for her, I thought, but didn't say anything.

Steve stood up, paced the room for a minute, then said, "What would you say if I told you I was gonna ask your mama to marry me?"

Oh, god, no. Not this asshole. I couldn't speak, and I couldn't breathe, because I knew she'd say yes. Not my mom from six months ago. She wouldn't let some guy like Steve mow our lawn. But Mom had changed, and Steve had all but moved in with us, and the thought of him being my stepdad made me want to hang myself with a guitar string.

"Well, what do you think?" Steve asked again.

"I don't think …"

"You don't think what, boy?"

"I don't think Mom would ever marry you, when there are so many more eligible bachelors in the Rubicon County Jail."

Steve was out of the chair and in my face in an instant. He shoved a grubby finger into my chest and said, "You listen to me, you little piece of shit. Me and your mama are gettin' hitched. That's happening, 'cause we're meant to be. So you'd better get used to the idea, or you can go back to Texas and live with your daddy, if he'll even have you."

I tried to stand, but Steve pushed me back hard on my bed. "Choice is yours, boy. But just know I don't give a shit, and me and your mama would be a lot happier if your ass weren't around."

Then he slammed the door and left, and I sat on my bed and cried.

Chapter Twenty

"Mr. Brinks, you're like, famous."

"I've been famous for twenty years, but that doesn't change the fact that it's almost Thanksgiving and we're not even through Act III. Now come on, folks, focus. We're talking about the naivety of Brutus."

"Yeah, but you were like nineties-famous; now you're now-famous."

I ignored this and said, "Brutus didn't question the motives of others because he believed everyone was as honorable as he, and in the end, this cost him his—"

"Did Ms. Walsh like her song?" asked the curly-haired girl near the door.

They'd been doing this for nearly an hour and a half, and since there were only a couple minutes left in class, I gave up, closed my book for the day, and said, "Yes. She liked it."

"It was so romantic," said the short blonde by the air conditioner.

"Uh … thanks," I said.

"Mr. Brinks, my YouTube video of your song already has over two million views," said the guy in glasses by the wall, "and YouTube pays people a dollar per view, so I'm going to be crazy rich."

"I don't think that's how YouTube—"

"They don't pay people, dumbass," said the guy behind the guy in glasses, after slapping the back of his friend's head. "You pay them a dollar per view. How do you think they make money?"

"Oh, shit," said the guy in glasses then pulled out this phone to remove my video, I suspect.

"Mr. Brinks, is your band getting back together?" asked the mousy-looking girl up front.

"No, I don't think we're—"

"Mr. Brinks, are you and Ms. Walsh getting married?" asked the curly-haired girl by the door.

"What? No. I mean … I don't know … maybe."

I blushed at my classroom's collective, "Aww," and thankfully the bell rang and they all left for second period. Well, all of them except for Kyler, who was asleep in the back of the room. I threw my pen at him but missed then walked over and shook his shoulder and said, "You don't have to go home, Kyler, but you can't stay here." He looked up, confused, and stood to leave. I followed him to the door, and we were both a little shocked when Jackson walked in.

"Oh, hey, Coach," Kyler said, suddenly more awake than he'd ever been in my classroom.

"You been sleeping, son?" Jackson snapped. "Is Mr. Brinks' class not stimulating enough for you?"

"No, Coach, it's great," Kyler said, then moving faster than he ever had on the field, added, "Gotta run or I'll be late for biology."

Jackson shut my door and sat on my desk and said, "He's a good kid."

"Who, Kyler?" I asked. "Jackson, he's the worst."

Jackson laughed despite himself. "Okay, he's a little shit, but he's the best quarterback ever to come through Rome. Would you believe college coaches are already calling me about him? Division One coaches, and that kid is just a freshman."

"Wow," I said, "too bad he'll never graduate from high school."

184

Jackson stood up and walked over to my window to look out at the Colosseum. "Well," he said, "that's what I came to talk to you about. You see, Brinks, Kyler is doing well in every class this semester. Every class but yours."

"Wait, you're telling me Kyler, the same Kyler who thinks the Riverton Little Caesars was built by the ancient Romans, is doing well in every class this semester but mine?"

Jackson turned around and nodded, and I said, "Jackson, that's bullshit."

My old friend forced a smile, but I could tell he didn't find the situation funny. I glanced out the window on my door to see students lining up for second period, but no one dared enter with Coach Crowder in the room, and Jackson wasn't in a hurry to leave, so I said in a lower voice, "There's no way that kid is doing well in every class but mine. I've never met a lazier student in my life, and I went to school with Fletcher Morgan."

Jackson shrugged and handed me a slip of paper. On it were Kyler's grades for the semester. An A in Alabama history, a B-minus in biology, another A in algebra, and an F in English literature. I shook my head and said, "Jackson, we've had two tests and two short essays this semester. Kyler failed both tests in spectacular fashion, and he didn't even bother to write the essays. The only reason I gave him an F is because they won't let me give him a G."

"The kid has a lot of pressure on him, Brinks," Jackson said. "Academically, athletically, socially. And as you can see, he's excelling in his other classes. So maybe it's …"

"Maybe it's what?"

"Well, maybe the two of you just don't …"

"Are you suggesting I'm the reason Kyler has an 18 in literature? Jackson, I'm the easiest teacher in the history of Rome. Half the answers on my multiple-choice tests are Star Wars jokes. Simple deduction and guessing should be enough to get half the answers right, and he doesn't even come close to that."

"Well, I don't know what to tell you, Brinks. He's shining in every class but—"

"Yeah, I heard you. But I'm having a hard time believing you. There is no way Kyler has an A in Silas's algebra class."

Jackson sighed and walked over to put a hand on my shoulder. "Dammit, Brinks," he said in a low voice, "of course he doesn't. Are you gonna make me say it? Silas wants Kyler on the team as much as me or anyone else in Rome. Do you think his offense would put up those numbers without Kyler? Of course not, but he's not going to lose his quarterback just because the kid can't solve for x, and I'm not going to lose him just because he can't find the energy to write a paper for your stupid class." Jackson turned to leave but stopped and over his shoulder said, "Brinks, you know I'm the reason you got this job, don't you? Your mama called the school back in the summer, and Trajan came to me, and I told him to hire you. I know about your mama's debt, and I know you're broke as hell, and I'd hate for you to lose this job. Particularly over some alleged inappropriate sexual conduct that you'd never be able to disprove."

"What the hell are you—"

Jackson turned around and held up his phone. On it was a selfie of me and the crazy girl I'd thought was a big Dear Brutus fan. She was making a kissy duck face. He pocketed his phone and said, "I've got fifty of these, Brinks, but I don't want to release them. That would just be too much to put on your poor mama in her dying days. So help me out here. I want us to be friends."

He slipped his phone back into his purple windbreaker while I stared at him with a mixture of disbelief and rage. Deacon was right, and I wasn't sure I wanted to live in a world where Deacon was right.

"Well," Jackson said, snapping me back to the present.

"I'll ... I'll think about it," I muttered.

"I'm sure you will," Jackson said and walked out the door

~ ~ ~

"What are you going to do?"

"I guess I'm going to change his grade. But I'm not giving

him an A. He can have a C-minus and nothing more."

Becca and I were in a booth at Pantheon Pizza, eating dinner and discussing my conversation with Jackson. Well, the part about changing Kyler's grade, not the part about blackmailing me with inappropriate selfies. I'd seen her, for at least an hour, every night since the homecoming dance. We were in love, I think, though we'd been rather good at avoiding all talk of our future.

Becca smiled across the booth and said, "I know it's a tough choice."

"It shouldn't be, though. People should be able to live in this town without having to join Deacon's stupid crusade or change Jackson's stupid quarterback's grades. This shouldn't be a binary decision."

"Well," Becca said, "you've lived in Rome long enough to know things are always more complicated than we want them to be."

I picked up a breadstick and said, "Oh, I know. But is it wrong to think that kid deserves to face the consequences of his actions?"

"He's the quarterback, Marcus; unless it's an interception, they never face the consequences of their actions."

"You're probably right. But don't you think it would be better for Kyler, long term, to feel some repercussions now, in hopes he'd grow up to be a productive member of society later?"

"Not really," Becca replied and sipped her beer. "Look at Deacon. He felt plenty of repercussions and still grew up to be the sleaziest man in Rome."

An older couple stopped by to say hello and ask about my mother, and once they'd left, I said to Becca, "But Kyler's parents don't have the money to set him up with a chain of check-cashing stores. What's he going to do in the real world, when people stop changing grades for him?"

"If he's as good as everyone says, people won't stop changing grades for him until he's the quarterback of the Dallas Cowboys."

I sighed, poured myself another beer from the pitcher, and said, "I'm still pissed that Jackson would even ask me."

"And you don't think Coach P asked teachers to change grades when we were in school?"

"I guess. I don't know. I never really thought about it." I stared out the window and watched the delivery boy leave with a stack of pizzas then said to Becca, "But don't you think it's a dick move that he put me in a situation where if I do the right thing, and Kyler missed the Carthage game and the playoffs, everyone in town would hate me?"

"Since when did you start caring what everyone in Rome thought of you?" Becca asked with a smile.

I reached across the table and put my hand on hers and said, "I still don't care what they think, but if I end up hanging around here for a while, it would be nice if everyone didn't hate me."

It wasn't a proposal, and it wasn't a confession of love, but it might as well have been both, and Becca pulled her hand back and asked, "So you're really thinking ... even after ... if your mom ..."

"Yeah," I said. "It wouldn't be my first choice of places to settle down, but someone very special lives here, so ..."

Becca sighed and wiped a single tear from her eye and, with a sad smile, reached back across the table, squeezed my hand, and said, "Well, Marcus Brinks, if you're even thinking of hanging around here for a while, you're definitely doing the right thing."

~ ~ ~

Since 1994, when Rome broke their thirteen-year losing streak to Carthage, the series had evened considerably. In the last twenty-two seasons, Rome won twelve games, Carthage ten, with neither team winning more than two games consecutively. People who vote on this sort of thing voted Rome-Carthage the third greatest rivalry in Alabama high school football. Rome fans took great pride in this, Carthage fans a little less, considering the large disparity in the two school's enrollments—something Rome fans reminded Carthage fans of whenever possible.

This year's game was at the Colosseum, and six of the *Riverton Times'* ten experts picked Rome to win and avenge last season's overtime loss. "If Kyler Barton is taking snaps, there may not be a team in this state, regardless of classification, that can beat Rome," said one expert. And of course, Kyler would be taking snaps. I'd seen to it. But during warmups, sitting next to Becca and her parents, who were actually quite nice and had possibly forgotten they caught me in their daughter's bedroom twenty-three years ago, I hated myself a little for giving in.

"Where are all the students?" I asked Becca as the team made their way to the locker room for prayer and a *Braveheart*-esque pep talk from Jackson.

"I forget sometimes you were gone so long," she whispered. "There's a new tradition for the Carthage game. You'll see."

"Okay," I whispered back, "but why are we whispering?"

Becca shushed me and pointed toward the gymnasium, where I saw the students walking single-file from the building. They held candles and wore togas and entered through the gate at the North end zone. Silently they crossed the field, forming a human tunnel in the South end zone, where the cheerleaders raised the victory banner, this week's featuring a pack of wolves devouring an elephant in graphic fashion.

The doors to the field house flung open, and the backlit silhouette of Jackson Crowder emerged as usual, but this time, he did not charge through the banner. He marched slowly, his team behind him, and as they reached the disturbing mural, a cheerleader handed Jackson her candle, and he touched it to the banner, which went up in flames. The team now followed their coach through the smoldering ashes and the human tunnel to their sideline, and while the students returned to the bleachers without a word, the team captains went to midfield for the coin toss. Rome won the toss, elected to kick, and once the captains rejoined their teammates on the sideline, a bass drum sounded. Every Roman—players, students, parents, and teachers—shouted and jumped as one. Another bass drum, another jump and shout, then another, and another, and by the time Rome's kicker raised his hand to ready the kickoff team, the Rome sideline and bleachers were absolute bedlam.

"Was that Jackson's idea?" I asked Becca after the kickoff and compulsory shout of "Victory or death!"

"Actually no," she said, "that was all Coach Pumphrey's doing. Carthage beat us the year after we graduated, and I think Coach P feared another long losing streak to them. The next season, he promised the students, if we beat Carthage, there would be a huge, unchaperoned party in the gym after the game. It's called *Ludi Romani*, and this very moment, the gym is set up for the party. Food and drinks and a band. If we win, the students and team will take off running for the gym, but if we lose, they'll send the band home and a homeless shelter from Riverton will come pick up the food."

I shook my head and said, "That's some serious motivation. But why didn't anyone mention this at school all week?"

"Because it's bad luck to talk about *Ludi Romani*," Becca said and covered her mouth.

The game began in less than ideal fashion for Rome. A poor pass from Kyler was intercepted and returned for a touchdown, a punt was returned for another, and by halftime, Carthage led 21-0, and their fans taunted us with chants of, "No taxation for fornication," which Becca explained referenced Rome's previous mayor, who was currently imprisoned for using city funds to pay for call girls.

Rome took the second-half kickoff and marched the length of the field, cutting the lead to fourteen, then scored again early in the fourth quarter, but trailing by seven with just over two minutes to play, things looked bleak. The Rome defense stiffened on a third and short from their own ten, holding Carthage to a short field goal that would all but ice the game.

"Block that kick," Becca screamed with the rest of Rome while crushing my hand in hers, and a Roman defender did just that, scooping up the ball in the ensuing melee and racing out to midfield. Rome was in business, and the home crowd came so unhinged Kyler had to motion for them to take it down a notch.

Silas called one brilliant play after another, and with the clock running under twenty seconds, he rolled Kyler out to the left with a run/pass option. The quarterback tucked the ball like he meant to run, and just as Becca shouted, "He's open," Kyler pulled up and lobbed a pass into the back of the end zone. Touchdown Rome, and the Colosseum shook.

Now only an extra point stood between Rome and certain overtime with their rival, and when the holder, Kyler, took the snap, the crowd held its collective breath, then lost their collective shit when he flipped the ball over his shoulder to the kicker, who was racing toward the goal line.

"It's a throwback," I said as the kicker stopped and, just before the War Elephant defenders swarmed him, threw a wobbly pass all the way across the field where Kyler stood waiting, all alone.

I turned and saw Silas pump his fist in the most nonchalant fashion before Becca tackled me and we fell into the family sitting in front of us. The Rome students, in their delirium, forgot there were still six seconds to play, and it took the referees ten minutes to clear the field so Rome could kickoff. Once they did, Carthage attempted several laterals until one was intercepted by a Roman defender who raced into the North end zone, past the statue of Jackson Crowder, and out the gate, followed by his teammates and the rest of the student body toward the gymnasium and *Ludi Romani*.

Jackson met the Carthage coaches at midfield to shake hands then turned, arms raised in triumph, toward the home fans who chanted his name. He applauded them back, hands over his head, and when he saw me, he pointed and gave me a quick salute before running to the locker room.

"See," Becca said, squeezing the life out of me with one last celebratory bearhug, "you did the right thing."

"I guess so," I said and wondered why it made me feel like shit.

"Marcus Brinks is hitting the books. According to Dear Brutus bassist Kyle Craven, the enigmatic frontman has enrolled at Harvard University. After rumors of rehab and a very public breakup with actress Rachael Leigh Cook, it appears Brinks has landed on his feet. When reached for comment, Brinks, through his publicist, replied, 'Beat Yale!'"

—*Entertainment Weekly*, "Music News,"
September 10, 1999

Chapter Twenty-One

Starting quarterbacks have always roamed the hallways of their high schools with impunity, their letterman's jackets acting as faux leather diplomatic plates. Crimes that would send mere mortals to the principal's office never earn quarterbacks more than a slap on the wrist—their non-throwing wrist, obviously. Even before his amazing eighty-yard run in the mud to defeat Carthage, Deacon was the undisputed king of Rome. But when he dragged that final War Elephant defender into the end zone and broke the thirteen-year losing streak, he ascended to levels of privilege known only by rulers who also doubled as their subjects' local deity. How popular was Deacon after the fall of Carthage? Now he even had license to pick on other popular students. In particular, a funny, good looking guy with Becker muscular dystrophy.

"I was just taking a piss, which isn't the easiest thing to do with these crutches, but I've gotten pretty good at it, and was almost done when they came in," Silas told Jackson and me as we sat in his garage after school on the Wednesday before Rome's first playoff game. "Fletcher watched the door, Marshall took a shit, and Deacon kicked one of my crutches out from under me." Silas pointed to the bandage on his chin and said, "I hit the urinal going down. Took four stitches to close it up."

"What did we ever do to these guys that made them so violent?" I asked and Jackson shrugged.

"I tried to get up, but Deacon pushed me back down and kicked me in the ribs. That's when he noticed all the blood from my chin. I think he sort of freaked out, and they left."

"What did you tell the nurse happened to your chin?" Jackson asked.

"That I tripped in the hallway. Now I get to leave all my classes three minutes early to avoid the rush, so it's not all bad."

Jackson and I started a game of Bill Walsh's on Sega—neither of us would play Silas anymore—and after flipping through an Eastbay catalog, Silas stood in front of the television and said, "I'm ready to join your coup, if you'll have me."

Jackson paused the game, and we looked at each other then at Silas.

"Holy shit, that could really work," Silas said after we'd shared our plan.

"Of course it could work," Jackson said, unpausing the game.

"Our problem is Jackson's parents never leave the house," I said, "and I never know when Mom will spend the night at Steve's. What about your house?"

"Yeah, right. My parents haven't spent a Saturday night out since 1979. I've got an idea though, and it might solve all our problems at once, but it's going to cost us. How much money can you two get your hands on?"

"I have a hundred bucks leftover from my last birthday," I said. "So that, plus whatever I can slip from Mom's purse."

"I've got two hundred dollars," Jackson said, "but I'm saving it to buy a bass cannon and some Vega woofers from Crutchfield."

"Well," Silas said, "you can either play your shitty music loud or bring down Deacon. The choice is yours. I've got a small fortune saved for the car Mom and Dad wouldn't let me buy, so I'll match whatever you guys come up with, and that should be enough."

"Enough for what?" Jackson asked.

"Enough to bribe my smokehound brother," Silas said.

~ ~ ~

The next three weeks passed with glacial urgency. School sucked, not only because Deacon had reached new levels of assholery while maintaining dictator-level approval ratings, but Becca was his once more and had been since that kiss after the Carthage game. But when Deacon fell, all bets were off, and I would be ready. I spent countless hours before and after school playing my guitar and preparing for the talent show. I'd settled on Big Star's "Thirteen," Becca's favorite song.

Rome defeated Mytilene at the Colosseum, 35-7, in the first round of the Alabama state playoffs. Then the team traveled north to Ocasek and defeated an overmatched team 49-0. In the third round, Southern Cherokee visited Rome, bringing with them two defensive linemen who'd start for SEC schools as freshmen the very next season. The game was close, but Rome prevailed, 17-10, setting up a semifinal matchup with Brother Maynard, a wealthy Catholic school from Mobile.

"It's got to be this weekend," I said to Silas at lunch on the Monday before the Brother Maynard game.

"It is," he said. "I talked to Paul last night. He's coming home Friday."

Paul was Silas's slacker older brother. He was in his third or fourth sophomore year at Troy State and came home once a month so his mother could do his laundry. We checked the calendar and knew he'd come home the weekend of one of Rome's playoff games, but we didn't know which one. He ran out of clean underwear just in time.

"He said he'd do it for two hundred bucks, which leaves us plenty for booze."

Silas and I bumped fists, and Jackson sighed and said, "Shit."

"What?"

"I don't know," Jackson said. "It's just we're only two wins away from the state championship now, and it would be really cool to get a ring, you know?"

"Jake Norton is just as good a quarterback as Deacon," Silas

195

said. "Besides, Brother Maynard is the best team in the state. If we beat them, the championship game will be cake, with or without Deacon."

"You think so?" Jackson asked.

"I know so," Silas said, and Jackson nodded resolutely.

"Okay," I said. "We should spread the word today. If we wait till Saturday, no one will know about it."

"Good call," Silas said. "I'll tell Mandy and MeghanJennifer; Jackson, you tell the team; Brinks, oh wait, you don't have any friends besides us."

I flipped him off, even though he was right.

~ ~ ~

Despite my insisting earlier that entire towns did not travel to away football games, when Rome faced Brother Maynard in the state semifinals, everyone in Rome did just that. Well, everyone except me. Since Mobile was six hours away, most people planned on spending the night and not returning to Rome until Saturday afternoon, but I needed to be home early the next morning when Paul arrived to earn his two hundred dollars.

The big AM station in Riverton broadcast the game, and I listened in bed while practicing guitar. The game was close, and Brother Maynard was good. Better than Rome honestly, and they led 14-10 at the half. But Rome came back, in part to a rumbling fifty-yard fumble return by Marshall Ford and, with less than a minute to play, led 23-21. But Brother Maynard completed a long miracle pass and, with only seconds to go, lined up to kick the game-winning field goal.

I was standing on my bed now, mumbling, "shit, shit, shit," over and over, because I wasn't entirely sure what I even wanted to happen. Part of me wanted Rome to lose so Deacon could taste defeat, but I needed Rome to win; otherwise, there was no use in getting Deacon kicked off the team.

"Maynard's holder puts a knee down at the twenty-two-yard line," said the play-by-play man as I turned up my radio. "A thirty-two yarder for the win. Good snap, hold, it's in the air, it's

… wide left! Wide left! Rome wins! Rome wins! Rome is going to the state championship game! The students are pouring onto the field here in Mobile. Rome wins! Rome is going to the state championship game!"

I sat down on my bed, listening to the screaming fans through the radio and realized I was about to cost my high school a state championship.

Oh well.

~ ~ ~

Silas's brother Paul arrived around eight the next morning, and when he rang the bell, my mother shouted for me to answer it, so I went downstairs and opened the door and Paul said, "Hey man, we're like working on your gas or something, so you need to spend the night somewhere else."

He was wearing the grey Dickies coveralls we'd bought him, with a homemade Alagasco patch over his heart, and I whispered, "Dude, you need to tell my mom, not me. And try to act professional, you know, like you work for the gas company."

"Whatever," Paul said, and I went to get Mom.

I waited in the kitchen while she spoke to him, and after an excruciating minute, she walked in and said, "Do you think one of your friends will let you spend the night tonight? Alagasco is working on a gas leak, and we need to be out of the house until noon tomorrow. I can stay with Steve, but—"

"I can stay with Silas. It's not a problem. I'll go pack a bag."

Two hours later, my mother was out of the house, and I was back inside, staring at the hundreds of dollars' worth of alcohol Paul delivered.

Phase one complete.

~ ~ ~

Silas and Jackson came over at six, and the three of us sat in the living room, drinking beers and watching SportsCenter and wondering if people would actually come.

"No one is coming," I said. "This was a terrible idea."

"The party doesn't start until seven," Silas said. "Why would anyone be here now?"

"But what if *he* doesn't come?" I asked.

"Then it wasn't meant to be. But at least you'll have thrown a straight bangin' party, which couldn't hurt your social standing."

"He'll be here," Jackson said. "What else would he do?"

"I don't know. Rest? The announcer said he was limping after the game."

"He limps after every game," Jackson said. "It's all for show."

MeghanJennifer arrived at seven sharp, followed by Maggie Duncan and Rachel, then Chase Malone and two dozen members of the Marching Legion. Brent Holdbrooks and Darryl the atheist came together, and then Jake Norton, second-string quarterback who had no idea how much his life was about to change, showed up with his girlfriend, Tabatha Thompson. Rita Bell rode with Mandy Duke, and Mark Porter and some other freshmen who lived within walking distance strolled up too. By eight, when Marshall and Fletcher arrived, there were over two hundred people in my house, and our street was jam-packed with cars. I knew my neighbors would call the police soon, if they hadn't already.

At half past eight, I found Silas bumping and grinding with Mandy Duke while "Flava in Ya Ear" blasted through my mom's stereo system. I pulled him away and whispered, "He's not coming. I'm telling everyone to go home."

"The hell you are," Silas said. "This is the best party I've ever been to. He'll be here, Brinks. Just relax."

I went upstairs to my mother's bathroom and splashed some water on my face, and when I came out saw two sophomores going at it in my mother's bed. I cursed and walked downstairs and there he was, with Becca Walsh on his arm. Someone handed Deacon a beer, and he downed it in one gigantic gulp, then Jackson handed him another, and he chugged that one too.

Deacon left Becca to mingle with his worshipers, and I walked over to her and said, "Hey."

"Hey Marcus," she said, hugging me. "Thanks for throwing the party."

"Yeah, no problem," I said. "Do you want a beer?"

"Not tonight," she said, pointing at Deacon. "I need to make sure that one gets home safe."

"Cool," I said then stared at my feet before saying, "I haven't really talked to you lately. How've you been?"

"Oh good," she said. "And I'm sorry about my parents the other day. I'm sorry about every—"

"Don't worry about it," I said. "We're cool, I promise."

"You're the best," she said, squeezing my arm, and out of the corner of my eye, I saw Deacon follow Silas through the kitchen and into the garage. I told Becca I needed to kick some sophomores out of my mother's bedroom but went into the garage, where Deacon was already sitting in the back seat of my Mazda.

"Brinks," he said, when he saw me. "This party is the shit. You are the shit, man. I love you so much. How many ... shit—"

He passed out onto the back seat, and Silas shoved his legs into the car and slammed the door.

"Holy shit," I said, "how much of that stuff did Jackson put in his beer?"

"Just a drop," Silas said. "Paul said that's all it would take."

"What was it again?"

"He told me I didn't want to know."

"Shit. Okay. We've got to leave."

My driveway was blocked, but we managed to get out through the yard then made the ten-mile drive to Carthage. We parked downtown, near city hall, and when we were sure no one was around, we pulled the hibernating quarterback from the back seat and, with considerable effort, placed him on a bench.

"He looks so peaceful," Silas said then emptied a can of beer on Deacon's head, and we jumped in my car and raced back to Rome, not breathing again until we passed the city limits sign.

There were now cars in the yard blocking my way into our garage, so Silas and I parked down the street and walked to my house where the party had reached new levels of insanity. A skater dude I recognized from gym was on our roof, literally howling at the moon. Someone had pulled our front door from its hinges, and it lay in the yard where Jackson, who'd apparently drunk his weight in vodka since we left, was pissing on my neighbor's Dachshund.

"Dude," I shouted at Jackson, "you were supposed to keep this under control."

Jackson looked at us, then at the Dachshund, and fell over laughing hysterically. I shook my head and went inside. I found some sophomores from the Marching Legion playing tennis in my living room, and they'd already broken two picture frames when I screamed at them to stop. In the kitchen, Mark Porter and some freshmen were microwaving a ball of aluminum foil to see what would happen; spoiler alert, it caught on fire, and when I went upstairs, I found two more couples had joined the first one on my mother's bed. Running back downstairs, I bumped into Becca, who looked more panicked than me.

"Have you seen Deacon?" she asked. "He's wandered off and—"

"He left with some girls from Carthage," I lied. "I heard them say something about a party back in the fire roads."

"That shit," Becca said. "I'm going to kill him. Marcus, can you—"

The buzzer on my mother's oven clock went off, and Fletcher Morgan punched it, shattering the glass.

"Becca, I'm sorry. I've got to—"

"Police!" someone shouted, and red and blue lights lit up the windows as Romans ran in every direction. Kids were jumping out windows and hiding in closets, and before I could even move, a Rome police officer entered the hole where our door used to be and shouted, "Who lives here?"

I stepped up and said I did, and he asked, "Son, are you a member of the football team?"

"No sir."

The officer sighed in relief. "Thank God," he said, then he shouted, "Everyone go home, now!"

The crowd quickly dispersed, leaving me alone with the officer and his partner, who sat me down on the couch and were offering detailed descriptions of the juvenile detention center where I'd soon live, when Marshall Ford and two sophomore cheerleaders emerged from the downstairs guest bedroom.

"Good evening, officers," Marshall said then passed my mom and Steve on his way out our doorless front entry. When I saw Mom's face, I knew juvie was a fate too kind.

I was a dead man.

Chapter Twenty-Two

"I hate to tell you this, Coach, but he's worse now than when we spoke back in the summer. No, I agree, what he's done here is nothing short of amazing, but I can tell you, it's taking a mighty toll on him. Next season? No, Coach, I don't think so. I'm not sure if he has four more weeks left in him. Hell, every Friday he's in the booth I count as a miracle. I honestly can't see a way he's still doing this next season. This'll be his last rodeo, and I'd love to send him out on top."

I was in Jackson's office on the Monday following his first playoff victory as Rome's head coach, a 63-17 destruction of E. O. Smith High School. He'd summoned me, I assumed, to change another football player's literature grade, but when I walked into the room, he was on the phone, and he raised a finger to say he'd only be another minute. I took a seat across from his desk and checked my email and pretended not to listen to his conversation.

"Hey, you too, Coach. Thanks for calling. It's always good to hear from you. Who, Kyler? Sure, Coach, just send the material to me, and I'll hand it to him personally. But I've got to tell you now, so you don't get your hopes up, we're talking about a five-star recruit here. Alabama, Michigan, Southern Cal, they're all after him. Of course, Coach, you too. Take care now."

Jackson hung up his phone, scribbled on a note pad in front of him, then said to me, "Coach Thompson, from Newberry College."

"Silas's alma mater?"

"Yeah," Jackson said, standing up and looking out his picture window onto the Colosseum below. "He called me two seasons ago, wanted to hire Silas as an offensive analyst."

"No shit," I said.

"Yeah, but he had concerns … about his health. I told him Silas wasn't well, and I doubted he'd make it through the season."

"Wait, why'd you—"

"He was calling to check in, see how Silas was doing. He still wants to hire him, but—"

"But what?"

Jackson sat back behind his desk and said, "But I can't afford to lose him."

I jumped up and said, "Hold on. You're telling me a Division I football program—"

Jackson scoffed. "They're DII, Brinks; don't be dramatic."

I glared at him. "You're seriously telling me an honest-to-God college football program wants to hire Silas, our friend, Silas, who's dreamed of being a college coach since we were kids, and you lied about his health so he'd be stuck calling plays for this stupid high school team forever? God, Jackson, you're such a dick."

Jackson shrugged, and after I sat back down, he said, "Brinks, in this job, you've got to be a dick sometimes, and what Silas doesn't know won't hurt him. Besides, one day he will be too sick to coach. If not next season, then the next or the next."

"Maybe, but that's not your call to make, you asshole."

Jackson smirked. "But it is my call to make, Brinks, and I just made it." He picked up his cell phone, held up a different photograph of that crazy girl and me, and said, "And I trust you won't talk to Silas about it either."

I stared at Jackson hard until he smiled and said, "Come on, Brinks. Let's not argue. Besides, I called you in here to say thanks. Without Kyler, we'd have never beaten Carthage. And you saw what we did to E. O. Smith Friday night. We're rolling, and there isn't a team in the state that can stop us now."

"Oh, go to hell," I said. "Kyler is eligible because you threatened me."

"Well, all the same," Jackson said, "thanks."

I stood up to leave and Jackson said, "Hold on, Brinks. Let's not leave this on such a sour note. How's your mom?"

"Dying."

"Okay," Jackson said, "well how about you and Becca? Things are good, or so I hear."

"We're fine."

"Just fine?"

I bent down to pick up a football off the floor and said, "What do you want me to say, Jackson? That I'm thinking of buying her a ring? That the only reason I changed your dumbass quarterback's grade is because I want to stay with Becca in this shit town, and it would be impossible to live here if everyone thought I cost them a state championship?"

Jackson laughed and I said, "What?"

"Brinks, I don't know what sort of ideas she's planted in that head of yours, but that girl ain't the settling down type."

"Fuck you."

Jackson raised his hands and said, "I'm just trying to save you from some heartache, friend."

I tried to throw the football through his window, but it was military-grade Plexiglas and bounced off toward Jackson's desk, knocking his coffee mug into his lap. He was shouting at me as I burst out of his office into the weight room, where a group of football players completing their morning workouts looked on in meat-headed bewilderment.

~ ~ ~

Rome defeated Mytilene in the second round of the play-offs, a 35-0 victory I did not attend because the game was in

Mytilene, and try as you might, you cannot get to Mytilene from Rome. The next week, Mansfield came to town, and I went to the game because Becca went to the game and I wanted to be with her. Rome won big again, this time 42-14, and it set up a semifinal with Gaul, the team we'd faced in the state championship game my senior year. Rome hadn't played Gaul since 1994, and I knew the excitement of a semifinal, combined with a week of town-wide vomit-inducing nostalgia over the last meeting, would have the Rome Quarterback Club panicked about what the future might hold.

Deacon caught me in the high school parking lot on the Monday before Thanksgiving, the Monday before Gaul. He had on his uniform, dark jeans and a camelhair blazer, but he looked like he'd slept in them, and I almost felt sorry for him that this stupid game was stressing him toward a massive cardiac event. Almost.

"Good morning, Brinks," Deacon said, hopping out of his truck as I made my way from my car toward the school.

"What do you want?" I asked.

"Now Brinks, is that how you talk to friends?"

"Friend? You had Darryl trick my dying mother into giving him an interview because I wouldn't help with your stupid little coup. Now what do you want? I've got to get to class."

Deacon put a paw on my shoulder and said, "It's not what I want, Brinks; it's what I don't want. And I don't want Jackson leading that team into Tuscaloosa next week to win the state championship."

"Well, I don't play for Gaul, so I'm not sure how I can help you there."

He squeezed my shoulder hard, and I jerked free and turned to walk away. "Good God, Brinks," Deacon said over my shoulder, "why do you even care? This town doesn't mean shit to you, and neither does the team or Jackson. When your mama dies, you'll leave here and never come back, so why don't you help me out? I heard you need money. I've got plenty. Just say a number."

I turned to face him and said, "You're right. Jackson is an asshole." Deacon grinned until I added, "But so are you, and not only that, you're wrong about me. I'm staying in Rome for good."

"Wait, because of Becca?" Deacon asked, the wheels in his head turning slowly.

"Yes, for Becca."

Deacon thought for a second then reached out his hand and said, "All right, Brinks. I had no idea things between you two were that serious."

"They are," I said, reluctantly shaking his hand.

"Well, I still wish you'd help us out, Brinks," Deacon said, "but I understand if you don't want to rock any boats." Then he slapped me on the back and said, "You and Becca have a Happy Thanksgiving," and drove away, leaving me to wonder what exactly he was up to.

~ ~ ~

Becca asked me to Thanksgiving at her parent's house then immediately took it back, saying, "Sorry, I know you wouldn't want to leave your mother alone."

"You could come to our house for dinner that evening," I offered, without consulting my mother, and Becca accepted, arriving around six carrying half a dozen Tupperware containers full of sweet potato casserole, green beans, cranberry sauce, and whatever else she could scavenge from her parents' lunch. These, combined with the ten-dollar turkey I purchased at the Riverton Publix that morning, made up the Thanksgiving dinner we shared around my mother's hospice bed. It was about as awkward as it sounds, and Becca and I picked at our food while my mother ignored hers completely.

"I know you must love having Marcus back in town," Becca said to my mother at one point, to which my mother replied, "It beats dying alone." I choked on my grape salad and, after recovering with a swig of sweet tea, tried to change the subject. "Mom, what has the paper said about Gaul this week? Can Rome beat them?"

"They've got a running back that's already committed to Georgia," Mom said, "but if we can stop him, we should be okay. Six of their so-called experts picked us to win; the other four idiots picked Gaul."

"I remember playing Gaul all those years ago in Montgomery," Becca said, and my mom snapped, "I bet you do."

Becca looked at me, confused, and I stared at my mother, trying to shut her up through sheer force of will, but she wouldn't look my way, so I said to Becca, "Sorry, her medicine makes her talk out of her head sometimes."

"The hell it does, Marcus Brinks," my mom said. "You take these dishes and go wash them up. I'd like a word with Ms. Walsh … in private."

I looked at Becca, and she handed me her plate and flashed a reassuring smile. "It's okay," she mouthed, and I gathered the rest of the plates and went downstairs.

In the kitchen, I scrubbed dishes and listened upstairs for shouts or perhaps a gunshot but thankfully heard neither, and after half an hour, the stairs creaked when Becca came down. I met her in the living room and asked if everything was okay, and Becca kissed me on the cheek and said, "Marcus, you have a sweet mother, and she loves you very much."

"She threatened you, didn't she?"

Becca smiled. "No, we had a nice talk. Now, do you need any help with the dishes?"

"They're done. Now seriously, tell me what you two talked about."

"Marcus Brinks, you heard your mother. Our conversation was private. But I bet she'll share some of the highlights later. Now, are you sure you don't want to go with us to Gaul tomorrow night?"

"Yeah, I should stay home with Mom, but I'll see you Saturday, right?"

Becca kissed me again, this time on the mouth, and said, "Of course you will."

Upstairs, Mom was asleep, so I sat in the chair in the corner of her room and read for an hour until she woke up and asked, "Did Becca go home?"

"She did. Now, what the hell did you two talk about?"

With effort, Mom sat up in bed and coughed for half a minute before saying, "We talked about you, and Rome, and the past."

"You didn't bring up—"

"No, Marcus, that's between the two of you. We talked about my past, and my mistakes, and then I asked her about her intentions with my son."

"Oh, God, tell me you didn't," I said, rubbing my temples.

"I did," my mother said. "You'll be alone soon, with no one to look after you, and—"

"Mom, I'm forty years old. I can look after myself."

"I was forty-three when we moved back to Rome. You're never too old to screw up, son."

"Fair enough."

"Now, I've spoken to Rebecca, so why don't you tell me your intentions with her?"

"Because that would be awkward."

Mom glared at me until I said, "Fine. I didn't come home with any intentions. When you called and said you were dying, I figured I'd come home, help out as best I could for a few months, then sell your house and move back to Jamaica until that money ran out too."

My mother shook her head. "Son, you don't have to say everything you think out loud."

"Sorry," I mumbled then said, "but I didn't come back here to awaken ancient feelings. When I saw her in the gym at that first pep rally, every part of me wanted to run, but I couldn't. So we talked, and then we hung out, and, well, I think she's the one, Mom. She's always been the one. And I hate to shock you in your fragile state, but I want to stay here, in Rome. I want to marry Becca and live in this house and grow old. God, it's all I've ever wanted."

My mother was crying, and after she wiped her eyes, she said, "Son, Becca is a sweet girl. She's single in a small town, so people say things, but I don't believe any of it. Not anymore. If you can give her the benefit of the doubt, then so can I."

"Thanks," I said and walked over to sit on my mother's bed, and as I held her hand, she said, "I'm proud of you, son. After everything with your dad and Steve, I shut down. I was stupid, and I didn't want to get hurt again, and you know what? I never did. But I've paid a terrible price. I've lived a lonely life, Marcus, and it broke my heart watching you go down the same road. But you're risking the pain to love again, and I cannot tell you how happy that makes me."

With considerable effort, my mother sat up to look me in the eye and said, "I can't see the future, son. I don't know if things will work out between you two. But I can die knowing you won't make the same mistake I made. You're going to grow old and happy with someone. I just hate I won't be around to see it."

I was crying now too and hugged my mother and said, "Me too, Mom. Me too."

"After graduating from Harvard, and spending a month in the Metropolitan Correctional Center for assaulting a NYC equine officer named Caesar, Marcus Brinks has spent the last six years living in a suite at the Sandals Royal Caribbean in Montego Bay, Jamaica, where he reportedly interacts with fans and plays a mean game of beach volleyball."

—*SPIN*, "*The Beige Album,* 10 Years Later,"
November 22, 2007

Chapter Twenty-Three

"Wait, how long?"

"I don't know. She said it was incalculable, which I took to mean a long-ass time."

My mother, like all accountants, was a spreadsheet junkie. She created spreadsheets for everything, from our family budget to when she needed to buy me new underwear. For my thirteenth birthday, along with fifty bucks and a sweet Bo Jackson T-shirt, she presented me with an absurdly complex spreadsheet, laminated no less, detailing the length and breadth of punishment any particular infraction would earn me during my teenage years. If I missed curfew, all I had to do was consult my spreadsheet to know my punishment was the loss of my next weekend. Disobeying my parents cost two weekends, lying four, bad grades (B-minus or worse) meant six weekends under house arrest, assuming of course that my grades rebounded, and drinking alcohol was the biggie, a whopping twelve weekends in the can. Whenever I'd screw up, Mom would consult the spreadsheet, which she hung on my door next to a poster of Hakeem Olajuwon and, with detached coolness, read aloud my punishment. No debate. No appeal. My punishment had always been there, in black and white, so I had no excuse.

However, since she'd left my dad, moved us to Rome, and hooked up with the biggest piece of shit east of the Mississippi, my mother rarely punished me for anything. By November, if I came home by curfew, it was only out of boredom. I disobeyed my mother more than I obeyed her. I lied to her frequently, my grades had tanked, and unless she'd mysteriously lost her sense of smell (and she was still with Steve, so maybe she had), she ignored smelling beer on my breath half a dozen times. But standing in her living room, ankle-deep in Solo cups and the stuffing from her couch cushions, my mother unleashed months of built-up parental justice in a ten-minute screaming display that I'm certain, had the police not been present, would have ended with my premature death at the hands of whatever blunt object she could find in her purse.

My punishment, doled out on the spot without trial by jury or consulting the spreadsheet, which we'd left in Texas, was eternal grounding. Perhaps this seems a little excessive, but Mom told me when I was thirteen that, if I committed a crime so grievous that she hadn't even bothered to list it on the spreadsheet because she knew I'd never be stupid enough to do it, her punishment would be swift and painful. And no, hiring a stoner to impersonate the gas company so I could throw an insane party that resulted in the destruction of most of my mother's property was not on the spreadsheet. Looking back, I'll admit, the punishment fit the crime.

"Well, at least she didn't kill you."

"True, but she's reserved the right to shoot me later if she finds another condom in her bedroom."

We were at lunch on Monday, meatloaf day, and Silas and I sat across the table from Jackson, whispering about the same thing everyone else in school was whispering about: My party and the fall of Deacon Cassburn.

"Did you guys see the paper?" Jackson asked, and when we shook our heads no, he said, "Here, I cut this out of the library's copy." He slid the *Riverton Times* clipping across the table, and we read it.

Carthage, Alabama—The Carthage Police Department announced the arrest of a juvenile offender, found intoxicated and nude on a park bench near Carthage City Hall, shortly before midnight on November 27, 1994. Carthage police officers discovered the juvenile while responding to an alarm at Carthage Flowers & Gifts. It is not clear if the two incidents are related, and due to the juvenile status of the offender, the Carthage Police Department cannot release additional information, a spokesman said.

Silas and I looked at each other then back at Jackson and burst out laughing.

"Keep it down," Jackson said, and we tried. Then he whispered, "Why did you take his clothes off?"

"We didn't take his clothes off," I said.

"He must have done that on his own," Silas added, and we burst out laughing again.

Jackson shook his head and said, "This isn't funny. In homeroom, I heard MeghanJennifer say Deacon is in federal prison."

"He's not in federal prison, you dumbass," Silas said. "They don't send drunk teens to federal prison. I bet they took him in, scared him with a bunch of juvie bullshit, then called his parents to pick him up. They'll just make him do community service or something."

"Will he get to play on Friday?" I asked.

"Nope. No way," Jackson said. "Coach P is crazy strict about discipline stuff. He tells us every spring, if we get into trouble with the law, we're off his team. If he let Deacon play, it would go against everything the man has ever said."

"So the state championship is Jake Norton's to win or lose," Silas said, and Jackson nodded.

"Shit, and now you're second string?" I asked, and Jackson nodded again then looked like he might spew meatloaf against the wall. I'm not sure we'd even considered that taking down Deacon Cassburn would leave Jackson one sprained ankle away from quarterbacking Rome in the state championship game. I can't blame him for looking sick.

"Deep breaths, dude," Silas said to Jackson. "It's gonna be okay. You won't see the field."

"I've lost my appetite," Jackson said, and as he stood to throw away his food, a couple sophomore girls walked up to tell me how much fun they had at my party. Then the skater guy from gym class who'd spent the night on my roof, howling at the moon, walked by with a fist bump and said, "Brinks, my dude, kick-ass party."

"Thanks," I mumbled, and Silas said, "See, my dude, I told you throwing a party would only help your social standing. You're now as popular as some third-string football players."

He was right, though I'd worried over the weekend that people would somehow blame me and my party for what happened to Deacon. But as word spread that he left my party with some Carthage girls, consensus was the dumbass got what he deserved.

"Speaking of football," Silas said, sliding an index card across the table, "I've added a throwback option to 'Convulsion'; this play is literally unstoppable now." I pretended to look at the squiggly lines on the card, and he said, "By the way, I got *Madden '95* yesterday. You up for an ass-beating this afternoon?"

"Eternal grounding," I reminded him.

"Oh right, sorry."

"Sorry about what?" Jackson asked, returning to his seat.

"Brinks's eternal grounding."

"Will your mom let you go to Montgomery Friday?" Jackson asked, picking up Silas' index card and saying, "Oh nice, a throwback option."

"I doubt it," I said.

"Shit. Sorry," he said, and I shrugged. I had bigger things to worry about than missing a football game. The talent show was just three days away, and with Deacon out of the way, Becca was all but mine.

"No biggie," I said as Becca walked by with her lunch tray. "I've got a feeling it's going to be a really good week."

~ ~ ~

216

Deacon returned to school on Tuesday, shooting holes in MeghanJennifer's federal prison story, but he was now persona non grata, which is Latin for a person no one gives a shit about. The football team shunned him because he'd let them down and possibly cost them a state championship. The rest of the school shunned him for the same reason and because, at some point in the last four years, he'd been a dick to each and every one of them. But most importantly, Becca shunned him. She no longer sat by him in class, or spoke to him in the hall, or acknowledged his existence in any way. The door was open.

On Thursday, I was up by five, cramming in all the last-minute practice I could cram, and around seven, I went downstairs for breakfast. Steve was there, as always, and he stared at me from the kitchen table while I poured a bowl of Fruity Pebbles.

"You would eat Fruity Pebbles, you little fruit," Steve said, and I tried to ignore him. He'd always sucked, but since the party, he'd reached all new levels of dickheadedness. He pointed at my guitar case and asked, "What the hell are you taking that to school for?"

"Talent show," I muttered.

Mom was next to Steve at the table, but she hadn't looked up since I entered the room. She'd been crying.

"Well, hell," Steve said, getting to his feet. "I'd forgotten all about that guitar of yours. I tell you what. I'm gonna take it down to Riverton Pawn and see what they'll give me for it."

I grabbed my case and said, "What the hell are you talking about?"

Steve moved toward me and said, "Way I figure it, you owe me about five hundred dollars in damages, boy."

"What damages? Mom, what is he talking about?"

"I kept some clothes in your mama's closet," Steve said, "and somebody at your party stole 'em."

"No one at my party would want your clothes, you idiot."

He was in my face now. "I kept some pills in there," he said, "and those are gone too. You owe me, boy, and you're gonna pay."

217

Ignoring half-hearted protests from my mother, Steve reached for my guitar case, and when I pulled it away, he stumbled and fell because he'd had Jack Daniels for breakfast. "You little shit," he said and this time came at me swinging. He caught me on the side of the head with a surprise left, and I dropped the case and stumbled back into the fridge before falling. Steve grabbed my case and said, "Back in an hour, Bev," and I watched him walk out the front door.

Up until that point in my life, I'd never been in a fight. Well, not a fight where both combatants actively participated. I'd never even thrown a punch, but this pathetic excuse for a grown man was going to keep me from winning Becca's heart, and something in me snapped. I caught him in the front yard, tackled him from behind, and somehow ended up straddling him on the ground, hitting his ugly face with both fists as hard as I could. I know I broke his nose—he tried to sue me to pay for plastic surgery years later, and we settled out of court for two hundred dollars, no joke. I'm not sure how long I sat there punching him, it felt like hours, but Steve eventually got away and ran to his car, peeling out of our driveway as fast as his piece-of-shit Mustang could manage.

I tried to open the case to check out my guitar, but my hands were still shaking with anger, so I just sat in the yard and cried. When I finally looked up, I saw Mom sitting on the front steps. She was crying too, but I didn't care. This was all her fault for bringing that asshole into our home, so I picked up my guitar and left for school without a word. It wasn't until fifteen minutes later, after the adrenaline rush passed, I realized I'd broken my hand on Steve's stupid face.

For the first time in my life, I skipped school, a four-week grounding per mom's spreadsheet, like such things mattered anymore. In the parking lot, I tried to see if I could still play, but my hand was so swollen I couldn't open the damn guitar case, so I drove to Eckerd and the pharmacist sold me a wrist splint and a bottle of Advil and told me to go see a doctor, but instead I drove around Rome for a couple hours then went home.

When I got home, Mom had scattered all Steve's belongings across the front yard, and I found her at the kitchen table, staring into her coffee mug.

"Marcus, your hand, what hap—"

"I broke it on Steve's face," I said, and she started crying again.

I sat across from her, and she said, "Marcus, I'm so sorry. I really messed us up."

I was mad at her, but I couldn't stand to see her cry, so I said, "Mom, this isn't all your fault. If Dad hadn't—"

"Marcus," my mom said, wiping her eyes but not looking at me, "there's something I need to tell you. Steve … Steve was my boyfriend in high school."

"Yeah," I said, "he told me the same night he said he was going to marry you and send me back to Dad."

My mother sighed. "I'm so sorry, Marcus. I truly am. Steve … do you remember last October, when I came here for my twenty-five-year class reunion?"

"Yeah," I said. "Dad and I stayed in Houston because we had Oilers-Bengals tickets."

"That's right," Mom said. "Well, I ran into Steve at the reunion, and he was … I know you won't believe this, but Steve can be very charming."

"What are you talking about?"

Mom rubbed her bare ring finger and said, "Your dad and I, we were in a rough patch then, and I don't know …"

"I'd rather not hear any more of this," I said.

"No, you need to hear this. Steve and I began talking on the phone two or three times a week, and when we were here visiting Grandmother last Christmas, I snuck out to see him a couple times. I told your dad I was leaving him in January, but he wanted to work things out. So I tried, I really did, but in June, he told me he'd started seeing his secretary, so I packed up our things and we left."

I stared at my mom for a full minute and finally said, "So Dad didn't leave you for his secretary."

"No, your dad had an affair, but—"

"But only because you told him you were leaving him for a redneck asshole. God, Mom, I've spent the last five months hating Dad, and he didn't do anything wrong. I didn't even call him on his birthday because I thought he was the reason we … but it was you … he didn't—"

"Your dad's not entirely innocent here, Marcus. I told you we were in a rough patch, and—"

"And you thought hooking up with the biggest asshole in Alabama would somehow make things better?"

"No, Marcus, I thought … I thought that …" Mom rubbed her eyes and said, "You never get over your high school love, Marcus. One day, you'll understand."

I stood up and said, "Here's what I understand. You're a selfish woman, and you destroyed our family, and I will never believe another thing you say as long as I live."

"Marcus, wait," Mom said as I stormed upstairs, but I didn't stop.

I didn't speak to her again for ten years.

Chapter Twenty-Four

My mother died in her sleep two days after Rome defeated Gaul 28-27 to advance to the state championship game in Tuscaloosa. She took a turn for the worse on the Friday morning after Thanksgiving, and though we listened to the game together in her room that night, she slept through most of it.

"Did we win?" she asked me Saturday morning, while I drank my morning coffee and read the *Riverton Times* in her room.

"Yeah, Mom, we won," I said, holding up the front-page photo of Kyler celebrating his game-winning touchdown pass. "We play Middlesboro next week in Tuscaloosa for the state championship." She managed a smile before fading again.

Becca stopped by around noon and talked me into going to the WigWam for lunch. I suspect Rita called her because she knew I was in for a long night and would need my sustenance. By evening, Mom's breathing became shallow, and I sat next to her in bed, wiping the sweat from her head with a cool washcloth and singing songs from an old hymnal she kept on her nightstand. I dozed off sometime after midnight, holding my mother's tiny hand. I was still holding it when she slipped away. Rita woke me up around four and told me she was gone.

I squeezed my mother's hand one last time then asked Rita, "What do I do now?"

Rita hugged me and said, "You don't have to do anything, Marcus. I'll call the funeral home when you're ready. They can be here in an hour."

"When I'm ready?"

"I thought maybe you'd want to spend some time with your mother first."

I looked at my mother's body then back at Rita and said, "Nope, I'm good."

Rita laughed through her tears and said, "Your mother told me you'd say that. She also made me promise I'd tell you to shave for her funeral or she'd come back as a ghost and shave you in your sleep."

I smiled and said into the air, "That's not terrifying at all, Mom. I'll shave, geez."

Rita put her hand on my shoulder. "Why don't you go to bed now, try to get some sleep. It's gonna be a long couple of days, but you don't have to do anything. Your mama has had everything planned for months. All you'll have to do is wear a suit and hug every neck in Rome."

"And shave," I said, standing up to stretch.

"Right, please don't forget to shave," Rita said.

I went to my room and collapsed into bed but couldn't sleep, so I took a shower instead then made myself a cup of coffee and sat on the front porch swing. It was a warm night by November standards, and I watched a car pass, tossing newspapers into the driveways of the few people who still subscribed. I wondered if I'd have to write my mother's obituary or if she'd taken care of that too.

The funeral home van arrived just as the sun rose, and the driver met me on the porch and began asking questions about my mother's makeup and clothes, but Rita came to my rescue and took them inside to answer all their questions. Half an hour later, they took my mom away, and I called my dad. He told me he was sorry before he said hello—I usually called him on Saturdays, and he knew the Sunday morning phone call meant Mom was gone. We talked for ten minutes, and he got choked up telling me the story of the first time he saw Mom on the concourse at Auburn. Then he told me he was sorry he couldn't make the funeral. I called Becca next, and she pulled up ten minutes later with a warm hug and breakfast from Krispy Kreme.

In Mom's kitchen, over donuts and coffee, Becca said, "You're getting a break because it's Sunday."

"What do you mean?"

"Well, all the little old ladies have Sunday school this morning, then they'll attend the service, and then they'll go to lunch. I suspect no one will show up at your door with a casserole until three at the earliest."

"Wait, people are just going to come over uninvited?"

"Yeah, but when you see the food, you won't mind."

Becca was right to the minute. Norma Porter, mother of Methy Mark, arrived at three sharp, hugged me, and handed me plastic containers full of sweet potato casserole, sautéed green beans, something pink that tasted better than it looked, and an entire pumpkin pie. For the next three hours, a steady stream of blue-haired ladies shuffled through my door, leaving casseroles and pies and bread and jug upon jug of Milo's sweet tea. I hugged necks and stacked the food in Mom's fridge, and Becca, God bless her, did most of the talking for me. However, once when three mourners all arrived at once, a little old lady cornered me and said, "You know, Marcus, your mama is in a better place now."

"The morgue?"

Again, Becca came to my rescue, saying I was thankful my mother was in heaven and no longer suffering, but I suspect not before the woman made a mental note to add me to the heathen section of the church's prayer list.

My mother's visitation was Monday night at Rome First Baptist, and though she'd already planned everything, I still had to meet with the funeral home director that morning to go over the paperwork. Kitts & Sons Funeral Home and Crematory was in Riverton, close to the R&R Tire plant, and the director, whom I suspect was either Kitts or one of his sons, was a touch pushy. I sat across from his desk, and after I signed my name a few times, he said, "Now, Mr. Brinks, your mama only paid for basic funeral services tomorrow, but if you'd like to upgrade to one of our premier services, I've got a price sheet right here." He slid a laminated sheet across the desk, and I stared at the letters and numbers without reading them before handing the sheet back and saying, "No, thank you. Rita said my mother planned this the way she wanted it, so I'd hate to change anything."

"Of course, Mr. Brinks," the director said, "of course. I gotta ask though, 'cause it's my job, but do you think your mama might have only bought the basic package because she hated to spend money on herself?"

He slid the laminated sheet back across his desk, and I said, "Look, Rita Bell said my mother knew exactly what she wanted, and she threatened to haunt anyone who changed a single thing."

The director pulled his laminated sheet back and said, "Well, we don't want that. But look, we do offer a la carte services. Have you considered having a bagpiper graveside or perhaps a bugler? No? Okay, well, do you think your mama would like the logo of her favorite college football team added to her coffin?"

The great thing about grieving is you can call people money-grubbing assholes, and they don't even get upset at you. The funeral home director just stood up, shook my hand, and said, "All right, basic package it is."

~ ~ ~

My job during that evening's visitation was to stand next to my mother's body and accept handshakes, hugs, and condolences from half of Rome. At my mother's request, her logo-free casket was closed, because she didn't want, in her words, "a bunch of blue-hairs from church standing over my dead body going on about how peaceful I look." Rita told me Mom even threatened to turn into a zombie and bite everyone in the church if we left the casket open, something I relished relaying to the funeral home director.

Becca stood by my side for the duration of the two-hour visitation, providing moral support and whispering people's names before they hugged me. Every member of Sunday's casserole crew came through the line, as did Marshall Ford, who tried to squeeze the life out of me with a bear hug then told me a weird story about how his dad wanted his head frozen like Walt Disney so they could bring him back to life with a robot body in the distant future. "I just keep it out back in the deep freeze," Marshall said then slapped me on the back and added, "Sorry 'bout your mama, Brinks."

Silas came to pay his respects, as did Darryl Loder, Melvin the high school janitor, MeghanJennifer, who'd married twin brothers from Weepel and lived next door to each other, Brent Holdbrooks and Mandy Duke, now Mandy Holdbrooks, and even Deacon, who for some reason picked then to ask if I knew of a discreet veterinarian who'd take a look at Diana's sore tooth.

"Is Diana his dog?" Becca asked after he left.

"His wolf," I said, but I don't think she believed me.

Fletcher Morgan brought his mother, who told Fletcher she'd never heard of me when he mentioned I used to be in a band, and then some of my students came through the line.

Karl, the small, thoughtful boy from my second-period class pulled me aside and asked, "Mr. Brinks, do you know that man?"

"Yeah, Karl, that's Fletcher Morgan," I said.

"Mr. Brinks, he keeps sending me snaps of naked women and invitations to a party at his house Thursday night called eXXXtravaganza."

I rubbed my temples and said, "Karl, he's a very disturbed man, and he's trying to get members of the football team in trouble before the big game Friday. Please tell the rest of the team so they'll know not to go."

Karl said he would, and I was about to tell Becca what Fletcher was up to, when Jackson and Amy walked in. They arrived just before the doors closed, I suspect, to avoid the crowds who'd want to talk about the Middlesboro game. Jackson hugged me, said he was sorry, then talked to Becca while Amy quoted Leviticus and inquired about my mother's eternal salvation. Just for fun, I told Amy I'd found a Koran in Mom's nightstand.

Mother's funeral was at ten the next morning at Rome First Baptist, and Brother Shawn asked me to meet him in his office beforehand for a time of prayer. I didn't want to go, but Becca said she'd go with me, and we waited on a couch in the church lobby until Brother Shawn entered with a knockout blonde. Becca and I stood, and Brother Shawn shook my hand and said, "Good to see you, Marcus, Becca. I hope you know your church family is here for you in these tough times."

We followed Brother Shawn into his office where he introduced the blonde as his wife, Tiffany. I shook her hand, and she asked, "What year did you graduate from Rome, Marcus?"

"I was only here for fall semester in '94," I said.

"Oh, okay," she said. "I finished in '92, but you might have known my little sister. Tabatha Thompson?"

"Tabatha Thompson," I repeated then said, "that name sounds familiar ... so you were ..."

"Tiffany Thompson."

Holy shit. I looked at Becca who, in wide-eyed terror, told me to shut up with an almost imperceptible shake of her pretty head.

"That ... doesn't ring a bell," I said through gritted teeth then, for the duration of Brother Shawn's five-minute prayer, fought back laughter and the mental image of his wife wearing nothing but Mississippi State socks.

"You should have warned me," I whispered to Becca, still fighting back laughter as Mom's service began.

"I'd honestly forgotten," she whispered back. "She's been back in town so long people don't really talk about it anymore."

My mother's service was short and beautiful. The Rome First Baptist choir sang "Amazing Grace" and "Morning Has Broken" then Brother Shawn read Mom's favorite psalm before, with tears in his eyes, he spoke briefly about the special role Beverly Brinks had played in the life of his church. And as the pianist played "Let It Be" and the pallbearers, men I didn't even know, came forward to carry my mother to the cemetery behind the church, I understood how special this fellowship had been to my lonely mother through the years. At the graveside, in the cold November rain, Brother Shawn read, "I am the resurrection and the life ..." and then it was over. There were more handshakes and hugs, and we left the workmen to bury my mother in the red Alabama dirt on a hill overlooking Rome.

Becca spent the rest of the day with me, and I was thankful, because our house had never felt emptier. Hospice had already removed the bed and equipment from my mother's room, and there was more food in the kitchen than I could eat in a year. We fixed ourselves either an early dinner or a late lunch and ignored the food for half an hour until I stood to throw away our paper plates. And as I caught myself thinking I should ask Mom if we should store some of this food in her deep freezer, it finally hit me she was gone. A flood of questions I'd never get to ask her rushed through my mind—What was her favorite childhood toy? Who was her first kiss? Where did Dad take her on their first date? Hundreds of questions I'd never be able to ask her because she was gone, and her memories were gone with her.

We spoke for the first time in ten years the day I turned twenty-eight. I'd thought, or hoped maybe, that I, like so much rock royalty before me, would die at twenty-seven. But when I woke up on my birthday alive and somewhat sober, I called my mom, and I'd called her every Sunday night for the last thirteen years. Over the years, we'd worked through some of our issues, ignored others, and usually talked about much of nothing for half an hour each week. Of course, I'd left things unsaid, unasked, but I always thought we'd have more time. Turns out, it was later than I thought.

Maybe it's always later than we think.

"Oh god," I said and caught myself on the counter because I felt dizzy, then I sat on the floor and cried for the first time since Mom died. I cried until there were no tears left to fall, while Becca sat next to me on the floor, holding my hand and telling me it would be okay.

I needed out of the house, so we went for a walk late that afternoon, but it didn't help much. I don't know why, but I'm often overcome with anxiety in the fall. Maybe the distant drums of practicing marching bands call to mind an invading hoard, or perhaps I suffer from some undiagnosed seasonal affective disorder, but on chilly autumn afternoons, I'm often overcome with a low-level apprehension. A feeling like my friends are all somewhere without me, and now it's too late for me to go. I felt the familiar pang of dread that day as we walked the darkening streets of Rome, listening to the Marching Legion practice across town.

Becca squeezed my hand and said, "It was nice of your students to come today."

"It was," I said, "though I suspect they just wanted to get out of class."

Becca smiled. "I'm sure they'll miss you."

"I'll see them tomorrow," I said.

"You're going back to school tomorrow?"

"It's either that or sit in an empty house all day, and as you saw, I'm not handling that very well."

Becca started crying, and I asked, "What's wrong?"

"It's just … I thought … I was sure you'd leave, now that …"

I put my arm around her and said, "When I came back that was my plan, but … but I'm happy, Becca." We stopped, and I looked her in the eyes and said, "I'm happy for the first time since I was a kid, because of you. And I want to stay here, because of you."

"But we wouldn't have to stay here," Becca said. "We could go anywhere. We could run away."

"I'm through running away. Besides, your life is here; your parents are here."

"My parents wouldn't even notice if I left."
She was sobbing now, and I squeezed her tight. "You deserve so much better than me, Marcus. Better than this town. You …"

I held her by both arms and said, "This is where I belong. It's where I've always belonged." She wouldn't look at me, and for a moment, I feared I'd misread the last few months entirely. "But look," I said, "I don't want to pressure you. If you … if we … if this isn't what I think it is …"

She wiped her eyes and hugged me for a long time, and when she finally pulled away, I said, "I love you," and through her tears, she said she loved me too.

We walked back to my mom's house and sat on the porch, and I held her close against the evening chill. "I've always loved this old house of your mother's," she said after a while.

"I haven't always loved it," I said, but it's a sweet old house. "Needs some paint, and I'd like to redo the bathrooms, maybe update the kitchen one day. There are plumbing videos on You-Tube. How hard can it be?" Becca laughed, and I said, "But I don't think I'll teach next year. I'm terrible at it."

"Marcus, that's not true."

"Yet it is. It's almost Christmas, and I still haven't learned most of my students' names." She laughed again, and I said, "This may sound crazy, but I'm thinking of opening a recording studio in Riverton. With all the publicity we've gotten lately, Geffen wants to reissue our album, and that should make me enough to get things started. After that, there are plenty of local bands to keep it in business, and I could give guitar lessons to make a little extra on the side. I still have friends in the industry too. You know, we could have a music festival here in the summer. Hold it at the amphitheater on the Coosa River and people could bring blankets or even listen from their boats. I can think of a dozen bands right now who'd come if—"

Becca looked at me and smiled, and I asked, "What?"

"I just like seeing you excited," she said and kissed my cheek, and we sat on the swing and dreamed until she said it was late and she needed some sleep before school in the morning.

I sighed. "I'm not sure if I can sleep in this big empty house tonight."

Becca grabbed my hand and said, "Then why don't you stay with me?"

I never slept in my mother's house again.

"Hey, fellow Brutes, I tracked down Chris Hollingsworth, MB's freshman roommate at UT. He's a pharmacist in Odessa. Anyway, I called the CVS where he works and he told me MB didn't date a girl named Fiona freshman year. Not only that, he said MB didn't date anyone freshman year. I think this proves CryHAv0c97's theory that a high school girlfriend inspired the Beige Album, not some girl MB dated in Austin. Thoughts?"

—Message board post by 2theBr!nks
on www.dearbrutusfans.net
November 30, 2013

Chapter Twenty-Five

I didn't go to school on Friday, and my mother didn't even bother to knock on my door and ask why. I slept till noon, ate three bowls of cereal for lunch, then laid back down to sleep the afternoon away, when Silas called.

"Dude, you're alive! I thought your mom might have found another condom in her bedroom and justifiably murdered you."

I laughed for the first time in two days then asked why he wasn't at school.

"They let us out at noon," he said, "because of the game. Gaul is three hours away, and the team has to get there early. Seriously, where've you been the last two days?"

I told him everything. About Steve trying to pawn my guitar, and me kicking his ass in the yard, and how my parents split up because my mom cheated on my dad, and not the other way around.

"Holy shit," Silas said, "and you broke your hand on his face?"

"I think," I said. "I lost myself for a minute there, so it's possible I kept punching the ground after he ran away."

"Well, that's awesome, about Steve I mean, not about your folks. That sucks."

"Thanks," I said. "How was the talent show?"

"Lame. Chase Malone did magic tricks, Mandy Duke sang

"Can You Feel the Love Tonight," four freshmen calling them-selves Nuns N' Moses performed a Christian version of "Para-dise City" that literally made my ears bleed, and Maggie Dun-can squirted milk out of her eye."

"Wait, what?"

"Yeah, it was totally gross. She won in a landslide."

"I hate I missed that."

"No, you don't."

I asked what else I'd missed, and he said, "Not much. We had a special candlelit pep rally first thing this morning, but it was weird. I'm not sure if everyone was nervous or half-asleep, but it felt like a strangely peppy funeral. Oh, and you should see Jackson. He's been walking around with an I'm-about-to-puke face for the last two days. He told me he had a dream where Jake Norton broke his leg in the first quarter, and when Coach P told him to go in, he couldn't find his helmet, so he had to play without one."

"I could actually see that happening," I said.

"Yeah, no kidding. Let's see … what else … oh, they asked about you today."

"Who?"

"Deeez nuuuts!"

"I'm hanging up now."

"No, seriously, Becca asked about you today."

"Really?"

"Yeah, she wanted to know if you were going to the game tonight, but I told her I doubted it, since NASA scientists are still trying to calculate how long you're grounded." I laughed, and he asked, "Are you going?"

"I don't think so," I said. "Technically, I'm still grounded in perpetuity, but I wouldn't let that stop me. I don't particularly give a shit about anything my mother says anymore."

"Well, if you change your mind, let me know and you can ride with me and my folks. We're not leaving until three."

I told Silas I'd think about it, with no intentions of thinking about it, then turned on my Sega but couldn't even hold the controller with the stupid wrist splint on. So I just sat in bed, listening to Morrissey's *Vauxhall and I* on repeat, because it was the saddest sad bastard album I owned. I'd listened to it seven times when the sun began to set, and sitting in my ever-darkening room, I started feeling anxious, which inevitably led to thoughts of Becca. She'd asked about me, which meant she was thinking about me, and if she was thinking about me, maybe I still had a chance. It was ten till five, and Gaul was three hours away, so I could be there before halftime if I left now, plus I'd have 180 minutes to come up with some romantic speech for Becca. This could work, and if it didn't, I could keep driving. I didn't have to live with Mom. I could drive all the way back to Texas. I thought about packing up my stuff but didn't have time, so I tossed a change of clothes into a paper sack, along with the book Becca gave me, then quickly showered because I hadn't in two days. Mom was on the couch when I went downstairs, and I walked past her without a word. A minute later, I was in my car, driving toward Gaul.

There were a few hiccups in my hastily organized last-ditch effort to win Becca's heart, one being Friday evening Birmingham traffic. I-459 was a parking lot, and I sat in my Mazda, cursing commuters and listening to the game, because thankfully, Birmingham sports stations were broadcasting all six state championship games simultaneously.

Rome scored first on a short touchdown pass from Jake Norton to Fletcher Morgan, but in the time it took me to drive a quarter of a mile, Gaul had tied the game. I merged onto I-65 South just as Gaul kicked a short field goal to take a 10-7 lead into the half. I'd planned to be in Gaul by now, but I was still over an hour away and stuck in traffic. Thankfully, the interstate began to move again a few miles south of Birmingham, and it was time to see what my Mazda could do.

Eighty-six miles per hour is what it could do, which isn't impressive but was twenty-one miles per hour over the speed limit, according to the state trooper who pulled me over near Clanton, costing me precious time and $153. Twenty minutes later, I was back on the road, but by then I'd lost the Birmingham station, so I scanned the dial until I picked up a faint Montgomery broadcast of the game. Through the static, I pieced together that Rome led 13-10 early in the fourth quarter, and as the signal grew clearer, I realized I didn't exactly know where Gaul was, so I stopped at a gas station for directions then continued on, observing the speed limit for the most part.

When I pulled into Gaul, it looked like the set of a post-apocalyptic movie. I think I saw a tumbleweed blow across the street. There were no people, no cars, only a single blinking red light that I ran on my way toward the glowing lights of the stadium on the edge of town. I parked a mile away from the stadium because every car from Gaul and Rome was there, and just before I killed my ignition, the man on the radio said, "Jake Norton back to pass on third and long, sets up to throw, and—oh my, he is hammered from behind! The ball is on the ground! It's scooped up by a Gaul defender at the forty. He's at the thirty, twenty-five, twenty, he's running away! Touchdown! Touchdown, Gaul! The Celtics lead 16-13 with three minutes to play! The Celtics lead, and Rome's quarterback is still down!"

"Oh shit," I said and shut off my car but could still hear the Gaul fans roaring in the distance. I ran the mile to the stadium in five minutes flat, fake heart condition be damned, and passing through the gates where ticket takers no longer took tickets, I saw that Gaul's extra point had pushed their lead to 17-13, and somehow, they already had the ball back.

"Brinks," Silas said, making a show of checking his watch, "get here when you can, man."

I joined him on the front row of the student section and, fighting to catch my breath, said, "What did … why … how does Gaul have the ball again?"

Silas shook his head. "They knocked Jake Norton out cold, and …"

"Oh shit, Jackson?"

"Yeah," Silas said. "We ran the damn kickoff back to their ten, but Jackson fumbled the first snap."

"Shit."

"Shit indeed," Silas said.

Gaul tried to run out the clock and rushed their fullback up the middle on first and second down.

"First down here and it's over," I said to Silas.

"It's been over," he said, but on third down, Marshall Ford broke through the line of scrimmage and hit the Gaul running back so hard the ball and his green helmet flew in different directions. Fletcher Morgan recovered the helmet, and Darryl Loder fell on the ball inside Gaul's ten-yard line. With twenty-six seconds to play, Rome had a shot.

Jackson scrambled on the sideline looking for his helmet, which he'd thrown in anger after his fumble, and Silas grabbed me and shouted, "Convulsion!"

"What?"

"My play, Convulsion! Brinks, it would work here! We've got to talk to Jackson!" Silas jumped over the railing and fell to the concourse below. I jumped behind him and helped him up, and we ran to the fence and began yelling at Jackson. He was in the huddle, listening to Coach Pumphrey's last-minute instructions, and when Jackson ignored him to look our way, I thought Coach P would tear his head off.

"Jackson, get your ass over here!" Silas screamed, and our friend, the starting quarterback, left the huddle and ran over to us.

Coach P, equal parts confused and enraged, ran toward us screaming, then realizing the play clock was running out, changed direction and sprinted onto the field to call his final time-out. As he did, the rest of the offense made their way over to Silas, who barked out instructions.

"Jackson, make sure you tell the head referee what's going to happen. If he calls the play dead, we're toast." Jackson nodded, and Silas turned to Marshall and said, "Marsh, you've got to sell this shit. Say it loud so the entire defense will hear. And remember, guys, the clock will be running on the last play, so don't let it run out. Hands in, here we go." Silas reached a hand and a crutch over the fence, and together he and the offense shouted, "Victory or death!"

The players ran onto the field, past a furious Coach P, who shouted instructions his team completely ignored.

The referee placed the ball at the six-yard-line and blew his whistle, setting the play clock in motion, but Jackson showed little urgency. With the clock ticking, he turned to have a word with the referee, leaving the offense standing around looking confused. Marshall Ford took off his helmet, laughed at his own quarterback, then shook hands with the Gaul defenders. Everyone in Rome would later learn Marsh was congratulating them on their state championship, pointing at Jackson and saying, "Our third-string quarterback is a damn joke. Guy has a panic attack and fumbles every time he steps under center. Congrats, boys, y'all got this won."

Jackson finished talking to the referee and rushed to the line of scrimmage, shouting at his players to get into formation, and just as Silas planned, he fumbled the snap and quickly fell on the loose ball.

"Clock's ticking; get them lined up, Jackson," Silas muttered as the referee reset the ball, and noise from both sidelines rose in a crescendo. Marshall Ford screamed at Jackson just for show, and Jackson screamed back before shouting nonsensical instructions to the rest of the offense.

Eighteen seconds. Seventeen seconds.

Jackson stepped under center. There were three wide receivers bunched to the near sideline, and Jackson looked their direction then barked out signals.

Twelve seconds. Eleven seconds.

Jackson stood up, put his hands over his earholes, then lurched toward the far sideline.

Eight seconds. Seven seconds.

Jackson began to shake and convulse before falling still on the line of scrimmage. The Rome linemen stood to look at their fallen quarterback but did not move their feet. Gaul defenders stood as well, and one defensive back even started toward Jackson to check on him.

Two seconds. One second.

The center snapped the ball to the running back, Brent Holdbrooks, who raced toward the near sideline as the game clock expired. The Gaul defenders, who'd been watching the opposing quarterback lie motionless on the ground, reacted late but still managed to cut off Holdbrook's path to the end zone, and that's when he stopped, looked back across the field, and lofted a wobbly pass toward the far sideline, where Jackson Crowder stood all alone.

From our spot along the fence, I could tell the ball was overthrown. I saw Jackson turn and race toward the back corner of the end zone but lost sight of him as he dove. The pass fell to earth as thousands of prayers rose to the heavens, and every Roman inhaled the last breath they'd take in a world where Jackson Crowder was just a mere mortal.

No one believes me when I tell them this, but I swear the roar of the Rome fans blew Silas and me over the fence like a bomb blast. I don't remember climbing the fence, so that has to be what happened. I don't remember a lot, to be honest, mostly because the entire Rome student section trampled me on their way to the end zone where Jackson waited on his teammates' shoulders, one hand raising his helmet to the heavens, the other still clutching the football that changed his life forever.

Chapter Twenty-Six

"As you can see, this is a beautiful stone. Excellent cut. Virtually colorless. Flawless clarity."

Everyone from financial planners to therapists recommend putting off major life decisions for at least six months while grieving the death of a loved one. So obviously, I was in the Riverton Mall, buying Becca an engagement ring, two days after burying my mother. With a surgeon's care, the man behind the glass counter placed the diamond on the black velvet cloth in front of me, and I stared at it, pretending it didn't look exactly like the first ten he'd shown me.

"And how much is this one?" I asked.

The man made a show of checking his price sheet then in a lower voice said, "This stone is $24,750." When I coughed that number back to him, he said, "Of course, one cannot put a price on these things."

"Oh no," I said, "I've put a price on it. The same price I told you ten minutes ago when I walked in. Now, do you have anything smaller than the Hope Diamond, or should I check out Riverton Pawn?"

I knew the fine folks at Harrell's Diamonds would try to play me with the, "Nothing is too expensive for the love of your life" line, and I also knew I'd fall for it and give them every dollar I had in an attempt to prove my love for Becca to some stranger. That's why I'd booked our flights to London the night before, along with our room at Claridge's. If I hadn't, I'd have bought Becca a much bigger diamond but would have proposed to her at Winona Falls, which, while lovely, is not Tower Bridge.

Her parents knew that I was taking her to London but not that I'd bought a ring—I'd talk to them about that later. I spoke to Becca's mom the day after my mother's funeral and inquired about their Christmas plans. She invited me to spend the holiday with them, which wasn't exactly why I called, but I appreciated it, nonetheless. Plus, I found out Becca was free after the 27th[th], and school didn't start back until January 8th. We'd spend New Year's in London and come home engaged. The confirmation email from Delta was in my glove compartment. I planned to surprise her on our drive to Tuscaloosa Friday for the state championship game.

The rest of that school week was a complete waste. After first period on Wednesday, when the curly-haired girl near the door, who openly despised football, announced she was freaking out she was so nervous about Friday's game then proceeded to vomit in the garbage can, I gave up any thoughts of finishing the third act of *Julius Caesar*. At one point during second period on Thursday, I even left my classroom unattended and walked down the hall to see Silas.

His classroom was no different. Students played on their phones while Silas sat behind his desk, nervously going over plays on his iPad.

"Are you ready?" I asked, pulling up a chair and sitting next to him.

"Beyotch, I was born ready," Silas whispered.

"I can't argue. You did draw up a game-winning play when you were seventeen."

"Yeah, but I should have had Brent throw the ball to Fletcher instead of Jackson. What a different world that would be."

"Oh god, I think we're all lucky not to be living in a Fletcherocracy."

"Honestly, it wouldn't be that much different," Silas said.

"More spitting, that's all."

He motioned for me to lean in, and when I did, he said, "Keep this on the low, Brinks, but I applied for the offensive analyst job at Newberry."

"That's awesome," I said, trying to act surprised.

"Yeah, I applied two years ago, but they went another direction. I gotta think, though, with the numbers we've put up this year, and if we can cap it off with a state championship, I've got a real shot of working on a college staff next year."

"No one deserves it more than you. You know I'm rooting for you, man."

I patted his back, and he said, "Thanks, homie."

"Okay," I said, "let me get back and make sure they haven't set my room on fire."

"Will you be there tomorrow?" he asked.

"Wouldn't miss it," I said and left his room feeling like shit.

~ ~ ~

At Rome High School, a wall of cubbyholes in the lounge served as teacher mailboxes. There was never anything in them worth reading—a check stub each month, the occasional newsletter from the Alabama Education Association, advertisements for teacher conferences Rome couldn't afford to send us to because the school was saving for a high-definition video scoreboard. Over four months, I checked my box five times at most and often wondered how things would have played out had I not checked it that day. I pulled out the envelope addressed to "Markuss Brincks," whoever that is, and opened it to find a handwritten note.

Brinks,

I know you think I'm an asshole, but I have something very important to show you tomorrow morning. Something that will change your mind on a great many things. Meet me at The Pindarus Motel in East Riverton, room 100, tomorrow morning at 6:15 a.m. I promise, Brinks, things between us will be different in the morning.

Jackson Crowder
P.S. Don't tell anyone else you are coming, even Becca.

I'm not sure how the note found its way into my mailbox, though I suspect Melvin the janitor played a part in its delivery. What I do know, with absolute certainty, is that Jackson Crowder did not write it. So who did? The owner of The Pindarus Motel in East Riverton.

Deacon Cassburn.

~ ~ ~

"You don't have to get up yet, babe. It's just five-thirty."

Five days a week, Becca woke up early and went to the Riverton YMCA to work out. Five days a week, I did not.

I sat up and wiped my eyes, and said, "I need to, though."

"You're coming to work out with me?" she asked, with what I mistook for excitement.

"What? God no."

Becca laughed, and I lied, "I need to run by Mom's house before school and find some paperwork the attorney asked about." I hated lying to her.

She kissed me on the head and said, "I'll see you at the pep rally then. Love you."

"Love you too," I said, and she was gone.

I showered, made the short drive to East Riverton, and parked beneath the flashing vacancy sign of The Pindarus Motel. The parking lot was mostly empty, but I saw Jackson's truck parked in front of what I assumed was room 100, so I stepped out of my car into the cold December morning and walked that way. There was an envelope with my name on it taped to the door, and I opened it to find a key card to the room. I held the card up to the lock, saw the light blink from red to green, opened the door to the dark room, and flipped on the light.

Have you ever walked into your garage at night, turned on the light, and watched cockroaches scatter? Well, it's not much different, really, than walking into a seedy Riverton Motel, turning on a light, and watching the love of your life and your former best friend do the same thing.

I turned around without a word while they scrambled for sheets and clothes, and by the time I reached my car, Becca was in the door, shouting my name, but I ignored her and drove away. She called thirty seconds later, and I declined the call, then she sent a text, and another, and another, and I turned off my phone without reading them. I don't remember driving to the school parking lot, but that's where I was, screaming and beating my hand on the dashboard, when Deacon Cassburn pulled up next to me.

If I'd had a gun, I'd have shot him. And sure, technically, I'd be shooting the messenger, but there can be some therapy in that. I didn't have one though, despite Rome's insane open-carry policy, and when Deacon climbed down from his truck and leaned through my open window, I stared straight ahead.

"Howdy, Brinks," he said, patting me on the shoulder, "seen anything interesting this lovely morning?"

I squeezed my steering wheel until my knuckles popped, and Deacon backed up a few steps out of precaution.

"It's funny," he said, "the whole town had heard the rumors about Becca and Jackson, but nobody could prove 'em. Then, lo and behold, they booked a room in the wrong damn motel. If you want to know what sort of man your friend Jackson is, he made Becca pay for the room."

I turned to face Deacon, and he shook his head with something resembling pity. "Look, Brinks, I don't like this any more than you, but you needed to know the truth. The truth has set you free, my friend. You're free to go now. You can get the hell out of Rome, and you can bring down Jackson while you're at it. Hell, I would do it, but I'm stuck here, and you know how these people can get about their football. So what do you say, you ready to help me take care of Jackson once and for all?"

I had a decision to make. I knew pain waited just below my rage. Pain that wanted to harden my heart and send me right back to where I was before I returned to Rome, before I fell in love again. The same sort of pain that cost me half my life, and cost my mom half hers. The pain I knew I was risking when I asked Becca to dance on the boardwalk behind Trevi's, and when I wrote a new song and sang it for her at the homecoming dance, and when I moved my toothbrush to her house. I knew I'd hurt soon, the same way your hand starts to hurt hours after punching the dashboard or your mother's boyfriend, but sitting in my car, I decided this time would be different. This time I would be stronger. I would be the man my mother thought I'd become. I would mend my broken heart, move on, and one day, I would risk it all for love again. But first … I had to burn Rome to the ground.

"Brinks," Deacon repeated, "I asked if you were ready to help me take care of Jackson."

"You're right," I said, "about the truth, it will set you free. And the truth is, the night after Rome won the state semifinal in 1994, there was a party at my house. And at that party, Jackson Crowder spiked your drink with some drug his sister's DJ friend at Jacksonville State sold him. Then he drove you to Carthage, poured a couple beers on your head, and left you for the cops to find."

Deacon stared at me for an eternity, and I thought perhaps he was about to shoot me, but instead, he shook my hand and said, "I appreciate you telling me, Brinks." Then he got in his truck and drove away.

~ ~ ~

"Mr. Brinks, are you okay?" asked the short blonde by the air conditioner ten minutes into first period.

"Fine," I said, without looking up from my phone.

The last two days I'd at least made a show of trying to teach before letting the students spend the class period playing on their phones, but that morning, I hadn't said a word, and at least a couple of them seemed genuinely worried about me, which was nice.

244

"What are you doing?" asked the curly-haired girl by the door.

I looked up and said, "Sending emails."

"To Miss Walsh?" asked the mousy-looking girl on the front row, and the room giggled until I glared at them and they stopped.

"No," I said and, turning back to my phone, added, "I'm sending an email to Darryl Loder at the *Riverton Times* with proof I changed Kyler's grade to keep him eligible." The rest of the class looked back at Kyler, but he was asleep at his desk, so they turned back to me, and I said, "And I'm sending an email to the ACLU to see if they're interested in baptisms on public school property. And I'm sending an email to the Federal Bureau of Investigation office in Birmingham to let them know Rome Quarterback Club members sent pornography to underage students in an attempt to lure them to a party with alcohol. And I'm sending an email to Rubicon County Animal Control to let them know Deacon Cassburn keeps an adult wolf in his backyard as a pet. And I'm sending an email to the head coach of Newberry College to let him know Silas Carver is more than capable of serving as his offensive analyst. And I'm sending an email to that attorney from Hornby with all the billboards, Lucian Figg, to let him know about a violation of the Americans with Disabilities Act and the opportunity for a huge cash settlement. And I'm sending an email to Harrell's Diamonds in the mall to enquire about their refund policy. And finally, I'm sending an email to Amy Crowder to let her know that her husband and my girlfriend have been breaking the seventh commandment in the Pindarus Motel."

I looked up from my phone, and the entire classroom was staring at me wide-eyed, so I stood up and said, "Now if you'll excuse me, I need to talk to Coach Carver."

~ ~ ~

Silas was in his room, ignoring his students, and when I opened the door, he smiled until I said, "Silas, I've got something to tell you, and I want your students to hear so they'll know what sort of asshole coaches their football team."

The students, who'd been talking and playing on their phones, now all looked my way, and I said, "Newberry College wanted to hire you two years ago, but Jackson told them not to. Not because he thinks you couldn't do it, but because he wants to keep you here, at Rome. That selfish son of a bitch knows he can't win without you, so he lied to keep you here. Silas, I was in his office last month when Newberry's coach called again. They still want to hire you, but Jackson told them you weren't up to it, physically, even though he knows you are more than capable. I'm sorry, man. I'm sorry I didn't tell you. I've been a shitty friend, and I hope you'll forgive me for waiting this long to say anything."

Silas nodded in a way that let me know we were cool, so I apologized to his class for the interruption then went back to my room and waited until the morning's pep rally when fan and shit were destined to meet.

"*The Beige Album* was somehow both before and after its time. A masterpiece demanding our undivided attention, misfortune paired its arrival with the internet boom of the late nineties and the onset of our collective ADD. Drop it five years earlier and we'd talk about it the way we still talk about *Nevermind* or *Slanted & Enchanted*, but, alas, few heard it through the noise. And yet, listening to this album again twenty years later, sonically, it remains a glimpse into the future. The genius of Dear Brutus is still there for those who find it, and as Marcus Brinks's voice cracks and fades on the final note of the coda "Release (No One Can Hurt Me)," a new generation of fans are left to wonder—what could have been?"

—*Pitchfork*, 10.0 review of *Dear Brutus: 20th Anniversary Reissue*, November 23, 2017

Chapter Twenty-Seven

What does it mean to be a fan—of a team, or a band, or anything? To be a fan is to latch on to something bigger than yourself and to attach personal meaning to that thing's performance and, if you want to get scientific about it, to receive a mind-altering rush of dopamine when that thing succeeds. Our brains remember the euphoria of celebrating a game-winning field goal or singing along with ten thousand others as our favorite band belts out their greatest hit. We chase that feeling, we anticipate it, and that's why we're physically ill when our team loses in the final seconds or our favorite band breaks up and the lead singer punches a horse. But on the flip side, there is bliss beyond all measure when our team comes through in an unexpected way. An otherwise unknowable ecstasy when, say, a third-string quarterback, who only seconds before lay helpless on the ground, leaps and makes a diving catch in the back of the end zone to win a school its first state championship.

In all the commotion, I didn't even think to look for Becca until sometime during the trophy presentation, which took place on Gaul's field amid the horde of celebrating Romans. By then, I'd lost Silas and was still looking for him when Coach Pumphrey, sitting atop Marshall Ford's shoulders, raised the trophy over his head and the crowd chanted, "Victory or death!" Then Coach P passed the trophy to Jackson, who was still on the shoulders of his teammates, and the crowd roared as he too raised the trophy in triumph.

After singing the fight song, then the alma mater, then the fight song twice more, the Roman crowd began to disperse, and I found Silas talking to the players involved in that final, magical play. Well, all but Jackson, who was giving an interview to WBRC Fox 6 from Birmingham. I stood back as the players hugged Silas in turn, Brent Holdbrooks tousling his hair and telling him repeatedly, "You da man, Carver! You da mother effin' man!" And after they'd all made their way toward the locker room, I walked up to Silas and said, "Nice call, coach."

Silas smiled, and I hugged him and said, "I still can't believe Jackson caught it."

He shook his head and said, "I know. I think the bad throw helped. He didn't have any time to think. If all he'd had to do was stand there and catch a perfect pass, the ball would have bounced off his face mask."

We stood there for a moment, soaking it all in, then he said, "Everyone in Rome is staying at the same hotel in downtown Montgomery tonight. You're coming, right? It's going to be the party of the millennium."

I told Silas I'd see him there, but after walking the mile back to my car, I realized I didn't know the name of the hotel where everyone was staying. So I drove toward Montgomery and spent an hour lost downtown before finally passing a tall building where roman candles shot from a tenth-story window. I knew then I'd found the place.

I parked in the deck across the street and walked into the hotel, and though time and occasional recreational drug use has perhaps distorted and exaggerated my memory of that night's events, the first thing I remember seeing was Mr. Galba, our straighter than straight-laced history teacher, with what appeared to be a very fresh and crudely done *SPQR* tattoo on his chest, splashing shirtless in the lobby fountain. Kool & the Gang blared from a boom box someone had set on the front desk, and the parents, teachers, and coaches of Rome danced with an inhibition rarely seen in anyone over the age of four. Coach P was at the bar, surrounded by cheering fans and a dozen empty shot glasses. I watched him down another shot to loud cheers then fall off his stool. Some of the adults had removed the sheets from their hotel beds and constructed togas that did not even remotely cover all their body parts that needed covering. Try as I might to forget, I can still see Mrs. Nerva, her breasts bared, climbing the lobby ficus tree for no apparent reason. I even saw Steve, slumped in the corner, with two black eyes and an empty whiskey bottle at his feet. Rumor was, he cleaned up, found Jesus, and now manages a McDonald's in Hornby, but I never cared enough to investigate.

By now, the hotel staff had given up and were either hiding in the manager's office or had abandoned ship entirely, and as I stood at the front desk, ringing the bell and looking for someone to ask what room the students were in, Mrs. Nero stumbled into me.

"Marcus, it's you," she said and kissed me on the lips.

I backed away, wide-eyed, and said, "Uh ... hi, Mrs. Nero."

"You call me Tonya," she said and hiccupped.

"Okay, Tonya," I said. "Hey, do you know where the students are?"

"Yes. I. Do," Mrs. Nero said slowly, touching her finger to her temple after each word.

"Can you ... uh ... tell me?"

"Sure, Marcus," she said, putting an arm around me and pointing toward the elevators. "The top two floors are reserved for students, but you are more than welcome to stay down here."

I told Mrs. Nero thanks, but no thanks, and she slapped my ass as I walked away toward the elevators. I punched the button for the ninth floor, and as the elevator rose, the sound from the lobby party faded but was soon replaced by the sound of an even louder party above. Seconds later, the elevator dinged, and the doors to Sodom and Gomorrah slid open.

I stepped onto the landing where someone had busted the glass to the snack machine, and Mark Porter and a few of his freshman friends sat gorging themselves on an endless supply of free candy bars.

"Brinks!" they yelled in unison when they saw me, my new-found popularity from hosting what was now the second greatest party in Rome history, apparently not yet faded.

"Hey guys," I said, and one of the freshmen, his face covered in chocolate, said, "Brinks, a girl at your party showed me her boobs."

"Good for you," I said. "Hey, have y'all seen Becca Walsh?"

They shook their heads no, and one of them offered me a Twix. "No thanks," I said and walked down the hallway in search of Becca.

The door was open to the first room I came to, and inside, kids danced under a strobe light. I pushed my way inside but didn't see any familiar faces then pushed my way back out, stumbling into the room across the hall, where the drum major, Chase Malone, sat wearing nothing but boxer shorts and his band helmet. Chase said he'd seen Becca in room 920; of course, he also said he'd seen Mahatma Gandhi in room 920, but I felt obliged to follow any and all leads.

Water was pouring out from under the door of the next room I passed, and out of curiosity, I peeked inside to see a mini horse, ankle-deep in water, because someone had left the tub faucet running full blast. I turned it off and left the door open in case the horse wanted to leave then walked down to room 920, which was a large, two-bedroom suite and apparently home base for the senior class. Inside, MeghanJennifer line danced on the kitchenette bar, and below them, Mandy Duke and Rita Bell, both wearing Rome football helmets, violently head-butted each other. Darryl the atheist was passed out on the couch, and Maggie Duncan was writing Bible verses all over his body with a permanent marker while her friend Rachel watched and giggled. A line of people holding Solo cups stood outside the bathroom, and when I looked inside, I saw Brent Holdbrooks mixing hunch punch in the bathtub. "Brinks," he yelled when he saw me, dipping a cup into the tub, "you've got to try this shit. It's nasty!"

"No thanks," I said and walked into one of the bedrooms where Marshall Ford was standing on the balcony rail, naked from the waist down and holding a cup of punch in each hand, while screaming the words to "God Bless the U.S.A."

"Brinks!" Marshall shouted, falling off the rail and back into the bedroom. "The flag still stands for freedom, Brinks!"

"He knows that," Fletcher Morgan said, walking out of the bathroom smoking a joint. "You know the flag still stands for freedom, don't you, Brinks?"

"Uh … yeah," I said and passed on the joint before asking if they'd seen Becca.

"Try the tenth floor," Fletcher said then, holding back laughter, added, "but knock first."

The tenth floor was quiet, most doors were closed, and apart from two sophomore girls spraying each other with fire extinguishers, the students in the hallway had passed out. I knocked on the first door I came to, and after a minute, Silas answered wrapped in a sheet.

"Brinks," he said, bumping my fist, "I didn't think you'd make it."

"I got lost," I said then asked, "Have you seen Becca?"

"In the lobby earlier but not since," he said then looked back over his shoulder into the room and said, "Hey man, Tabatha is waiting on me."

"Jake Norton's girlfriend?"

"Yeah," Silas said with a shrug, "he's in the hospital getting his concussion checked out and—"

"—And all's fair in love and football?"

"You know it, homie," Silas said, and with another fist bump, he was gone.

I continued down the hall until I came to an open door and found Deacon Cassburn inside, drunk out of his mind, sitting on the bed watching SportsCenter alone. I tried to leave before he saw me, but I wasn't quick enough, and he said, "Brinks, have a seat. They're about to show Plays of the Week."

"Sorry, man, I can't stay. I was looking for …"

"Becca?" he asked.

"Uh … yeah. Becca. Have you seen her?"

"Yeah, she's next door," he said then turned back to the television without another word.

I walked next door to room 1049 and knocked on the slightly ajar door, but there was no answer, so I let myself in. I heard a girl's voice and muffled laughter, and I was about to call out to Becca as I rounded the corner, when in the lamplight, I saw Jackson lying in bed, half-covered by a sheet.

Next to him, wearing only his Rome jersey, was Becca Walsh.

Stumbling backward, I left before they saw me and collapsed into the hallway. "No, no, no," I muttered to myself over and over then briefly considered storming back into the room and kicking Jackson's ass and/or confessing my love to Becca. I still had one good hand to break his face with, and on the drive to Gaul, I'd basically written a sonnet for Becca, most of which would later appear in our song, "Pale Eyed Girl, Pt. 1." But Jackson thought I was over Becca. I'd told him as much. And Becca wasn't going to leave the new king of Rome. Not for me. I'd missed my chance. It was over, and I couldn't breathe, and I needed out of that hotel immediately.

Deacon looked up as I passed his door, and when I shook my head in disbelief, he shrugged and returned the gesture. I stumbled to the elevator landing, where Mark Porter and friends were now raiding the tenth-floor snack machine, and while they asked about my next party, I beat on the down button with my splint. An elevator rose slowly from the basement—second floor, third floor—but I couldn't wait for it. I was suffocating. So, I found the stairwell and ran down ten flights, pushed my way through the lobby full of drunk adults, and burst into the cold December night where I screamed at the top of my lungs.

High above, roman candles exploded, and as I staggered across the street to my car, the tears came. I was still crying when I hit the Louisiana border four hours later. I'd only just stopped when I banged on my father's door at ten the next morning. He let me in, and I crawled into my old bed, praying when I woke up my fall in Rome would have all been a bad dream.

Chapter Twenty-Eight

Keeping with tradition, Rome scheduled a special candlelit pep rally at ten Friday morning, leaving the team and town ample time to make the journey to Tuscaloosa for the championship game late that afternoon. They even used real candles again, not wanting to jinx anything. I'd already sent Principal Trajan an email informing him of my resignation, effective immediately, but out of morbid curiosity hung around for one last pep rally. Becca caught me outside the gymnasium, her eyes puffy from crying all morning.

"Marcus," she said, reaching for my hand, but I pulled it away. "I've been calling and texting all morning. You have to let me explain. Marcus, this morning—"

"There's nothing to explain," I said. "You fooled me twice; the shame's on me this time."

"Fooled you twice? Marcus, what are you talking about?"

"Jackson," I snarled. "I walked in on you and Jackson in that Montgomery hotel after the state championship game twenty-three years ago."

Students making their way into the gymnasium stared at us, and Becca pulled me away from the entrance and, looking genuinely confused, repeated, "You walked in on Jackson and me after the state championship game? Marcus what are you talking about?"

"I loved you, Becca," I said, pulling at my hair in frustration. "I've loved you from the moment you walked into Mr. Galba's class wearing that Weezer T-shirt, and I was going to tell you that night, but then I saw you in bed with Jackson. You're the reason I left Rome that December. God, I never should have come back."

"Marcus," Becca said, putting a hand on my arm that I shrugged off. "I honestly don't know what you are talking about. I hardly even remember that night. I was drunk out of my mind. Everyone was. Three teachers got divorced after that party. Maybe I did make out with Jackson, but I'm pretty sure I made out with MeghanJennifer at one point too. Wait, is that why you kept asking why I didn't go to prom or the Christmas dance with Jackson? Marcus, we were never together. It was ten minutes of drunk kissing, and you walked in at the absolute worst time. I swear to god."

"I seem to keep doing that," I said.

"Yes … no … Marcus, what you saw this morning … that started a year ago, before you came back. Things got so compli-cated … and I never thought you'd actually stay in Rome … I was going to tell Jackson this morning it was all over, and that you and I—"

Becca froze as Amy Crowder walked by, glaring at Becca before entering the gymnasium with ill intent.

"Dammit," Becca said. "I've ruined everything. I always ruin everything. Marcus, please—"

She was right; she did always ruin everything. Honestly, that's all I really knew about her. For half my life, I'd been in love with a face, with the idea of a girl that only existed in my mind. Based on nothing more than careless flirting and shared taste in music, I'd convinced myself she was my soul mate, when in fact all she ever did was break my heart, and when I finally realized this, I felt a beautiful release.

"You know it was you, right? You were the girl, Becca. Every song I ever wrote was about you."

"Marcus, I—"

"You were all I ever wanted, but now, if you don't mind, I'd rather not see your lying face ever again."

I turned and walked into the candlelit gymnasium, where students, cheerleaders, and the Marching Legion waited patiently for their heroes, and found a spot along the wall next to the crazy old man who always screamed about Middlesboro, and Deacon Cassburn, who smelled like bourbon and was so drunk he'd brought a cup of whatever he was drinking into the school with him.

"Brinks, my friend," Deacon slurred, and when I nodded his way, he added, "Today's my birthday, Brinks. Ain't that some shit?"

A snare drummer beat out a cadence, and single file, the football team entered the gym through the door to our right, making their way toward the stage. The assistant coaches followed, and as Jackson entered the gym, Deacon pushed past me, knocked Jackson to the ground with a right cross, then poured his cup on the coach's head before stumbling into the parking lot.

A crowd of students, fans, and two process servers closed in on Jackson, helping him to his feet and offering towels, and when the commotion cleared, Jackson held two summons notifying him of two lawsuits filed against him earlier that morning. Dazed, he continued toward half-court, where a microphone awaited, and as he took off his windbreaker and tried to dry off, the crowd watched in silence.

Principal Trajan's footsteps echoed as he crossed the court to have a word with Jackson, and as their hushed conversation grew louder, everyone in the gym heard Jackson say, "I'll text the pictures to your wife right now if you don't get your ass off my court, soldier."

Trajan hesitated then turned and walked away, and after Jackson wiped the blood from his mouth, he grabbed the microphone and said, "When you're successful, like me, the jealous losers of the world will always try to bring you down." The crowd applauded this because they'd always applauded whenever Jackson said anything. "Like Fletcher Morgan," Jackson continued, "who tried to sabotage all we've worked for. But I've learned the Rome police arrested Fletcher minutes ago on child pornography charges." More applause followed, though this time mixed with murmurs of confusion. "Fletcher came at the king and missed, and now he's paying the price. Like Deacon Cassburn, who wanted to bring me down but has now fallen so far he's shit-faced, stumbling around a high school parking lot at ten in the morning." Jackson held up the two summons, one a civil liberties suit, the other concerning the Americans with Disabilities Act, then ripped them to pieces and shouted, "The losers will try to tear down what we've built here. They will try, and they will fail!"

Jackson turned to address his team on stage and, for the first time, saw Silas, sitting front and center, wearing a purple windbreaker. "Oh hell no," Jackson said and turned to yell at Principal Trajan, who was now having a hushed conversation with members of the Rubicon County School Board. Jackson turned back toward Silas and shouted, "Clothes don't make you the king, you crippled loser. If you think I'm stepping down, I'll tell you what I just told Trajan. It's not happening. Not now. Not ever. I'm the only constant here. I'm the fucking northern star."

"Coach," Darryl the atheist shouted from across the gym, "any comment on the *Riverton Times* report that Kyler Barton is ineligible for tonight's game because he failed English literature? Will Rome forfeit all games he participated in?"

Jackson stared at Darryl, then turned and found me against the wall.

"You too, Brinks?"

"Me too, you piece of shit!"

I often wonder what Caesar thought when the first dagger pierced his side. If his life flashed before his eyes, did he see the miscalculations that would eventually lead to his bloody end in the Theatre of Pompey? If he had it all to do over, would he not cross the Rubicon? Would he stay in Egypt and settle down with

Cleopatra? Would he sleep in on the Ides of March? Or are men like Caesar, like Jackson Crowder, incapable of seeing their mistakes even with the benefit of hindsight?

Jackson scanned the gymnasium, looking for a single friendly face, but not finding one. When he hung his head and rubbed his temples, his state championship ring sparkled in the candlelight. His reign was over, he could see that at least, even if he couldn't understand why, and defeated, his footsteps echoed as he walked toward the exit. But then something inside him truly snapped, and he turned and charged me with crazed anger in his black eyes. Perhaps he intended to fight us all and I was just first, or maybe, in his sick mind, my return to Rome planted the seed of his downfall. Either way, I fully intended to go down swinging, until Diana bolted through the door and, smelling the wolf piss Deacon had just poured on Jackson, proceeded to rip my old friend to shreds.

Many things that go through your mind when you see your oldest friend and enemy being eaten alive by a snarling she-wolf, first and foremost, 'Thank god that's not me.'

I'd like to go on record here and say that arming educators is a terrible idea. I had teachers, and so did you, who shouldn't have been trusted with a letter opener, much less a handgun. And yet, had several teachers not been packing heat that day, Diana might have hurt a student, and that would have been truly tragic. But as it was, while the wolf snapped and growled and students screamed and ran and knocked over candles, fortune presented two dozen educators and administrators who Jackson had blackmailed over the years, along with a scorned wife with fervent Levitical beliefs on the appropriate punishment for adulterers, an opportunity they'd likely never have again. In the following days, a Rubicon County Sheriff's ballistics expert concluded they'd fired a combined sixty rounds at Deacon's pet wolf. Twenty-three hit the great Jackson Crowder.

In a desperate attempt to restore order, Silas shouted into his microphone, "Students, teachers, Romans, listen to me!"

259

But the stage curtain was now on fire, and by nightfall, Rome High School would lay in ashes. Rome's students would finish the school year attending Carthage, or Sparta, and when their school was rebuilt a year later, the Alabama High School Athletic Association thought it best they never field another football team.

Somehow, in the chaos of screaming and stampeding Romans, I found myself outside in the parking lot, watching flames lick the roof of the Ronald J. Pumphrey Gymnasium. And with sirens roaring in the distance and black smoke blotting out the cold December sun, I walked away from it all, past the statue of my old friend, across a field of fake grass.

THE END

Dear Brutus

From Wikipedia, the free encyclopedia

Dear Brutus is an American indie rock band formed in Austin, Texas, in 1996, consisting of Marcus Brinks (lead vocals, guitar), Porter Clayton (drums, xylophone, accordion), Wade Barker (guitar, zanzithophone, backing vocals), Kyle Craven (bass guitar, banjo, backing vocals), and Piper Van Pelt (piano, pipe organ, synthesizer, bullhorn, backing vocals).

After signing to Geffen Records in 1997, the band released its first album, an eponymous debut, known as the *Beige Album*, which sold over 500,000 copies, was certified gold, and hailed by *Rolling Stone* as "a gut-wrenchingly confessional, lo-fi power-pop masterpiece."[1] Widely considered to be inspired by *The Giver,* Lois Lowry's young adult dystopian novel, and by lead singer Marcus Brinks's high school crush, the *Beige Album* received universal acclaim and holds a perfect score of 100 on the aggregate review website *Metacritic*.[2][3]

The group disbanded in 1999, when Brinks, citing stress, abruptly walked off stage during an Amsterdam concert, though after months of eccentric behavior followed by years of reclusion, it is generally believed the lead singer suffered a nervous breakdown.[4]

In early 2018, Dear Brutus shocked fans by announcing the impending release of their long-awaited second album. According to the band's official Twitter account, the album, rumored to be inspired by the death of lead singer Marcus Brinks's mother, will be called *The Rome of Fall*.[5]

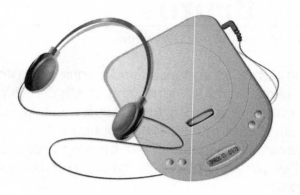

Acknowledgements

Thanks to my wife, Tricia, whose disdain of mushy public declarations of love leaves me with little choice but to quote "Buddy Holly" by Weezer. "Woo-hoo, but you know I'm yours. Woo-hoo, and I know you're mine. Woo-hoo, and that's for all of time."

Thanks to my sons, Linus and Oliver, who contributed nothing to the creation of this book, and in fact, hindered its completion by several months. Nevertheless, I love you both more than I knew possible.

Thanks to my family, Kim and Alan Gibbs, Karen and Harrell Day, Ashleigh and Beau Ashley, and Lori and Johnny Dorminey, for their love and support, and thanks to my nieces and nephews, Garrett Ashley, Morgan Ashley, Chandler Ashley, Ava Dorminey, and Jake Dorminey, who hopefully still think it's cool to see their names in my books.

Thanks to Becky Philpott for her many hours of editing expertise. If you enjoyed this book, thank Becky, if you didn't, just know it could have been much worse.

Thanks to everyone who read early versions of this book and didn't tell me to delete the manuscript and find a new line of work, including Jess Parris, Ava Dorminey, Deb Rhodes, Joseph Craven, Jessica Buttram, J.T. Hornbuckle, Karen Day, Mary Grace Powers, Lori and Johnny Dorminey, and Shay Baugh.

I listened to a lot of '90s music while working on *The Rome of Fall*, including, but not limited to, Beck, Blur, Beastie Boys, Blues Traveler, Green Day, Mazzy Star, Nirvana, Dr. Dre and Snoop Dogg, Pearl Jam, The Jesus and Mary Chain, Pavement, Warren G, Lisa Loeb, Oasis, and Weezer. Thanks to all these artists for making the music that defined my high school years, and again thanks to Tricia, for not saying anything when I briefly began wearing my Kurt Cobain flannel shirt again.

No thanks to the Glencoe High School class of 1996 for choosing "Love Me Tomorrow" by Chicago as our prom song over "Fade Into You" by Mazzy Star. Seriously guys?

And finally, thanks to everyone who read my first novel, *Two Like Me and You*. Your kind reviews and notes of encouragement sustained me while I worked on this book, and I do hope you enjoyed it as well.

TWO LIKE ME AND YOU

EDWIN GREEN'S EX-GIRLFRIEND IS FAMOUS

We're talking cover-of-every-tabloid-in-the-grocery-store-line famous. She dumped Edwin one year ago on what he refers to as Black Saturday, and in hopes of winning her back, he's spent the last twelve months trying to become famous himself. It hasn't gone well.

But when a history class assignment pairs Edwin with Parker Haddaway, the mysterious new girl at school, she introduces him to Garland Lenox, a nursing-home-bound World War II veteran who will change Edwin's life forever.

The three escape to France, in search of the old man's long-lost love, and as word of their adventure spreads, they become media darlings. But when things fall apart, they also become the focus of French authorities. In a race against time, who will find love, and who will find more heartache.

"A smashing debut that's both intimate and epic."
—*Kirkus Reviews (starred review)*

"... beautifully original and engaging."
—*IndieReader*

"... a laugh-out-loud, hearwarming story that fans of John Green will adore."
—*YABooksCentral*

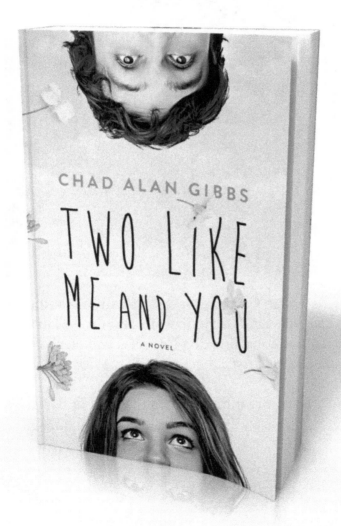

For more information or to purchase please visit www.chadalangibbs.com

Chad Alan Gibbs is the award-winning author of *Two Like Me and You*. He lives in Auburn, Alabama with his wife, two sons, one dog (we miss you Harper), and an embarrasingly large collection of Star Wars action figures.

For more information and email updates,
please visit www.chadalangibbs.com

CPSIA information can be obtained
at www.ICGtesting.com
Printed in the USA
LVHW050736210620
658569LV00006B/1032